So I
Lied

So I Lied

A THRILLER

Chelsea Ichaso

THOMAS & MERCER

Text copyright © 2025 by Chelsea Ichaso
All rights reserved.

Published by Thomas & Mercer, Seattle

www.apub.com

Amazon, the Amazon logo, and Thomas & Mercer are trademarks of Amazon.com, Inc., or its affiliates.

ISBN-13: 9781662521690 (paperback)
ISBN-13: 9781662521706 (digital)

Cover design by James Iacobelli
Cover image: © metamorworks, © Rytis Bernotas, © yuriyzhuravov / Getty

Printed in the United States of America

To Courtney, Leah, and Bethany

NOW

The scream rings out beside me, piercing my ears, tearing through the whistling wind. I feel my friend's arms on me, her face buried in my neck. Even as her fingertips dig through the fabric of my coat and her tears wet my cheek, I can't console her. The leather boots I purchased just for this trip are frozen in place, as if nailed to the moss-laden forest floor. My lips are paralyzed in their parted half-moon state. I want to shut my eyes, but it's as if my lids have been pried open with forceps.

I can only stare at my other friend—the one whose body lies sprawled on a bed of twigs and pine needles, unmoving. Blood soaks the wool of the scarf she bought in town only two days ago. Her lifeless eyes are open, and though it's dark, I can't help thinking that she's looking at me.

Accusing me.

CHAPTER 1
ROWAN

My chest is tight as I follow Jocelyn through Manchester Airport, Cadence hustling at my side. One of the wheels on my rarely used rolling suitcase is broken, and it keeps snagging and sticking every time I attempt to navigate around someone—roughly every two seconds. Between the sprinting and the claustrophobic terminal, I struggle to catch my breath. I'm not used to airports. I've never even traveled out of California; having a kid at twenty tends to put a damper on any extravagant travel plans. I'm not one of those *Oh, I'll just hop on a plane with my toddler*-type parents. Plus, there's the money thing.

Our baggage arrived late, so we're racing to catch the train departing to Conwy, Wales, in twenty minutes. If we miss it, we'll be stuck here until the next Conwy-bound train tomorrow. It isn't exactly how I imagined our peaceful girls' week kicking off, but Jocelyn swears that once we reach our destination, it will be worth the journey.

"Are you coming, Rowan?" she calls back to us.

Jocelyn travels all the time. For work, for pleasure. Money has never been an issue for her. At first, I was a bit disappointed when she pitched something quiet in the country. Fast and loud has always been my speed—at least before Molly came. After Molly, life became a series of a different sort of all-nighters. The kind where hangovers made way for a bone-deep fatigue that never faded, no matter how much I napped on weekends with that little bundle snuggled to my chest. In high school, I was the party girl of the trio—which wasn't saying much. Between prissy Jocelyn and prudish valedictorian Cadence, it took little to claim the spot as "the fun one." I've been a slave to my job and my kid for eight years; living it up for a week before Jocelyn's nuptials sounded like a fabulous idea. But Jocelyn has already done "all of that." She and her fiancé, Landon, recently traveled to Paris, and six months prior to that, she was in Bali for her wedding-planning business. Jocelyn hasn't been to the UK in *ages* (meaning it's been two years); however, her aunt and uncle run a bed-and-breakfast on the idyllic northwest coast of Wales. "What if we all just took it easy for a week?" she asked, though neither Cady nor I could've exactly disagreed, seeing how Jocelyn was not only the bride but was fronting the entire bill for the trip. "Sat around and drank good whiskey. Strolled the beaches?"

In the end, I had to admit that, as usual, Jocelyn's plan sounded good. Perfect, even, especially when I saw pictures online of the scenic towns in North Wales. Foggy coasts, rolling green hills full of grazing sheep, ancient stone castles. Considering that I'm finally comfortable leaving Molly for a week, some time in the quiet countryside with my oldest and dearest friends sounded like exactly what I needed. Maybe it will restore some parts of me that were left raw and damaged eight years ago.

We reach the end of the terminal, and Jocelyn halts, patting her jacket pocket.

I take the opportunity to hunch over my bag in an attempt to catch my breath. People continue to sweep past, grazing my clothes, bumping my behind. "You okay?" Cady asks, steering her suitcase out of harm's way.

"Mm-hmm." I would joke about the fact that I haven't exercised since obligatory physical education in high school, except I don't have the lung capacity for it.

Then I realize she was talking to Jocelyn.

"Yeah," Jocelyn says, smiling. She looks different, though still gorgeous today without any makeup on. Apparently, she only uses moisturizer and lip balm on flights due to the drying effects of the airplane filtration system. "Makeup only ends up all over your face after tossing and turning on a travel pillow," according to her. It sounded like rich-people bullshit to me, especially since I don't own a travel pillow. But I catch my reflection in my phone's camera and confirm that, as usual, Jocelyn Elliott was right. Mascara is smeared under my eyes, my foundation is flaking off along with my now dehydrated skin, and my dark-brown curls are stringy.

Jocelyn, on the other hand, looks radiant. Her freckled cheeks practically glow, and her shoulder-length auburn hair is flawless after our two flights to get here, plus a sprint through the terminal. "Just thought I'd lost my passport. Forgot I put it in my bag."

I let my backpack slide down my shoulder and reach for my water, when Jocelyn says, "This way." She's off again, Cady already close behind.

I take a deep breath of body odor–filled air and yank my broken suitcase along. This is the way it's been for almost a decade. Those two, always a little closer. Me, always trailing slightly in their dust.

I'll admit I was surprised when Jocelyn invited me on this trip. We've hardly been the trio of old, not since Molly came along.

Not since a little before that, if we're being completely honest.

We met freshman year of high school in English class. Our teacher, Mrs. Harris, had grouped us together for a project. We soon discovered that, thanks to my artistic skills, Cadence's knack for the English language and academics in general, and Jocelyn's organizational abilities, we had the makings of an A-plus team when it came to crafting posters about Emily Dickinson.

After our presentation was done and we'd earned our As, we found ourselves inventing new reasons to hang out. And we never stopped inventing them. Despite our different interests—Cady's in academia, Jocelyn's in event planning, and mine in art—we all ended up at UC Santa Barbara. Far enough from our homes in Southern California to truly experience college life, but close enough that Jocelyn's parents could stop by to lavish expensive gifts and dinners on the three of us.

Then, in the spring of sophomore year, I could no longer hide my pregnancy. With a baby to consider, I had to find a steady, full-time job. I dropped out of school while the other two continued at UCSB, living the life I wished I had.

Maybe if things the previous fall had gone differently—if it hadn't been clouded in black—everything would've gone as planned. I might've had the support to make it all work.

But that wasn't the way things turned out.

We reach the corner of the terminal, containing a gift shop, a bathroom, and an open restaurant packed with customers. Cadence stops at the bathroom, her sandy-blond hair coming loose from its ponytail and falling into her face. "Hold on, Joss!"

Jocelyn pivots, looking annoyed. "There's a bathroom on the train."

"Sorry," Cadence says, shoving her suitcase toward me, "but train bathrooms are gross, and I'm going to pee my pants. Anyone else need to go?"

Jocelyn checks the time on her phone again, lips pressed flat. "Might as well. If we're late, we're late." She abandons her suitcase beside Cadence's. The two of them push toward the bathroom, leaving me as a human luggage rack.

A few feet away, a window spans the entire length of the restaurant, and I spot the city of Manchester through it. Stools line a counter beneath the window, some filled with diners grabbing a quick meal. For the first time, it hits me that I'm in a different country.

The realization should spark awe and wonder; instead, it triggers something like anaphylaxis, wringing my throat tighter.

I've never been apart from Molly for even a weekend in Palm Springs, much less flown to another continent for an entire week. Yet here I am, an ocean away from my baby. I attempt to shake the thought off. She's with my parents, whom she loves dearly. We only left last night. I can't break down already, not in front of two people who have absolutely no idea what I'm going through. Jocelyn and Cadence are my closest friends, but they don't have children. They're expecting the Rowan who hitchhiked all the way to San Francisco for an art show when I couldn't afford a plane ticket. They're not expecting mommy drama. They'll regret inviting me, and Jocelyn's entire bachelorette trip will be wrecked.

But trying not to panic only forces my breath shallower, my vision darker. I spot a black coat draped over one of the stools, no owner in sight. If I don't pick up my feet and move, the feeling will swallow me whole, a monster gulping down its victim. Without thinking, I take a few quick steps into the restaurant. I slip behind the stools as if I were merely on my way to purchase food up at the counter. Once the coast is clear, I snatch the coat.

I tuck it beneath my arm, and immediately, a cool rush of air reaches my lungs. I weave through the diners, that slight, adrenaline-inducing fear pumping through me. But the fear only speeds my steps, pushing me out into the terminal.

Jocelyn and Cadence emerge from the bathroom just as I shove the coat into my backpack, zipping it up inside. When I hand over their luggage, my collar feels looser, my limbs steady again.

CHAPTER 2
CADENCE

We nearly miss the train again, thanks to Jocelyn's organizational skills, or lack thereof. When we finally reach the platform, she grabs her leather travel wallet from her bag, only it's unzipped. The entirety of its contents spills onto the bacteria-infested ground. Papers fly everywhere, behind trash cans, under travelers' feet. Luckily—with the help of an elderly gentleman who finds Jocelyn's passport under a bench—we manage to collect it all, locate the tickets, and jump in the closest train car before the whole thing chugs away from the station.

The ride from Manchester to Conwy, Wales, takes roughly two and a half hours. I planned on napping for most of it since I'm exhausted, thanks to the middle-of-the-night layover at JFK and jet lag. But I'm unable to tear my eyes away from the view out the window. Rowan's gaze is equally fastened on the scenery: miles upon miles of green hills and pastures full of grazing sheep, cut only by long, narrow stretches of vacant coast. Occasionally, we pass a little tract of homes or pause at a miniature station to let a few travelers out. From the terrain to the fog, it's nothing like home, and I can't wait to explore.

Jocelyn wants to spend the week relaxing, but there's so much to see. I have a list of sights bookmarked on my phone as well as a very tentative itinerary: castles, national park, the highest peak in Wales, a small isle—not to mention all these charming seaside towns with their restaurants and historic city walls. The last time I was on a trip like this was when Jocelyn took me to Rome to celebrate our college graduation. She was the same way back then, wanting to sit in a piazza and sip wine and eat gelato all day. Trust me, we made it to the Colosseum, the Forum, the Sistine Chapel—you name it, I dragged her there. We still had time to eat plenty of gelato, and deep down, I know she's grateful I pushed her.

I did my best to let Jocelyn handle the arrangements for her bachelorette trip; she's paying for the travel expenses and meals, after all. It's *her* aunt and uncle who are graciously providing lodgings. So when I noticed that Conwy Station isn't the closest one to our bed-and-breakfast, I only asked once if she'd run the itinerary by her aunt and uncle. She assured me that she didn't need to bother them; she'd been her own travel agent for two decades. "Thanks, but we don't need a valedictorian on this job, Cady."

I smiled, silently fuming the way I always do when she and Rowan call me that, since they know good and well that I lost the title and was extremely bitter about it for far too long. Then I backed off. Sometimes, it's better to simply let things run their course, to accept the consequences, rather than call Jocelyn Elliott out.

When the train creaks to a halt at Llandudno Station, I nudge Jocelyn, who's been sleeping on my shoulder ever since our stop at Crewe. "Hmm?" she asks, sitting up and rubbing her eyes.

"The next stop is ours." The train never pauses for long, so I gather my luggage from the overhead storage compartment. Our train car has completely cleared out, leaving us plenty of room. The girls follow suit, Jocelyn yawning and Rowan still fixated on the landscape.

Across the table, Rowan pulls a woven beanie from her bag and tugs it on over her curls. "Looks cold out there, doesn't it?"

I nod, sliding my arms into the sleeves of my khaki-green hooded jacket. "Definitely not the April of sunny SoCal." The train hisses and squeaks to a stop at Conwy Station, and water droplets begin to speckle the window. I pull up my hood and wheel my suitcase toward the door.

When I step down onto the platform, the wind sweeps my hood back, allowing the rain to pelt me in the face. The others join me, and the doors slide shut behind us, the train roaring to a start. It chugs away, its end snaking beneath a moss-covered stone archway. We back beneath the shelter to get out of the rain and collect our bearings, and I notice just how minuscule this platform is.

"Hmm," says Jocelyn, glancing around. "I guess we should head inside and ask about the car rental place."

"And a bathroom," Rowan says.

"Why didn't you use the one on the train?" I ask, trying not to sound like her mother and failing. But that is what I feel like. Only five-year-olds suddenly realize they have to go to the bathroom the moment it's too late. "Was it the germs?" I know that's the reason *I* didn't use it.

"No, I just kept picturing the train jolting to a halt and me falling over with my pants around my ankles."

Jocelyn laughs. "Still scarred from the motor home trip to Wyoming."

"Literally," Rowan says, referring to the summer after freshman year of college—when she emerged from the bathroom, she was bleeding from a gash where her forehead hit the sink.

We head around the building, dragging our belongings with us. Jocelyn approaches what we assumed to be a ticket counter, but it's merely an unmanned help point. There are no bathrooms, nothing else at all but a set of stairs leading up to the town.

Jocelyn shrugs. "I'll call the place." She starts up the stairs, and we follow, hefting our bags along. "I know it's somewhere nearby. We can probably walk."

As she pulls out her phone and wanders away, that awkward silence settles between Rowan and me. It's like being nineteen again and showing up to lunch at the cafeteria only to find out that Jocelyn couldn't make it. The meal would become a series of forced inquiries and shoveling food into one's mouth as quickly as possible to end the agony.

Rowan and I have always been friends, but it's the kind of friendship that often requires Jocelyn's third-party presence to function properly. Fortunately, this place is a conversation starter in its own right. Together, we take in what we can of the town. The air smells of fresh rain mingled with sea salt and grass—wholly unfamiliar yet completely intoxicating. I inhale it. We marvel at the stone walls that, according to my research, circle the entire town. "You can walk the whole thing," I say. "There are series of stairwells around it, leading up to the walls."

"Incredible," Rowan breathes, wrapping her arms around herself. She bends over to unzip her backpack, removing a jacket and shrugging it on. "That's better." She pulls the hood over her hat.

"It is chilly. That jacket your dad's?" It's not terrible, but the coat is big on her and definitely not Rowan Castillo's style. Though she's toned everything down since having Molly, Rowan has mostly maintained her quirky-artist-meets-cool-California-girl vibe. Bright colors, slouchy cardigans, sandals even in the rain. Her curly hair is always big and perfectly undone. The kind of hair you see on the street and covet.

Rowan reddens. "Yeah. He made me bring it. Says it's all-weather or whatever. 'For the hiking,'" she says, mimicking his gravelly voice. "The cute one's in my suitcase. Too much trouble."

I laugh; I can completely picture Rowan's dad saying that. He takes the outdoors very seriously. Before a camping trip back in high school, he gifted all three of us survival kits fit with a compass, bear spray, and a lighter. "Well, you may be grateful you brought it," I say. "It's always better to be overprepared. And you can fit some warm, chunky sweaters under it."

"I bet the locals are going to laugh at us, with our mittens and mountain jackets in the spring."

"Let 'em laugh. This has already been more rain than we see in a year."

A few yards away, Jocelyn's voice rises. "What do you mean it's booked for two days from now? I booked it for *today*, the fourteenth of April!" She holds the phone in her right hand, and with her left, she digs her fingernails into the skin at the back of her neck—Jocelyn's frazzled tell, the closest thing she has to a bad habit. During final exams senior year of college, she dug so hard she broke the skin.

"No other cars available until then? Are you kidding? What kind of place—okay, you know what? Just cancel the reservation. We'll rent from a place that actually has cars." There's a moment of silence, apart from the sound of Jocelyn's shoes pacing over the stone. "You're lying. This is absolutely unbelievable. You're a liar, and I hope you—" She flinches, as if the person on the other line reached through the phone and slapped her. I see the slow rise and fall of her chest as she lets the phone drop to her side, her eyes going distant.

Rowan and I dare to meander closer. "Everything okay, Joss?" I ask, though it's obvious it isn't. This is what I get for letting her handle the travel arrangements. She's staring down at her expensive leather travel wallet, and I get the distinct urge to grab it out of her hand, open it, and let the wind carry its contents out to sea. I picture the credit cards and itineraries hitching a ride on a swirling gust and Jocelyn's futile attempt to catch them.

She turns to us, frowning. Her hood is back, but she has that naturally straight hair that isn't bothered in any way by the elements. "There was a screwup with our car rental reservation." She throws a hand in the air. "So, now we have no transportation."

"Didn't you get a confirmation email a couple days ago?" I ask. It's not like I do much traveling, but that should be pretty standard, I would think.

"Yeah, maybe I just got the dates mix—"

"I'm sure we can rent a car somewhere else," Rowan offers.

"Well, if the asshole on the phone was telling the truth, the next rental place is in another town, and it's completely booked too. Apparently, everyone in northern England heads this way for spring vacation."

"What about an Uber?" Rowan asks.

I pull out my phone and start to search. "It only operates in Cardiff, down in the south. I'll get us a taxi. Once we're at the B&B, we can figure something out. I read that taxi is one of the main modes of transport around here anyway. We might not need to bother with a rental." To be honest, the idea of Jocelyn navigating unfamiliar routes on the opposite side of the road is a little unnerving. I smile and pull her in for a hug. "Everything's going to be fine."

She sighs. "You're right. The B&B might even be walking distance from everything we need anyway."

I nod, though I'm positive it isn't. When I looked up the Water View Bed and Breakfast, it seemed a pretty good distance from the other Conwy lodgings. Right smack in the middle of the woods.

A few minutes later, a black taxi pulls up. The driver, a ruddy-cheeked man with white hair, loads up our belongings. The three of us pile into the back seat, Jocelyn in the middle. When the driver asks for the address, Jocelyn digs through her travel wallet. "Sorry, just a second," she says, frowning. "Everything's all disorganized after—ugh." She gives up, letting the wallet plop into her lap. "I can't seem to find the address. Do you know the Water View Bed and Breakfast?"

"Oh yes, a lovely location," the man says in a pleasant Welsh brogue. "In the forest, edge of the river. We don't get many requests to go out that way."

"The forest?" Jocelyn asks. "I thought this was a beach town."

"It is," the driver says. "But your lodgings aren't in Conwy proper. You're out in Snowdonia. *Water View* refers to the river, not the ocean."

"How far a drive is it?" asks Rowan, who still hasn't peed.

"Maybe forty-five minutes."

She pales. "I might need to find a bathroom first."

"Closest one's the petrol station on the corner, but the toilet's out of service. Best to use the bushes." The man points to some shrubs off the road.

I dig a new pack of travel tissues from my backpack and hand them to her, but she waves me off.

"I'm a mom, remember?" Reaching into the small pouch of her backpack, she produces her own tissues as well as a travel bottle of hand sanitizer. Then she glances out the window, still undecided.

I put my tissues away, trying not to feel slighted. I've always been resident mother and nurse of the group. Even in our hall back at UCSB, people would come to me when they felt sick. I'd taken care of my mother while she battled cancer, sat by her side in the hospital countless times—including the time she developed a bacterial infection from that germ-infested place. Caring for her led to some of my own fears, but it also entitled me to a medical opinion. There were weeks when I visited Grace Ling down the hall every day before dinner. She'd torn her ACL playing soccer and counted on my visits during the recovery period. "Hey." I nudge Rowan. "You did it on the drive to Big Bear freshman year, and it was snowing."

She purses her lips. "Pretty sure my pee froze in midair."

Jocelyn whispers, "Urine crystals," and we break into a fit of giggles, just like we did back then.

The drive to the bed-and-breakfast takes more than forty-five minutes—fifty, to be exact. Joss is obviously still irked about the whole situation, but she refuses to accept the taxi fare Rowan and I offer. When her stomach rumbles, I hand her a bag of chips from my backpack, and she cheers up.

The views on the drive help too. The lush green hills, rocky crags, and bony trees lining the two-lane road have a calming effect. Rowan suggests we play a sheep counting game, which holds our interest for exactly one hundred and four sheep. We ask our driver—Phylip with a *y*—to stop at a little market so we can stock up on provisions to get us to dinnertime.

"Phylip," I call out after we return with our bag of goods. "How do you say 'thank you' in Welsh?"

"Diolch."

"Well then, diolch for stopping."

"Pass that over to me," Jocelyn says, taking the plastic bag from Rowan and removing the bottle of whiskey.

"You can't just drink that in here," I whisper.

"Sure you can," Phylip calls back. "Enjoy your vacation."

"Maybe you're right, Cades," Jocelyn says, popping the large cork off the bottle and taking a swig. "Taxis sound like the way to go. You want some, Phylip?"

I give her a warning look and mouth, *He's driving.*

"Oh no, I'm all right, thank you."

Jocelyn passes the bottle off to Rowan and squints at her phone. "Is anyone else getting service? I'm supposed to let Landon know that we arrived safe and sound."

I glance down at my own phone, disappointment unfurling inside me. "I haven't been able to get a signal since the train station."

"You won't get a signal out here," says Phylip. "Part of the charm."

Jocelyn's eyes grow in horror. "I'm sure Helen has Wi-Fi at the place," she whispers.

"Thought we were getting away from it all," I tease.

"We are. We don't need to be completely cut off from civilization, though. Don't you have—I don't know—work emails to answer or something?"

"Spring break, remember?" I graded my last stack of papers the night before we left. I'm free and clear for the entire week. I even took next Monday off so I could rest up after the trip.

"Well, some of us have people who need to get a hold of us." The words feel sharper than any physical prick. *Single Cadence.* Always alone. No one to love or be loved by, other than her mother. "I'm sure Rowan will need to FaceTime Molly."

I glance at Rowan, who stops sipping the whiskey. "Wait, you don't think we're actual—"

15

"Of course not," I say, though her bronze skin has gone pasty. "Even if Helen doesn't have Wi-Fi—which I'm sure she does—we'll get service in town." I reach past Jocelyn to take Rowan's hand. "You'll see Molly's adorable little face and hear her sweet voice every day. Promise."

She lets out a puff of air and passes the bottle to me. "Sorry. I just—I miss her."

"We know," Jocelyn says, throwing an arm around Rowan's shoulders.

But the gesture is as fake as her words. She has no idea how Rowan feels. Sure, Joss has been through hardship—perhaps worse than even Rowan—but she doesn't know what it's like to be away from her own child. Neither of us does; at least I don't pretend.

"Hey!" Jocelyn says, pointing across my lap out the window at a sheep farmer. "Isn't that your boyfriend?" she says, too low for Phylip to hear.

I roll my eyes. It's the same joke she's been using since we were teens, only back then, the target was the skinny kid with the Batman lunch pail or the ancient science teacher who couldn't remember to zip his pants. "You're not going to drink that?" she asks, not waiting for my response as she grabs for the bottle.

But I hold on to it, make her work a little to tug it from my grasp.

I let the fantasy play out in my head, as I have many times. I imagine myself raising the bottle high overhead. I can almost hear the whip of wind and the crack of her skull as the glass comes down on it.

CHAPTER 3
JOCELYN

We're deep in the woods when the trees clear. Sunlight pours into the space to illuminate the log cabin. It's three stories with a gabled roof and a few small balconies on the second level, overhanging the garden.

"Guess the rain stopped." Rowan leans forward in her seat to peer through the partially fogged windshield.

"It'll be back," Phylip says, navigating us along a windy dirt road to park behind the only other car.

"It's spectacular." Rowan unbuckles her seat belt and gets out of the car to help the driver with the bags.

I have to agree. The grand wood cabin is nestled among the pines, and from our vantage point on the road, you can just make out the sparkling blue water behind it. The sound of the birds and the rushing river drifts in through the open car door. The landscaping is pristine, the colorful spring flowers in full bloom. The location is a dream.

Just not the dream I'd envisioned. My aunt and uncle have been working on this place nonstop for the past two years, so they haven't gotten around to creating an actual website with photos of the B&B. Why didn't my aunt bother to mention that it was in the middle of nowhere? If I'd wanted to stay in the woods, I would've driven the mere hour and a half to Big Bear, not flown across the ocean and taken a train ride. I check my phone again, gritting my teeth at the utter lack of signal bars, and crawl out of the car.

After paying Phylip and taking my bag, I stop him again. "If we need a ride to town, are there taxis out this way? Or should I call you again?"

Phylip frowns and tucks his shirt in. "Oh no, you won't find taxis out here. I'll give you my personal number, and we can arrange something. I should admit, though, it'll be expensive. And I'd need to know in advance, so as I don't book another ride."

"Right." I take the number from him and stuff it into my jacket pocket. Having forgotten the Welsh word already, I thank him in English and head after the others along a cobblestone path leading to the front porch.

As Cadence reaches the steps, the door opens and Helen bursts through it. "You're here!" Despite my frustration, I flash a smile to match hers. "Here, here," she says, scuttling down the porch steps to help Cady with her suitcase.

"Oh, I've got it, Helen. Thanks. This place is absolutely stunning."

"Isn't it?" She hugs Cady, who she's met at various family functions over the years. My aunt's hair, normally dyed a rich chestnut, has grown out into its natural gray hue. It suits her, as does its shorter length and the sweater she's wearing, a burnt-orange shade that matches some of the foliage around us. She's leaner than I remember, hard labor around this place having toned her muscles.

"Rowan," Helen says next, her smile dimming. My aunt embraces Rowan, and I begin to dread my turn as her eyes fill with tears.

"Thanks so much for letting us stay here," Rowan says, wiping her own eyes as my aunt finally releases her. I guess that's the way it is when you last saw a person under tragic circumstances. You go back to how you felt in that moment. The last time the four of us were together was at a funeral, the feeling a sadness so intense it strangled me.

Helen's gaze moves to mine next, and I have to look away. I've seen her many times since my brother Jake's funeral. She helped out with my mother—her sister, Teresa—who was so trapped in her grief that she basically checked out of her life. My mother is still breathing, but she's not living.

Seeing Helen now brings it all back. Day after day of the two of us trying to force my mother to eat, to get out of bed, to remember she still had a husband and a daughter. Putting all of my effort into caring for her so I could avoid facing my own brokenness. So I could ignore the fact that I'd lost something so precious, so integral to my identity, that I'd never be whole again.

Helen had been there the day my brother died too. Back then, she only lived a few minutes from us, and rushed over the second she heard the news. I can still see the look on her face as she walked through the door. An expression that mirrored everything I felt: the horror, the grief. The utter realization that life would never be the same.

When Helen bought this place and moved out here, I was bitter at first. She'd finally given up on my mother and abandoned her. I was angry that she'd been not only willing, but able to simply decide to be done with all of that. She'd gotten a brand-new start, while the rest of us remained trapped in our grief. Of course, she claimed that she and Uncle Paul were simply on vacation when they'd fallen in love with the land and the culture.

All I know is that my mother had already lost a son, and then suddenly, she'd lost a sister too.

Maybe the bitterness—that resentment I've held against my aunt—is the reason I had to come out here. A chance to purge my soul of these feelings I've harbored for years. It's not like I can't afford my own lodgings.

The bitterness is also likely the reason I never asked many questions about this place. It's the reason we're now miles from any of the sights and restaurants, surrounded by trees instead of ocean and ancient city walls.

Helen moves closer, wrapping her arms around me. "Jossy," she whispers into my hair. "How are you, my dear?" I've missed her voice, that husky quality that reminds me of my mother.

"I'm well."

"And getting married." She pulls back to smile at me, her eyes red and watery. "I'm so happy for you. Now, let's get you all inside before the rain starts up again."

We enter the cabin, finding ourselves inside a rustic reception area. I breathe a sigh of relief. When I heard "bed-and-breakfast," I pictured those horrible Victorian-era places with rose-covered wallpaper. The simplicity of this room, however—the exposed brick fireplace off to the left, the white-paneled walls, the unfinished pine desk adorned with only a glass vase filled with wildflowers—it's perfect. My job as an events planner and interior designer has me constantly criticizing everything, but I'm having trouble finding fault with this space.

"Like what we've done with the place?" Helen asks, as if reading my mind.

"It's gorgeous," Cady answers for me.

"Better than I could've done," I say, to which my aunt laughs.

"Let's not exaggerate." She wanders back behind the desk and starts fiddling with her computer mouse.

"So, you do have Wi-Fi." I tug my phone out and navigate to the settings. "What's the password? I haven't checked in with Landon since the baggage claim—"

"Well, that's the thing." My aunt bites her lower lip. "We've been having some trouble getting it to work out here." My stomach drops. "It comes and goes. The guy was out here just yesterday and claimed it was fixed, but . . ." She squints at the screen. "Maybe one of you young people can figure it out." She throws her hands up, sidestepping out of the way as Cady slips into her place.

"Better get it to work, Cady," I say, "or we're stuck out here with no car."

"We do have a landline," Helen says, "but I thought you were renting."

"There was a mix-up with our reservation," Rowan explains, knowing I'm on the verge of a fit.

"Where are my manners?" my aunt says, slapping her palm against her forehead. "You must be thirsty and exhausted. Here, sit." She directs us to a bistro table set in front of the fireplace and scurries off through a door to the left. A few minutes later, she returns, setting a tray of waters and biscuits down.

Helen carries a glass and a biscuit over to Cady, who accepts them with a frown. "The tap water is safe to drink, I assume?"

"Jeez, Cady," I say with an eye roll. "My aunt isn't trying to poison you."

"No, I know," Cady says, cheeks reddening. "I usually research these things ahead of time, but I forgot."

"I assure you, the water is very safe," Helen says, wandering back to our table. "You know, it just occurred to me. Worst-case scenario, Paul can taxi you around, here and there."

"Where is Uncle Paul?" I'd assumed the car out front was his.

"On his daily route to town. He gets fresh produce and milk for breakfast."

"Are we your only guests this week?" asks Rowan, playing with something in her jacket pocket.

"You're not." Helen grins proudly. "All three rooms are booked for tonight. Some newlyweds arrived yesterday, and another couple is set to check in any minute."

A tendril of guilt weaves through me. When I accepted my aunt's offer of free room and board, I hadn't realized business would be booming. How the hell did she manage to complete the bookings with spotty Wi-Fi? "I'm happy to pay for our room," I say. "You obviously could've rented it out to paying customers."

"Don't be silly." Helen waves me off. "You're family. All of you."

"Any luck?" I ask Cadence, who's still working at the computer, her dishwater-blond hair draped over one shoulder.

"Not yet." She looks up from the screen, lips twisted. "Helen, where's your router?"

My aunt points to the corner. "So," she says, turning to Rowan and me. "What are your plans while you're out here?"

"We're hoping to lie low for the most part," I say. "Though Cady wants to do some sightseeing in Conwy."

"And Caernarfon," Cady calls from behind the desk. "And Snowdon."

"Oh." Helen glances out the window. "They're advising against Snowdon right now. Rain makes the path too slick. There are plenty of hikes around here or in the park, but the peak is a bit too dangerous."

"Thank goodness," I mumble at the same time Rowan whispers a sarcastic, "That's a shame." We stifle giggles and avoid Cady's glare.

"Are there any restaurants in walking distance?" Rowan asks. "We'd hate to bother Paul too much."

"There is a pub, through the woods and down the road a ways. Maybe a twenty-minute walk."

"Sounds like dinner plans," I say, relieved that we aren't entirely cut off from civilization.

"But I should warn you," Helen says uncertainly, tucking some gray hair behind her ear. "Be careful of the roads around here."

"Why is that?" Rowan asks.

Helen presses her lips flat, like she's regretting having spoken. "There was an incident this past week. Not *here*." She waves a hand as if to diffuse the terror. "It was in Chilham—that's a couple hours outside of London. But a foreign traveler went missing on a rural road."

"Are you saying there's some sort of killer on the loose?" I ask with a laugh.

"Of course not." She shakes her head. "I'd just as soon believe it was a gwyllgi, like in the tales that come from the east."

"A gwi-what?" Cady asks, pausing her work.

"Oh, the gwyllgi is a Welsh legend. The dog of darkness. A large black hound or wolf with red eyes that can breathe fire. In North East Wales, they say he haunts the lonely roads at night, stalking travelers. Just one look at him can paralyze a grown man, and some even say the beast is the devil himself." She lifts her brows playfully. "As far as I know, the creature doesn't get out this way, so you can sleep easy. But I can't help thinking"—she sobers now—"that if that girl last week didn't just run off of her own free will . . . just be careful, that's all I'm saying. Always stay together. Never walk alone on the dark, rural roads."

I share a look with Rowan, and she covers her grin with a biscuit. "We'll be careful, Helen," I say. "I'm sure Cady has studied the martial arts. We'll be fine."

My aunt inhales deeply, chuckling on the exhale. "Ignore me. I'm getting imaginative in my old age. Let's hear more about the wedding. You're finally marrying the man of your dreams! How do you feel?"

"Happy, of course." It's true. I've known Landon was the one ever since we met freshman year of college. He'd been seeing someone else back then. But it didn't take long for that relationship to unravel and for him to ask me out. We couldn't get enough of each other. If we weren't physically together, we'd be on the phone. I'd lie on the bottom bunk in my dormitory room, talking for hours and putting off my studies.

We've been together ever since. Other than Cady, he's been the one constant in my life, the person I could always count on. He was there for me when my brother, Jake, passed away. My grief was all-consuming, but he never shied away from it.

"How are the plans coming along?"

"Everything is set." I sip my water. "You know me. Planning weddings is what I do."

"It isn't harder, though, having it be your own?"

I smile wryly. "I've been waiting for Landon to propose for the past six years. There's been plenty of time to decide exactly how the day would go." I'd never quite understood his reasoning on the wait, to be honest. Yes, we both valued having a career. But we'd lived together for half a decade. He believed in the idea of marriage. He loved me—I knew that. I just couldn't figure out why he didn't want to marry me.

Over at the desk, Cady clears her throat. I know that deep down, she's never much liked Landon or our relationship. But she does her best to hide it; that's the sort of friend she is. "If you all want to get settled, I can sort this."

"You sure?" asks Rowan. "We can wait." She starts toward the desk. "Or I can have a look."

"Nah, it shouldn't take too long. By the time you're ready for dinner, it'll be up."

I shrug. "A shower sounds amazing, actually."

Helen grabs Cady's bag and points to the stairs at the back of the room. "This way, then."

She leads us up a winding staircase to the second floor. We pass a door marked ROOM 1, and she stops at the next one, labeled ROOM 2. "Here we are." Pulling a set of skeleton keys from her jacket pocket, she unlocks it.

Inside, the decor matches the reception area in its simplicity: dark wood flooring, a pair of full beds with matching white comforters, folded blankets piled at the foot of each. A rustic bedside table stands between the beds, and the door to the bathroom is off to the left. "This is perfect," Rowan says. "Thank you, Helen."

"It's a joy to have the three of you with us this week," Helen says, removing a key from the ring and placing it in Rowan's hand. "When you're all settled and have some time, I want to hear all about little Molly. Photos too, please."

"Of course." Rowan smiles as Helen leaves the room.

Alone together for the first time in ages, the unease rushes back. Rowan must feel it, too, because she begins rifling through her things without so much as a glance my way. "You can take the first shower," she says, removing her coat and folding it.

"Okay." Neither of us mentions the fact that there are only two beds, meaning two of us have to share. There's no discussion to be had.

Rowan and I were never as close after my brother Jake's death. We became constant reminders of that loss to each other. Me, his spitting image, from my hair color to the pattern of my freckles. My blue-green eyes that matched his. She hasn't been able to celebrate my birthday—*his* birthday—for the past eight years.

She, well, she's been that gutting reminder to me. In every family photo of Rowan and Molly, there's a hole beside them where my twin should be.

And let's not forget Molly herself. If you placed my second-grade school photo alongside hers, you'd be hard pressed to tell us apart. She's got my smile and my auburn hair—her dad's auburn hair.

But the reminders aren't the only reason we haven't been close. I suppose I've been a bit wary of Rowan since Jake's death. Not that she *did* something to him—I know Rowan couldn't hurt a fly, much less the boy she'd been in love with for two years. But I've wondered if she knew more about the circumstances leading up to the tragedy than she ever let on.

Or maybe I've been an idiot. Maybe I've only ever been suspicious of Rowan because of my own secret.

The one I could never tell her.

NOW

Sirens sound in the distance. Lights flash, little blazing beams dancing their way through the pines.

Helen, wrapped in her husband's embrace, chokes on a hysterical sob and glances up. "The police," she says. "Paul, show them where we are."

Her husband nods, taking his flashlight and striding off in the direction of the road.

When he's gone, Helen stands over the body, her tears mixing with the rain that's falling harder now. "I wish I'd done more. I'm so sorry, girls."

I try to answer, but the words get caught in my throat.

"What will we tell them?" my friend—the one who's still alive—whispers in my ear.

I cough, finding my voice but also triggering my gag reflex. "That we found her like this, just now."

"And the others?"

I nod. "We'll tell them all about the others." Then I wander over to a nearby shrub and vomit.

CHAPTER 4
ROWAN

While Jocelyn is in the shower, I dig my hand back inside the jacket pocket. Sure enough, it's filled with a wad of cash—close to two hundred pounds—and a train ticket to some Welsh town, dated today. That guilt that snaked around me downstairs when I felt inside the pocket tugs tighter now. I didn't just steal a jacket; I wrecked someone's trip.

The guilt always trickles in, eventually. I try to take things that can be easily replaced; I obviously missed the mark this time. Still, this guilt is better than the suffocating feeling—the one I'd be drowning in if I hadn't taken anything.

This is something I do. I take things that don't belong to me. I wish I didn't, but nothing else helps me to cope when the weighty thoughts press in. My friends don't know—they've never known. And they can never find out.

Because one time, I stole something irreplaceable.

The shower turns off. I grab the wad and stuff it beneath the contents of my suitcase, then drape the jacket over my bed and search for my toiletry bag.

The room door clicks open and Cadence enters. "Good news!" she says as Jocelyn emerges from the bathroom wrapped in a towel. "I got us a ride to the pub for dinner."

"Oh good!" Jocelyn says, rifling through her suitcase. "You fixed the Wi-Fi, then?"

"Well, no." Cady reddens. "I tried everything I could from this end. It's got to be the provider's issue. Helen says she'll call them in the morning."

Jocelyn grumbles under her breath. The heavy thoughts start to push in: *I've never gone an entire day without talking to Molly. She'll be in a panic if I don't check in. My parents will worry. Maybe I can use the landline, though I have no idea how much that will cost.*

"How did you manage a ride then?" I ask in an attempt to avoid the thoughts.

"A couple just checked in, and they've got a car. I got to chatting with them a bit. They're headed out for dinner anyway, and they have room."

Jocelyn, standing in a bra and underwear, shrugs on a paper-thin shirt and begins to towel dry her hair. "You're telling me you actually want to get in a car with two strangers, Cady?"

"I mean, no." She picks at her fingernails. "But I don't really want to take that walk down the lonely road at night either."

I see her point. Mythical wolf creature or not, I'd get in a car with two strangers if it meant avoiding that trek, especially after the day of travel we've had. "Maybe she's right."

"Oh, come on, Rowan," Jocelyn says in a bored tone. "*You're* not afraid."

It hurts a little because she's referring to the old me, her fearless friend. I'm not that person anymore. Motherhood has made me cautious. I'm no longer living for myself. I have a daughter who needs me.

Jocelyn, more than anyone, should understand that people change. After all, she used to be my most loyal friend, and the instant Molly came along, she bailed. "To be fair, both options come with risks."

"I'm not up for small talk with foreigners," Jocelyn whines. "It's not like some killer is going to attack all three of us on the road. That traveler girl was probably a stupid college student who wandered off on her own."

"Right." Cadence's cheek puckers like she's chewing the inside of it. "Well, I can go back down and tell them never mind."

A thump sounds from the next room over, followed by a door clicking shut.

"They're staying in the next room?" I ask.

Cady nods. "Yeah, should I—" She gestures with a thumb in that direction.

Rain pitter-patters against the sliding glass door, and Jocelyn crosses the room to pull aside the curtain. Frowning, she lets the fabric fall back down. "Maybe we could just stay in tonight."

"We don't have any food," I say.

"My aunt does."

"I don't know," Cady says. "She's already gone to a lot of trouble."

"She's family. She said it herself."

"This couple—they seem really nice." Cadence's smile is hopeful. "If they give you the wrong vibe, we can walk back."

"That seems like a reasonable offer," I say, gathering my toiletries. "You two decide." It's not like they're asking my opinion, anyway. I close myself off in the bathroom and let them continue chattering about our new neighbors.

By the time I've finished up, my stomach is growling. "It's all yours, Cady," I say, moving to where I laid out my clothes on the bed. "What'd you decide about dinner?"

They giggle. "We're going to take the ride, if that's all right with you," Jocelyn says.

"Good, I'm starving. What made you change your mind?"

"Oh, just hungry too." On the bed, she digs out her mascara and a compact mirror from her makeup bag.

"More like she saw the guy," Cady says, rolling her eyes as she retreats into the bathroom.

"What does that mean?" The room is chilly, and I rush to get my clothes on.

Grinning, Jocelyn leans forward conspiratorially. "He came and knocked on the door to see if we were ready." Her eyes widen. "Um, Rowan. It would've been a crime to turn him down. I mean, *hello*, I have two single friends."

"I thought Cady said he arrived with someone."

"Well, yeah. But he's not wearing a ring." She lifts her brows and begins to apply lip gloss. "It could be his sister, for all we know. And you saw how desperate Cady was to get in his car."

"Cady did all this because of a guy," I say flatly.

Jocelyn laughs. "Of course not. I'm surprised Cady got up the nerve to talk to a strange man, let alone a handsome one, at all."

I am too, to be honest. While Cadence is intelligent and successful at most things she attempts, she's never been particularly good with men. She's never had a boyfriend, and when she does allow Jocelyn to set her up, it never goes past one or two dates. Cady is picky, that much is clear. But she also sabotages every relationship that has an ounce of potential.

Not that I'm one to talk. I've had a handful of boyfriends since Jake. But they've never reached the stage where I'm willing to introduce them to Molly. Maybe I've gotten overly picky too; I have my reasons. Molly already missed out on having a father once. A really good one. At least, I know he would've been, if he'd had the chance. I refuse to bring someone into her life only to have them ripped away again. If I do allow a man into our lives, he will be *the one*.

"Trust me, Rowan. That accent." Grinning, Jocelyn feigns a shiver.

I shrug and root around for my own makeup bag.

Molly isn't here tonight, and we've come all this way to have a good time.

◆ ◆ ◆

When Cadence says she's ready, her hair is in a chaste braid down her back, and her face is bare and pink from the shower.

Jocelyn blocks the door. "Cady, there is an extremely hot guy in the next room. Go try again." She gestures toward Cadence's things, which are now neatly tucked away in her suitcase.

Cady glances down at her frumpy sweater that's pilling so badly I can see it from across the room. "I'm starving, Joss."

"Same," I say.

Jocelyn sighs dramatically and skirts around the bed. "It'll take two seconds. Where is your . . ." She tosses some items of clothing around the suitcase, and her hand emerges with a little bag. "Aha! Get over here." She pats the bed, and Cady, grimacing, marches over.

After a quick application of blush and mascara, Jocelyn declares her "good enough." We walk to the next room and knock. The door opens, and a tall, muscular man with blond hair and sparkling blue eyes appears. "Hello." He smiles at Cady, and then his friendly eyes rove over to me. He looks around our age. "I don't think we've met," he adds in an accent that could be Scandinavian. "I'm Magnus."

Jocelyn wasn't exaggerating. He's gorgeous.

"Rowan," I say, my face growing hot.

"Thanks so much for waiting," Cadence says shyly. "And for offering to drive us."

"It's our pleasure." He cranes his neck back. "Val, you ready?"

"Yes, coming!" a female voice with a Spanish accent says. A moment later, a stunning, dark-haired woman is at the door. She looks younger than Magnus, perhaps around twenty-five. "I'm Valentina." Together, they make a head-turning couple.

After introductions, the five of us head outside into the rain, squeezing inside Magnus's rental car. It's a Volkswagen mini that only sits four, so Jocelyn is essentially sitting on top of us. "Sorry about the space," Magnus calls back to us.

"It's fine," Jocelyn says. "We went to high school together, so it's nothing new. One time Rowan sat in my lap in the back of a MINI Cooper for two hours. Remember that, Ro?"

"Oh yeah. On the way to Pete's lake house." We'd managed to pack seven people into a four-seater.

"My legs kept going numb," Jocelyn adds with a laugh.

I'd never appreciated Jocelyn more than in that moment. I knew she was in pain, and it was too tight for us to switch places. But this creepy guy—Donny something—kept teasing that I should move onto *his* lap. Jocelyn grinned and bore the ride, then stuck to my side the entire weekend to make sure he couldn't get anywhere near me.

"I don't remember that," Cady says, and guilt knots up in my stomach. The lake trip was back when I had Jocelyn's favor and Cady was the third wheel. In fact, Cady hadn't even been invited on that trip because some of the guys thought she was too much of a prude. We'd gone without her, and Jocelyn, queen of lies, told her we were both stuck in bed with food poisoning.

"It was a long time ago," Jocelyn says. "So, Magnus and Valentina, are you going to be staying with my aunt for long?"

"Just three nights," Magnus says as the car emerges from the cover of the woods into a black void. His headlights shine onto the dark road, windshield wipers at full speed, the cold fogging up what little visibility he has. "We spent a few days in the northeast, seeing sights like Bodelwyddan Castle. Sorry, I'm sure I mispronounced it."

"Sounded fine to me," Jocelyn says.

"Anyway, just a quick stop here in the northwest, and on Wednesday, we'll take the ferry to Ireland."

"That sounds fun," Cadence says, perking up. "I'd love to see Ireland."

"You should come with us," Magnus says.

"Oh." Cadence titters nervously. "Well, we're only here for the week. I'm a teacher back in the States. I've got to be in class on Tuesday."

"Cadence is *very* responsible," Jocelyn says teasingly.

"Won't your students survive without you for a few days?" Valentina peers back to smile at Cadence.

Jocelyn was right. The relationship between those two is a bit confounding. If it's a couple's trip, why is Valentina so keen to have another woman in tow?

Maybe they're friends. Based on accents and coloring alone, siblings seems unlikely. I peer around Jocelyn's shoulder. "Where are the two of you from?"

"Argentina," Valentina says. "And Magnus is from Norway."

"That's so interesting." Jocelyn glances back at me deviously. "How did the two of you meet?"

"At a hostel in Switzerland," Magnus says. "A few weeks back."

"You only just met?" Cadence asks, failing to mask her horror.

Valentina laughs. "I'd been traveling alone for weeks already and was about to head back to Argentina. Then I met Magnus, who'd only started his trip when his companion had to fly home for a funeral. So, we got to talking, and he invited me to take his friend's place."

A little flurry of hope goes through me at this news, followed quickly by shame. I didn't come on this trip to find a man—certainly not a man most likely tied to a life in Norway.

"I work remotely anyway," Valentina continues, "for a marketing firm back home. So I figured, what the hell, you know? Why not extend the trip and see more of the world? You only live once." She reaches across the seat to run her fingernails through Magnus's hair, flashing a large rhinestone-studded butterfly ring, and any clarity I had is trampled by confusion again. There's obviously something there, no matter how shallow or new. I wonder how many beds are in their room.

She turns back to look at me now. "And you, Rowan? What keeps you from staying on?"

"Oh, I'm an administrative assistant for a bank." I wind a curl around my finger and clarify "a secretary" even though they didn't ask for clarification.

For a while, people would laugh whenever I gave out my job title, like I was joking. In high school, I'd been the one with the daring fashion choices and dreams of becoming a full-time artist. The multicolored hair alone didn't quite mesh with the image of a bank secretary. These days, people don't blink when I tell them. I'm this person now: Rowan Castillo, the administrative assistant. The woman who works ten-hour shifts in a stiff pantsuit, answering phones and following orders, then comes home just in time to put her daughter to bed. Painting? I can't remember the last time I held a brush. I want to believe my hand would still know what to do, that my soul would still breathe passion and color and life onto the canvas. I force a smile at Valentina. "The place barely runs without me."

"Helen said the pub would be around here somewhere," Magnus says, leaning forward to squint through the windshield. "On the right."

I can't see much, other than Cady on my right and Jocelyn's back directly ahead. The left window is a black blur. My body sways, and Jocelyn nearly topples off my lap as the car turns again before bumping along a dirt road.

"There it is," Valentina says, pointing. I can just make out the lights through the trees, and even in the small, stuffy space, any tension dissipates. "Park here."

Magnus turns off the engine, and we all spill out, pulling up our hoods as the rain beats down. I zip up my stolen jacket, pleased to find that it's keeping me nice and toasty despite the elements. A paved path leads up to the door, where two lamps illuminate the building's facade. The white pub is a little run-down, but fit with charm from its thatched roof to its Tudor-style dark trim.

Inside, the dimly lit pub is filled with music. Three empty tables dot the way to the bar, at which two elderly men sit, drinking beers. When we approach, their easy chatter in Welsh halts, and they turn to eye us.

"Good evening," Valentina says.

"Eve'nin," one of them answers. The other continues to stare as though a herd of buffalo just stormed through the bar door. Apparently, this pub doesn't receive many travelers.

The door behind the bar opens, and a younger man with messy brown hair and a five-o'clock shadow emerges. "Welcome," he says without smiling. He's wearing a gray button-down shirt with the sleeves rolled up, revealing his many tattoos. Jocelyn nudges me—because he's my type. "Take a seat at the bar, or if you prefer, the table at the corner is nice and private. Has a fireplace to get you warmed up."

"The fireplace sounds nice," Valentina says, glancing in the direction he pointed. I watch Jocelyn shut her parted lips and frown, used to being the voice of the group.

"What can I get you to drink, then?" asks the bartender.

"Two gin and tonics," Jocelyn answers before Valentina has a chance. "And . . ." She glances at me with a dumbfounded look; it's been too long since we've been out together.

"I'll have a beer," I say. "Something Welsh, please."

The bartender nods, and Jocelyn turns to our new friends. "You two? We're buying tonight. It's the least we can do."

Magnus shakes his head. "You don't have to—"

"I insist." Jocelyn waves him off.

Shrugging, he turns to the bartender. "Two of whatever beer she's having." I can't help but notice that he ordered for Valentina.

My gaze flicks to the men at the bar, who are no longer staring at us; instead, they're fixated on the television screen mounted over the bar shelves. It's a news story. The caption at the bottom of the screen reads, "Lisa Granger's Mother Speaks Up."

We get settled around the low table near the fireplace, and Magnus drags over an extra chair to make five. The bartender soon brings over our drinks and takes food orders. Jocelyn asks for the Wi-Fi password and immediately gets up to call Landon.

Cady glances down at her own phone, frowning. It must be hard always having to check in with her mother.

"So, what are your plans while you're here?" Magnus asks, leaning back in his chair, beer in hand.

Smiling, Cady navigates through her phone to pull up a detailed itinerary. "This is what I was thinking." She glances at the corner of the pub, where Jocelyn seems to be having trouble getting through to Landon. "But it's a relaxing girls' trip, so nothing's set in stone. Conwy tomorrow, then Caernarfon Tuesday. I wanted to hike to Snowdon, but Helen says that's not allowed right now."

"It's allowed," Valentina corrects, sliding her sparkly gold phone into her coat pocket. "Just not"—she pauses, lips twisted as if in thought—"Reco—what's the word?"

"Recommended," Magnus says.

"Right," Cady says. "We're not very experienced hikers, so we'll probably pick an easier trail in Snowdonia if the rain lets up."

"Val and I are going hiking tomorrow morning," Magnus says, stripping off his sweater. Down to a T-shirt, his muscular arms are on full display. "You should come."

"Oh, really?" Cadence brightens. "Which hike?"

"We can't," Jocelyn says, pulling back her chair and plopping down in it. "We've got Conwy tomorrow, right Cady?"

"I mean, that's what I put down. But I thought—"

"Well, if that's what you put down, that's what we're doing." She grins over at Magnus. "These two don't travel much, so we're really trying to make the most of our time here. You know, seeing as much as possible. Cady's a very thorough planner, so we let her lead."

Cadence blushes and takes a sip of gin and tonic. Apparently, it's too big a sip, and she starts to cough. "Sorry," she mutters, wiping her lips.

"Well, I think that's great," Valentina says. "Three good friends seeing the world. You are extremely lucky."

"We know." Jocelyn reaches out with both hands to squeeze mine and Cadence's.

It's slightly sickening, the way she can say one thing and mean another. She's taken every opportunity to whine in my ear about that itinerary—complaining she's already seen too many castles to count, that she'd rather sit back and relax before her big day. I'm surprised she even remembered the name of the town.

Either Jocelyn really hates the sound of a hike, or she hates the idea of sharing us tomorrow. That's the thing about Joss. She doesn't have a problem lying if she feels threatened or even slightly bothered. And the lies come to her easier than fish to a worm.

"I'm going to call Molly," I say. It's Sunday, so she's likely hanging out at home with my parents.

"Tell my niece how much I miss her," Jocelyn says in a sugary-sweet voice.

And there's another lie. In order to miss her niece, Jocelyn would need to have a relationship with Molly in the first place.

CHAPTER 5
CADENCE

When Rowan gets up to call Molly, the bartender returns with the food. I ordered the lamb soup, which comes steaming in a large bowl and smells divine. The others dig in, and Jocelyn starts a sidebar with Valentina. I know what she's doing. She's been doing it ever since we were teens: trying to create opportunities for her pathetic best friend.

I wish I could tell her the truth—that I don't need a man in my life.

It's not something I could ever share with Jocelyn, though, considering that the only man I've ever loved is the one she's about to marry.

I blow on my soup, then fold my napkin neatly over my lap. I should probably check in with my mother. I did call while we were waiting for our baggage, but she'll want to know that we reached the B&B. She worries about me. Actually, we worry about each other, ever since her cancer scare several years back. I'll call after I get some food in me.

I sneak a glance at Magnus, who catches me. "Looks good," he says, smiling.

I nod stupidly, the embarrassment and hot steam mingling to create my own personal sauna.

The Landon thing happened innocently enough. He and I met in freshman biology at UCSB. I fell in love with his smile and his green eyes. At first, I was confused. I was used to being the plain one, the invisible friend. My hair was straight and mousy blond, whereas

Rowan's was gorgeously curly and Jocelyn's was a vibrant shade of auburn that even movie stars would kill for. Rowan had a dazzling tan year round, while my skin was prone to acne. I was flat chested where my friends were developed, even back when we met at fourteen. My nose had a prominent bridge that made me self-conscious. I thought that, like all the guys in high school, this boy was only speaking to me because I was smart, especially when he invited me to his room to work on an assignment together.

But it turned out that he didn't need help in biology. He actually wanted to hang out with me. Without my prettier, magnetizing friends at my side, I'd suddenly become desirable. Landon and I fooled around, and when I went back to the dorm room I shared with Jocelyn and Rowan; told them I'd been with my new study partner. I don't know why I didn't tell them the whole truth—that I'd met a guy. Maybe I was afraid that if Landon ever saw my gorgeous friends, it would render me invisible all over again.

Maybe it was because I knew it was all too good to be true.

Landon and I spent more time together, and I fell for him harder. He fell for me too. He was the only person who never seemed annoyed by my endless, encyclopedic knowledge of random facts. "Some people have a fear of things like that," I said once, pointing out a wasp's nest behind his dormitory, where I'd asked him to meet me. "Trypophobia. It's a fear of holes that are closely packed together."

Landon smiled down at me, but not in the way that Joss would've. It wasn't an *Oh god, Cady. Here we go again* smile. It was something like fascination, which was quickly followed by his lips on mine. "Where'd you hear that?" he asked in a breathless voice.

"Oh, I must've read it in a book."

Sometimes, I swear he'd pretend to need a concept explained just so that he could say, "You're going to make a great teacher one day, Cadence." I confided in him about the valedictorian fiasco, and he looked angry enough on my behalf to make the three-hour drive to my school and punch out Mr. Pruit. That was when he told me about his own struggles with his dad. How the old man wanted Landon to end up at his law firm, to grow into a replica of himself. Landon wanted anything else.

One week, he came down with a nasty cold, and I got to nurse him back to health. I walked to the nearest CVS and stocked up on tissues, cough drops, and tea. "You're amazing," he said through a sniffle right before he fell asleep with his head in my lap, my fingers running through his hair.

We only ever hung out in his room or in the library. I didn't want the other girls to meet him yet, even though he'd started calling me his girlfriend.

Then one day, he stopped waiting for me after biology class. He stopped texting too. I asked if he wanted to study for our midterm together, and he replied, Sorry, this isn't working out.

I was gutted. But I'd known, hadn't I? It was the reason I'd kept so much of our relationship a secret from my roommates.

It wasn't until a few weeks later that I truly felt the depth of my devastation. That was the day that Jocelyn and Landon showed up at our dorm room, hand in hand.

Landon's eyes met mine, and I could tell he was just as stunned as I was. Jocelyn had told him about her roommates, Rowan and *Katie*—at least, that was the name he'd heard. Not *Cadence*, the name he'd come to know me by.

In that moment, we pretended to meet for the first time, cementing our history as this big dirty secret. It was already too late to come clean, so it would continue to sit in the backs of our minds, a haunting thing. Every time I saw the two of them together, it felt like one thousand needles jabbing me in the lungs. It showed me just how little I'd ever measure up alongside my best friend. Everything I'd believed about myself in high school became true again. I'd let myself entertain a fantasy.

The reality was this: I was ugly and pathetic. Nothing but a dirty secret.

If only I could've hated Landon for the way he cast me aside. If only I could've been grateful for the bullet I'd dodged. Instead, I continued to pine over him even as he held my friend's hand on a stroll across campus. Even as the two of them played footsie in the library. Even as he kissed her softly on the cheek right in front of me.

I kept waiting for them to break up. Jocelyn had had plenty of boyfriends, and none of them ever lasted long. Landon would be no different.

Except he *was* different. He never went. Only stayed and stayed. That black spot on my relationship with Jocelyn. The thing that made me hate her a little. The thing that made me hate myself even more. And at night, I continued to fantasize about him apologizing to me, admitting he'd made a huge mistake. About him kissing me softly, the way he kissed her.

When Jocelyn announced that they were engaged, I squealed with her, hugged her, took her out to celebrate. Afterward, I went home and threw up.

Jocelyn believes that because I can barely look at him or speak about him, deep down, I despise Landon. I'll never refute this. The truth—that I'm still in love with her fiancé after ten years—is so much worse.

I can see Jocelyn giving me looks from across the table. I still haven't engaged Magnus, and she's frustrated with how I've failed her, yet again.

There is one thing I'm genuinely interested in when it comes to our Norwegian neighbor, so I turn to him. "Sorry, we got interrupted before. Tell me more about tomorrow's hike."

"Ah, yes." He puts down his fork and dabs at his lips with a napkin. "The walk hits some of the stone formations in the area. It's become this strange . . . hobby, I guess you Americans would call it. Though maybe it's more of an obsession. You've heard of the Druid's Circle?"

"Only the little I read while researching for the trip. It's a misnomer, right? It's called the Druid's Circle, but it was actually constructed before the Celts even arrived in Britain, during the Neolithic period."

He smiles. "You're quite smart. And correct. There are several other prehistoric formations in the area. Some circles, some standing stones, even tombs. Everyone knows about Stonehenge, but in Wales there are many similar, though smaller, formations. No one knows exactly what they were used for, other than ceremonies or rituals, perhaps in an attempt to pacify the elements or to show reverence for the earth. Bones were discovered in many of them, indicating some sort of burial ritual, though they've likely been converted by various religions and people groups over the centuries—even now, modern pagans make the pilgrimage to the stones to practice worship."

"That's fascinating."

"We plan to drive out and make the trek to Druid's Circle as well as Circle 275." He finishes his beer and leans in. "I really hope your friend changes her mind, so you can join me."

I get a skin-tingling sensation, but it isn't just from Magnus's words. Across the table, the discussion seems to have gone silent. When I peek over, Jocelyn is still chatting away, but Valentina's brown eyes are fixed on *me*.

My face grows hot, and I look away. "Well, Jocelyn's sort of in charge. It's her wedding we're here to celebrate." I hear Valentina's staccato accent start up again and relax.

"That's right," Magnus says. "You mentioned that back in the B&B. And what about you? Any wedding plans in your future? A husband waiting for you back home?"

I busy myself with another spoonful of broth, finding it suddenly difficult to swallow. "Oh no. I'm single. No ties back home." I make the last part sound lighthearted, but the words pinch at my heartstrings.

"Really? A girl as beautiful as you?" He shakes his head. "Impossible."

I clear my throat. Guys don't often refer to me as *beautiful*. Girls either. I'm known for my brains. Being called *beautiful* by a strange man feels almost as fake as it does flattering. "My job keeps me busy. It's very fulfilling, teaching kids."

"Of course." He never takes his blue eyes off me. "A woman like you doesn't *need* a man."

I turn back to my soup. "How's the lamb?"

He laughs. "Sorry. I forgot all about it for a minute. It is delicious, though. Would you like to try some?" He brings a forkful of lamb across his plate, holding it up before me. Is he flirting with me?

Of course not. It's the gin and tonic talking. This extremely attractive man is not flirting with me. Not right in front of this gorgeous woman who's staying in his room tonight. Possibly even in his bed.

And yet.

"I'll let you enjoy it," I say as the marinade starts to drip onto the table. "I've got lamb in my soup."

He takes the bite himself, and when finished chewing, asks, "So, what do you like to do when you're not teaching? Or traveling to Wales."

"Oh, um . . ." I think about my free time, about what I do when I'm not inside the classroom or helping Jocelyn with maid-of-honor duties. I do have a hobby. An *obsession* of my own. But I can't share it with Magnus. I can't share it with anyone, actually. "I like to read," I blurt, racking my brain for the last book I've actually finished, in case he asks. "And crochet," I add. "I crochet all sorts of things."

Rowan sits down on my other side. "Cady is very good," she adds, examining her full bowl of beef stew. "She made my daughter the cutest hat for her last birthday."

It makes me sound like some sort of spinster, the single lady who sits at home alone, crocheting. It's better than the truth.

"And how old is your daughter?" Magnus asks her, though I catch his eyes trailing back over to mine.

"She's eight." Rowan's eyes light up the way they do whenever she speaks of Molly.

"And staying with her father this week?"

Her gaze drops to her plate, the light extinguished. "My parents. Molly's father passed away."

"I'm sorry." Magnus flushes. "You're raising her alone, then?"

Rowan nods, picking at her food. I'm torn between squeezing her hand and playing it off as no big deal to keep the attention off her.

Across the table, Jocelyn suddenly turns to us. "What am I doing? You're done with your drinks! I'll get more." Standing, she dusts a crumb off her sweater. "What are we having? The same?"

"Whiskey," Rowan says, though her beer is half-full.

"Yes!" Jocelyn throws a fist into the air. "Five whiskeys, then?"

I'm not a big whiskey drinker, and jet lag has me half-asleep as it is. But she's already halfway across the pub, and saying no to Joss is never quite worth it.

On our way to the car, I become aware of the light, empty feel of my coat pocket. "I must've left my phone back there!" I yell after the others, the rain swallowing my voice.

"What?" Jocelyn asks, sounding annoyed. "You really must be drunk, Cady." She's right; I'm rarely forgetful. "Check your pocket again!"

I obey, rain splattering me in the face as I pause. "It's not here." I start to turn when someone touches my back.

I spin around, squinting in the moonlight at Valentina's face beneath a dark-colored hood. "I grabbed it for you," she says, tugging my phone from her pocket.

"Oh. Thank you." Relief runs through me as I wrap my fingers around the case. But the feeling is soon replaced by disquiet.

It's true I had a lot to drink. I must've had my phone out on the table and simply forgotten it. But why didn't Valentina just give it back to me in the pub? Why did she wait until I remembered it was missing? On the ride back, I unlock my phone, going through the various apps. The insane thought that Valentina somehow went through it when I wasn't paying attention gnaws at my brain like an insect. I try to smash it or swat it away. It's ridiculous. My phone has a passcode.

When we return to the B&B, it's nearly 2:00 a.m. The rain is coming down so hard that just the dash from the car to the door has us drenched.

Inside, the reception area is dark and unmanned, Helen and Paul obviously having gone to bed. We hang our wet coats on the rack by the door.

Upstairs, I spot a note attached to Magnus and Valentina's door as we say our good nights. There's one taped to ours as well. Jocelyn takes it down, reading aloud as Rowan locks up. "'Sorry I missed you all. See you in the morning. If you need anything, dial seven. Love, Uncle Paul.'"

The heat is on, thankfully. Still, that chill from being wet and bone-tired won't be shaken until I'm safely beneath the covers.

Shivering, Rowan peels off her damp jeans and heads inside the bathroom. I change into my pajamas and wait for her to finish up. On the other side of the bed, Jocelyn, down to a T-shirt and some boxer shorts, is flipping through photos of her and Landon saved on her phone. When she giggles, I try to block it out the way I always do. But she tugs on my sleeve. "Well done, Cady. I honestly didn't think you had it in you."

I slide beneath the covers to warm up. "What are you talking about?"

"Magnus. The guy is like, *perfect*. And you engineered that entire thing, not only gifting all of us with his beauty, but a mode of transportation on a rainy night too."

"Well, I wasn't trying—"

"Oh, stop. He *likes* you. If the offer of a ride didn't prove it, whatever was going on in that pub certainly did."

Suddenly, the chill is gone, replaced by a burning heat. So, Magnus *had* been flirting with me. Embarrassment tangles with a sense of vindication. "He doesn't like me. He's with Valentina."

"I don't know about that." She wrinkles her nose. "The two of them don't really seem like a couple, do they? I mean, there's *something* going on. They're sharing a room."

I think of the possessive glare Valentina gave me back in the pub. Definitely something going on.

"But they also only just met," Jocelyn continues. "And they live on different continents."

"As do I," I say. "And even if he was interested, I'm not."

Her jaw drops. "You're *not interested* in a Norwegian god."

"Joss, I came on this trip for you, not for some guy."

"And I'm your best friend. I won't be offended if you find the love of your life"—she shrugs—"or even just get some action on this trip."

I know this isn't true. On the surface, Jocelyn oozes confidence, but the truth is she's completely insecure. Not many people can see it, but I do, the moment she feels displaced. If she were really fine with me going off with Magnus this week, she would've agreed to tomorrow's hike. "Forget it, Joss."

Rowan emerges from the bathroom, and I get off the bed. But she remains in the doorway, frowning. "The toilet's broken."

"Uck," Jocelyn says, looking down at her phone again.

"No, I mean, it's not like . . . *that*. But it won't flush."

"I guess we should dial seven," says Jocelyn.

"Oh, I'd hate to wake your aunt and uncle at this hour." Rowan glances back at the toilet uneasily.

"Well, it's their fault." Jocelyn slides off the bed. "If they had properly functioning toilets, they wouldn't get woken up." She moves over to the room phone on the bedside table.

"Maybe I can figure it out," I offer, leaving the comfort of the bed. "Is there a plunger?" I've lived alone long enough to know how to unclog a toilet. Frankly, I'm surprised Rowan doesn't. Though she rents and I own. She probably calls her landlord whenever an issue arises.

There's a knock at the door, and I startle.

"Who the hell is that?" Jocelyn glares at the door.

I tiptoe back to the bed as Rowan fumbles for some pants.

"It's Magnus," comes a deep voice. "Is everything all right in there? I heard something about a broken toilet."

My stomach drops. I look at Jocelyn, whose blue-green eyes are huge.

She scrambles to get up and open the door, not bothering to cover her pajama top, the thin fabric of which is completely sheer. She opens the door and lets him in. "You know how to fix it?" she asks, leaning against the door in a slightly provocative pose.

"I'm happy to take a look, if that's all right with you." He's changed into some sweatpants and a form-fitted black T-shirt. When Jocelyn moves aside to let him through, she mouths *Oh my god* behind his back and pretends to faint against the wall.

But my attention isn't on Magnus's physique. Our neighbors heard about the toilet through the wall.

What else did they hear?

CHAPTER 6
JOCELYN

In the morning, I wake up before the others. A faint light trickles in through the slit in the window blinds, painting highlights over the room. I attempt to slip out of bed without waking Cady when my gaze lands on the bedroom door.

It's wide open.

I double-check Rowan's bed, but she's dead asleep, dark curls splayed over her pillow.

"Cady," I say, reaching over to shake her.

With a groan, she starts to turn over. "What is it?" she asks, eyes still shut.

"Did you leave the door open?" I ask.

Now her eyelids spring open. She shoves the covers off her and sits up. "No, why would I do that?"

"Rowan," I hiss, too frozen to get up and shut the door. "Rowan!"

"Hmm?" she mumbles, rubbing her face.

"Did you leave the room last night?"

Cady moves to the bathroom, slowly inching inside to check it. A moment later, she calls, "All clear," before heading to the bedroom door.

"Rowan," I snap again. "Did you—"

"What are you talking about?" she cuts in, finally taking in her surroundings as Cady pulls the bedroom door shut. The lock clicks into place.

"So, none of you went anywhere last night? None of you forgot to shut the door?"

"No, of course not," Rowan says, her skin paling.

Cady shakes her head. "Maybe we didn't shut it all the way after Magnus left last night."

"But that . . ." I was so tired last night, I honestly can't remember.

Rowan grabs her phone off the nightstand. "We probably forgot to lock it, and it just came open."

"Yeah, I guess," I say, drawing out the words. "One more thing for Uncle Paul to take a look at."

"But what if . . . ?" Cady's gaze roves to the wall between our room and Magnus's, and she bites her lip.

"Shit," Rowan says, still looking at her phone. "It's eight thirty-five. Didn't your aunt say that breakfast ends at nine."

"Better get going," Cady says. But she isn't moving; her eyes are still on the door.

We throw on some clothes, brush our teeth, and head out. "I'm looking forward to some girl time today," I say as we hurry down the stairs.

"Even if it's at a boring old castle?" Rowan asks with a smirk.

"Even then." I elbow her like we're teenagers again.

But we reach the doorway to the breakfast room, and there they are.

Valentina waves us over. "Come sit with us," she calls out, though the tables only seat four. The room has a rustic-cozy vibe, like the reception area. A large window provides views of the woods, and the tables are each set with dining ware and a vase full of fresh yellow buttercups. The floral aroma mingles with coffee, sugar, and a hint of brine.

A couple occupies the table nearest the window, sipping coffee, their plates empty. They must be staying in room three. The woman looks to be midforties, with bleach-blond hair and heavy eyeliner. The man is much older, perhaps in his sixties, with salt-and-pepper hair and a gruff look to him. She's dressed in designer boots and a long, cream-colored coat—very British vacationer-chic—not the horrible, bulky jacket and ill-fitting jeans American travelers her age wear—but I listen in long enough to ascertain that they aren't speaking English; Welsh maybe, judging by the guttural sounds. The woman catches me staring and turns her head, just snagging my eye before I look away.

When I turn to my friends, they're already finagling the remaining table closer to Magnus and Valentina's table.

"How was your night?" Magnus asks, reaching for his coffee mug.

"We all slept fine," Cady says. "Thanks again for helping out with the toilet."

"It was nothing."

My aunt emerges from the kitchen, tray in hand. "There you are," she says, placing two plates of fried eggs, ham, sausages, tomatoes, and some sort of green patty in front of our neighbors. "Happy Monday."

"Sorry, Aunt Helen," I say. "We were out late."

"I hope you had a good time. I'll have to tell your uncle you're down here. But first, breakfast orders." She points to Valentina's plate. "This is a traditional Welsh breakfast. Of course, I can do toast and jam instead. I know how you American girls are about breakfast."

"I'd like the whole experience," Cady says. "It looks delicious."

Helen beams. "We grow and can the tomatoes right here on the property."

"And is that laverbread?" Cady asks, pointing at the circular green patties on Valentina's plate.

"It is," Helen says. "One of the reasons Paul drives to the coast every day. To get it fresh."

"And what is *it* exactly?" Rowan asks, squinting at it.

"A Welsh delicacy," Helen answers. "Made from laver seaweed. It's more of a fried oatcake than a bread."

"Sounds yummy," I say wryly.

"I'm excited to try it," Rowan says. "I'll have the same."

"Make it three." I fold my sweater and drape it over the back of my chair. "But you can leave the green stuff off mine."

Helen takes our drink orders and scurries back to the kitchen.

"So, you two slept all right?" Rowan asks our neighbors.

"Oh yes," Magnus answers. "We were up bright and early, walking in the woods."

"Bright and early?" I check my phone for a signal with no luck. "After the night we had?"

Laughing, Valentina runs her fingers through her long, dark hair. My eyes are drawn to the somewhat gaudy silver butterfly ring on her middle finger, her taste in jewelry apparently the closest thing she has to a flaw. You'd never know she'd barely slept last night. *Bitch.* The word doesn't even fit, though. She hardly looked me up and down the way most women do; instead, I'm the one scrutinizing her. I chatted her up in the pub, feeling out the situation with Magnus some more. Not that I actually think anything will happen between him and Cady. More because it intrigues me. A beautiful girl like Valentina, with a respectable career in marketing. Perfectly social, and yet alone in Europe. Surely, she has friends, yet she chose to travel by herself.

Until she didn't. She met Magnus, and suddenly, a companion suited her just fine.

Across the table, she and Rowan strike up a conversation about Molly.

Off to my left, Magnus leans an elbow onto the table to talk to Cady on my right. "We found something most interesting on our walk."

"Did you?" she asks as Helen returns with a pot of coffee.

"Remember those stone formations we were talking about? Well, we found one in the woods that doesn't seem to exist on any of the maps."

"Really?" Cady matches his posture, genuinely interested.

"Thank you, Helen," I say, busying myself with my mug while the two of them continue talking around me. "Do you know anything about this rock formation?" I ask my aunt.

"Here in these woods?" She pours another cup, frowning. "No, but that doesn't mean much. They're all over Britain."

"It's fascinating," Magnus says. "The stones we found don't seem to come from this area. One of the reasons there are so many formations in Pembrokeshire is because the large stones used are indigenous to the land. But they aren't found in this area."

"I wonder how they transported the stones all the way out here," Cady says.

"Some sort of truck?" I offer.

"In the Neolithic period?" Cady laughs.

The back of my neck starts to itch, just beneath the hairline. I scratch at it.

"Well, is it far? I'd like to check it out after breakfast." She looks at me, realization dawning. Maybe disappointment, too, that it's my trip, so I get the final say. And I do want to say no, just like I did last night. It's *our* trip, and we came to have some quality time together.

But I haven't been the nicest friend to Cady so far. As much as I should be encouraging her spending time with a handsome man—as much as I want to set her up—I guess part of me has always taken it for granted that Cady is single. And if she's single, I have her all to myself.

"I mean, if it's okay with you, Joss," Rowan adds.

"It isn't far, Jocelyn," Magnus says reassuringly. "Only a ten-minute walk."

"Sounds fun, doesn't it?" Rowan says, sounding like her old self, the one who was always up for anything. It reminds me of the time in ninth grade when I dared her to hop my cute neighbor's fence and write a note from a mysterious stranger, confessing her undying love. To my astonishment, she only grinned and started to climb. "I mean, only if you want to, Joss."

"Of course." I drop my hand and reach for the sugar as if I were the most easygoing person in the universe. "Why don't we all go? I could use the exercise if I'm going to fit into my wedding dress."

After breakfast, we change into more hiking-appropriate attire and meet Magnus and Valentina behind the cabin. The rain has cleared, but even at midmorning, the air has a bite to it. I stuff a beanie over my head and tug on my mittens. When we reach the end of the path and edge around the landscaping, I notice the large fenced-in garden on the side of the cabin. It must be the one Helen mentioned at breakfast. Various plants and sprouts grow on a raised bed, each with a little identification label poking out of the dirt—tomatoes, new potatoes, and parsnips. Beyond it lies a small orchard of what look like fruit trees full of white blossoms.

The river roars in the distance, but it isn't until we follow our neighbors through a small line of trees that the wide, rolling body of water comes into view. We snap a few photos, and Valentina offers to take one of the three of us on my phone.

Rounding the cabin in the direction of the mountain, we push through the trees, spotting a smaller cabin—though *shack* is a more accurate term for this box-shaped building. "What's that?" I ask. The log shack hasn't been updated along with the main cabin. Parts of it are rotted, and the windows are opaque from oxidation. Smoke puffs up through the chimney, however; a sure sign that the place is in use.

"It must be where the groundskeeper lives," Valentina says. "I saw him out front, tending to some plants. Kind of creepy-looking guy, but he does a nice job."

I did wonder how Helen and Paul managed to keep the landscape in such sparkling shape at their age.

We pass the shack, and Valentina leads the way to a small trail weaving through the dense pines. We take to it in single file.

"I love this scent," Rowan says dreamily. "The earth after rain."

"Petrichor," Cady says. "That's what the scent is called."

"Thank you, Valedictorian." I try to catch Rowan's eye, to share that glance we used to share whenever Cady spouted off useless facts. But she's ahead of me, apparently still enamored with the *petrichor*.

The path is monotonous: trees on the left, trees on the right. The terrain grows continually steeper, and my calf muscles pinch. I completely fail to understand the appeal of hikes. Yes, the sound of the birds and the pine scent is soothing, but the walk is tiring, not to mention boring.

Magnus comes alongside me, pressing a little too close for comfort on the thin stretch of trail. "I'm sorry," he says in a low voice. I look up to find a sheepish smile that's at odds with his chiseled jaw. "You wanted to relax on your trip. Val and I are getting in the way of that."

It's true; they are. But I grin back. "Not at all. I'm sure the views are spectacular, and I love a good walk." An innocent enough lie. Harmless, really, compared to some of the ones I've told over the years.

"And your husband-to-be?" He leans in closer. "Does he also enjoy a good walk?" The way his eyes are trained on mine sends a delightful shiver down my spine.

"Landon? Oh. Well, he . . ." For a second, I can't for the life of me remember what Landon likes and doesn't like. Lately, we've been spending most of our free time apart.

"He likes to walk," Cady says as she comes up behind us. "You two just walked all over Paris, right Joss?"

"Oh, right." I laugh, and Cady presses between us, moving to join Rowan and Valentina ahead. "Landon is very active. He likes the gym and plays basketball with his friends on Thursday nights."

"And what do you do on Thursday nights, when he's away?"

His gaze is as thrilling as it is uncomfortable. Landon used to look at me this way. Then, at some point, after years of asking and answering questions we already knew the answers to, the intensity left his eyes. He still looked at me, but not as if knowing me was this exhilarating, challenging puzzle of a feat. Magnus looks at me that way now, as if I were a mystery. I've missed this feeling.

My honest answer is so drab. I've been busy, running my own business. It's not just about choosing the right flowers or venue; there are thousands of hours spent behind the scenes, on my laptop, crunching numbers and generating spreadsheets. Pleading with banks. Things I don't particularly enjoy but do to keep afloat in this endeavor.

Other than that, I spend a decent amount of time with Cady, or bingeing bad reality television. I'm not quite sure how I became this person. "I find ways to keep occupied," I say coyly, determined to feed into the mystique.

"How did the two of you meet?"

"College. He was in my English class and pretended to need help with an assignment."

"Oldest trick in the book, right?"

"Right. And you and Valentina? Do you think you'll see her after your trip ends?"

He shrugs. "We'll have to see where things take us." It should be the confirmation I've been after, that there is something going on between those two. Only I can't help feeling like the *us* isn't referring to him and Valentina.

It's ridiculous, this flirting. I've never cheated on Landon, and I never would.

Still, I entertain the idea because it adds an edge to the dullness of this hike. "You said you came from the east, right? What were you doing out there?"

"More hiking—the scenery is wonderful. A national park that's basically an outdoor museum. We saw Flint Castle as well. Ruins from the thirteenth century. Just spectacular."

"Neat." My boots slosh in a mud puddle I didn't notice, casting a brown spray onto my jeans. *Shit.* Now I'll have to ask Helen about a washing machine.

"We'd planned on getting to London to see more sights, but we figured that while we were out this way, we should see all that North West Wales has to offer."

"My aunt said a girl went missing near London last week. Might be best to stay away."

"Yes, Lisa Granger. An American. It was all over UK news. Very sad. Though investigators now believe she's fine. At least, that's what they were saying before we left the east. I read a few articles. Apparently, when police questioned Lisa's traveling companions, they claimed she often spoke of disappearing."

"Really?" I try to imagine what could make a person so unhappy that they'd want to abandon their entire life. "Well then, let's hope that's the case."

Ahead, the others stop beside a large red-leafed shrub sprouting from the mountainside. Valentina calls back, "Magnus, do you remember where we left the trail?"

"Left the trail?" Cady asks, glancing at me. "Why would you do that?" Her voice squeaks the way it does when she's anxious.

"We sort of wandered off the beaten path," Valentina says. "Just to explore. There isn't any dangerous wildlife out here. It's perfectly safe."

"Helen spoke of a wild-dog creature," Rowan says, lifting her brows mischievously.

"The *gwish-gee*," Cady says. "It's a myth."

Valentina laughs. "Oh, we heard all about the gwyllgi last week. Especially when that girl went missing."

Magnus checks his phone. For a moment, I wonder how he's managed to get service. But I lean close enough to see that it's only a basic compass app—no signal required. "This way."

Valentina nods and pushes through the pine needles. Rowan follows without pause, a glimmer of her old self, up for a good thrill.

Cady and I remain on the path another beat. "You're the one who wanted to see these rocks," I hiss. Her eyes are narrowed, focused on the brush off the trail. I've known my friend long enough to see through her skull to all the concerns spinning around in her brain. There will be the poison ivy, of course. If she had service, she'd be googling whether or not it's a problem here. Then we'll have to watch for stray bullets if there's even the slightest chance that a hunter could be skulking through the land. And deep down, because she can let her imagination run off at times, there is a slight worry about the creature from Helen's tale, even though my aunt assured us that not even the myth is indigenous to these parts.

Sighing, she fiddles with her jacket zipper. "They're right. We have nothing to fear in these woods."

They probably *are* right. Still, it couldn't hurt to catch up to Magnus. Even a giant mythical dog wouldn't get past that guy. The forest ground squelches underfoot as we trek deeper, trudging through ferns and flowery shrubs. When we pass an old shack, even smaller and more ramshackle than the groundskeeper's, Cady stops. "Are we allowed to be out here? Is this private property?"

"Always the goody-goody," I say, though even *I'm* picturing a burly Welshman sprinting from the shack, rifle aimed at my head.

"It's abandoned," Valentina says. "We checked this morning. Isn't it fantastic?"

"If you say so," I mumble.

The others start ahead, and Valentina slows to keep pace at my side. "You should be careful," she says.

"Why?" I ask, my gaze darting to the ground. "Is there a snake or some—"

"I mean with Magnus."

"I don't understand."

"Just—I'd watch my back if I were you."

Heat flashes through me. What is that supposed to mean? Is she staking her territory, or is she saying I should be *wary* of Magnus? We pass the shack, and before I can follow up again, she says in an entirely different, easy tone, "So, Cadence mentioned you plan weddings."

"Oh," I say, experiencing something like whiplash as I try to come back from her cryptic warning. "Yeah, and some interior design work. I run my own business."

"That's impressive," Valentina says. "And surprising, actually."

"Why is that?" I nearly spit.

She laughs in a disarming way and pauses to admire a patch of wildflowers. "Just that Cadence made it sound like the business wasn't working out."

"What exactly did Cady say?" I ask, stooping to pick one of the blue blooms. This flower's name eludes me, only adding to my frustration.

"Just a little about your struggles to nail down a career. How you sometimes need your father to help out."

Cady said all that to this complete stranger? An ember of rage burns within me. "I guess Cady can comment, since she knows a lot about failure. You should ask her about *that*."

As soon as the words are out, I want to suck them back in. I tear a petal off the flower and watch it fly off with the wind. "Cady's wrong about my business. It's taking time, but all new ventures do." At least, that's what I'm hoping. That they go through rocky patches before finding the smooth, white sands of success. But it doesn't change the fact that I'll have to borrow more money from my father if I want to keep my company afloat. He'll hand over the money, but only after giving me the speech. The one about how I'm not living up to the Elliott name. And he'll leave it at that, even though he'll be practically bursting with disappointment and a list of things left unsaid.

Things about how the wrong twin left this earth far too soon. Things about how Jake never would've ended up thirty and still dependent on my parents. And I don't even have children to blame for my ineptitudes. Or a husband, for that matter.

I cast the now bare stem to the side of the trail.

"Of course," Valentina says, nodding along beside me. "I actually thought about starting my own firm a while back. I had all the top clients, and a few of my colleagues kept encouraging me." She lets out an airy laugh. "But I'm too comfortable where I am. Would I be here now, if I were head of an entire marketing firm?"

"I guess not." As much as I appreciate the sentiment, envy prickles up. Valentina is younger than me, yet sounds so accomplished.

A hot sweep of shame follows. Would I be more successful if I were home, working on my business, rather than gallivanting around Wales? I am spending more of my father's money when I should be working to pay him back.

"You'll succeed," she says with a nod, her brown eyes latching onto mine. "I can tell you're the kind of person who gets what she wants in life." She glances up just as the trickling sound of water drifts through the trees. "Ah, this way."

We reach the small stream, which Valentina and Rowan cross with ease. Cady and I tiptoe over the moss-covered rocks precariously. When she reaches the bank, I lose my focus and wobble. Shrieking, I start to fall, but Magnus grabs my arm and steadies me.

Catching my breath, I let out a nervous laugh. "Thanks. That was a close one."

"Not a problem," he says, a half smile on his lips.

"How much farther is it?" I ask, trying not to betray either the effect of his smile on me or my annoyance that we're still hiking. Then there's a new thought—the one Valentina just planted in my head. That maybe I shouldn't get too close to Magnus.

"We're nearly there."

Sure enough, a minute later, the trees give way to a small clearing. "This is it," Valentina says, pointing to where the sunlight streams through the trees to illuminate a series of standing stones. They form a circle, approximately twenty feet in diameter. The stones vary in shape and size: some flatter on top, some narrow and leaning, anywhere from one to three feet in height.

I move to the low stone nearest me. It's block-shaped, the surface rough and speckled with lichen. Grass grows up around it on all sides, and a vine is wrapped around the base.

"It's just like the Druid's Circle," Cady says, examining the next stone over. "Only on a smaller scale, I'd imagine."

"Yes," Magnus says. "There are forty-one stones in the Druid's Circle. Here, I count ten."

"And no one knows what these circles were used for?" Rowan asks.

Magnus shakes his head and wanders around the outside of the circle. "Not exactly. They likely had a variety of ceremonial purposes. I'm just wondering why this one isn't on any of the guides or Google Maps."

"We did leave the trail to find it." Valentina crosses through the center of the circle and stops, kneeling. "Magnus, come look at this."

He does, and the rest of us creep in closer as well. "This part of the ground is different, don't you think?" she says. "The grass is newer, lower."

"Almost like there was something in this spot at one time," Rowan says.

"Like what?" I eye the patch, unsure how they've ascertained all of this information from some dirt and grass.

"Maybe another stone," Magnus says. "These ones along the outside could've been seats of some sort, meant for viewing whatever was here in the center. Like some sort of burial tomb. Or even . . ."

He doesn't finish the thought, and I can't help but ask, "Or even what?"

"A sacrificial altar," Valentina says.

Something rustles in the trees behind me, and I jump. "Like, for animals?"

Magnus shrugs. "Maybe."

A chill winds up my spine. "Cady, don't we need to get a move on if we're going to see that castle?"

Cady looks up as if wrenched from a daze. "What? Oh yeah." She wraps her arms around herself. "We do."

"Sure you don't want to join us for the Druid's Circle?" Magnus asks. Cady's the one who cares about all of that, but his eyes are on me.

I smile, thinking again of Valentina's warning. "I think we've seen enough strange rocks to last quite some time. But thank you for the offer."

His smile falls, as if he's genuinely disappointed and not simply playing his part in my flirting game. "Well then, let's get you back."

His head flicks toward the trees before his back turns on me. Suddenly, I worry I've said the wrong thing.

"We did come for some quality girl time," I add, my feet crunching over dead leaves as I follow him. His steps are massive, and I struggle to keep up. "And I've been dying to see this castle Cady keeps talking about."

I catch Cady's eye roll. It's a lie, and she knows it. She's also used to it. These lies are who I am, part of my charm. Nothing to worry about.

As long as one lie in particular stays buried. *That* lie did cause harm.

NOW

Light darts through the trees like fireflies, followed by the sound of voices. The police swarm in my direction, shouting indecipherable commands and pointing flashlights. All I can do is freeze and throw my hands in the air, like the movies taught me. It makes me look guilty.

And I am guilty.

When they reach me, they tell me to move away from the body. That's when I get sick again. I apologize, explaining that I have to go back into the trees. They don't trust me, so they follow. They watch as I get sick all over the forest floor.

I apologize again, but one thought drowns out all others: my friend, who was living and breathing, warm blood pumping through her earlier today, is now being referred to as "the body."

"It's okay," says the female officer, only she introduces herself as Detective Inspector Collins. I am filled with dread; not only is this happening, but it's happening in a country where I don't know how to properly address the police. In the dark, I make out the woman's brown hair tied up in a bun, though her features are murky. "You were the one who found the body, then?" she asks.

I nod.

"And have you touched or moved the body?"

"No." I shake my head, too fast. *Guilty, guilty, guilty.*

"She was on the ground here, then?"

"Yes," I say as the detective inspector's flashlight makes the same journey mine did nearly an hour ago—from the body lying on the ground, following the red trail over the grass, and ending at the large stone soaked in blood.

"Do you have any idea who would've wanted to hurt your friend?" the detective inspector asks.

"Yes." I nod adamantly. "The man. The one staying in the room next to ours. He was everywhere, stalking us." I try to swallow, but the cold air and the horrors of this night have left my throat bone-dry. "He was dangerous."

CHAPTER 7
ROWAN

When we reach the B&B, I spot the couple from breakfast sitting up on the balcony, having a smoke. I wave, but they stand, the woman stretching as she spins around and the man putting out his cigar on the railing. They open the sliding door and slip inside their room.

"What do we think their deal is?" I whisper to Jocelyn.

She shrugs. "Isn't it obvious? He's a retired gynecologist, and she was his former patient, who married him for the money." She's speaking in what is definitely not a whisper. "Now, they just travel the world, bird-watching and"—she furls a hand—"tasting wine. The bad news for her is all that wrinkled, flabby skin. The good news is that she never has to leave the house to see a gynecologist ever again."

"That's disgusting," Cady says, but up ahead, Valentina starts to giggle.

"You were close," Magnus says, his face a bit flushed. "He's a plastic surgeon."

"A fine guess," Jocelyn says, "but I'm rarely wrong."

"You mean you're rarely *right*," I say with a laugh. We used to play this game at the mall when we were teens. Sometimes, I'd chat up our subject long enough to get the real answer, and then we'd argue about whose guess was closest.

"Except I spoke to him this morning," Magnus says, "before you all arrived at breakfast."

"Oh." Jocelyn presses her lips flat.

"You do have other gifts," I say, patting her on the shoulder.

In the reception area, we find Paul crouching behind the desk.

"Uncle Paul!" Jocelyn says, causing the poor man to bump his head on the desk.

"Whoops." He brushes it off, shaking what's left of his gray-white hair, and looks over at us. "Jossy! Hi, girls. How are you?" He skirts the counter to give his niece a hug, and I notice he's gotten rounder, his skin more creased since the last time I saw him.

I'm sure the same could be said of me.

In my periphery, Magnus and Valentina wish us a good day. I wave as they head up the stairs.

"Sorry I missed you all yesterday," Paul says.

"We're sorry too." Jocelyn pulls back from the hug. "It's so good to see you." But there's a layer of gloom beneath the surface of this joyful reunion. Jocelyn's ever-beaming eyes seem to dim the way they did when her aunt met us yesterday. Like all the light has been drained.

Paul moves to Cadence next. "Barely recognized you, missy. Or should I call you professor?"

Cady's eyes lower. "No, sir. Not a professor. Just a—"

"There's no *just* about it," I cut in. "Cady is a brilliant middle school science teacher."

"Oh." Paul frowns. "But I thought—"

"Change of plans," Cady says, and my chest tightens on her behalf. She apparently still hasn't fully recovered from the valedictorian debacle all those years ago. When it all went down, it set off a chain of events. Cady was turned down from UCLA, her dream school. Then she changed her major because UCSB didn't have the professors she'd had her heart set on. In the end, her entire career path altered.

"Hi, Paul," I say in an attempt to save Cady from a conversation she's always found excruciating.

"Hello, Rowan. You're looking lovely as ever. How have you been?"

"I'm good, sir. Your place is gorgeous."

"Aw, thanks. It's been a lot of hard work, but I'm blessed to be living such a dream in my old age." His gaze veers to the window's view of the woods. "And little Molly?" His bushy white eyebrows lift. "How old is she now?"

"Eight, sir." It isn't hard to remember if you can recall the number of years since Jake passed away. She was born a mere seven months after his death.

"I'm sure she's a spitfire, like her dad."

"That she is." A slew of stories bursts into my head: the time she punched a kid in preschool for making fun of her red hair, the time she got in trouble in second grade for stealing a kid's lunch— the lunch had actually belonged to Molly's friend, and Molly had simply taken it back. "I was going to share my lunch with Greta, Mommy," she'd said, tears in her eyes after her unjust stint in the time-out chair. "But I got so mad that I couldn't let him get away with it."

Joss would adore Molly, if she'd ever give her a chance.

I smile at Paul, and it's genuine; Molly's lively spirit is one of those things that always brightens my day, no matter how bittersweet the comparison to her dad. The memories of Jake start to pop up: all the times I pitched an adventure and he tried to outpitch it. If I said we should check out the hiking spot up north over summer break, he'd suggest Machu Picchu.

"Such a shame," Paul says, interrupting my mental spiral. "All that potential. All that life left to live." Then, remembering himself, he rubs his eyes and attempts to straighten his crooked back. "Well, girls, what are your plans for the day?"

"We were hoping to call a taxi to take us to the castle," Jocelyn says. "The, uh . . ."

"Conwy Castle," Cady says. "Any chance the Wi-Fi's fixed?"

"Sorry, no." Paul points toward the desk. "That's what I've been working on. The guy called this morning to say he can't get out this way until the afternoon now."

Beside me, Jocelyn sighs.

"You can use our landline, though taxi companies are pretty hit or miss out here."

"I have the number for the driver who brought us from the train station," Jocelyn says, digging through her jacket pocket. "I'll try him. You two can head on up. It'll give me a chance to catch up with Uncle Paul, anyway."

We acquiesce, and in the quiet of the stairwell, it becomes crystal clear how much our short conversation with Paul has dampened the mood. "I was dreading seeing them," I admit to Cady. "The last time I saw them was at the funeral."

She glances over at me. "I know." We reach the top of the stairs, and she slings an arm over my shoulder. Cadence has never been a particularly affectionate person, but right now, I need it so much that I don't care how forced it feels. "At least that's over."

It's a bit naive, but that's Cady too. To assume that all the bad thoughts about Jake are over now, when they've never left for even a day out of the past eight years. And it isn't just because the love of my life was stolen from me before our lives together had even begun. It's because something happened just before he died. Something inexplicable.

The day before Jake died, he broke up with me.

He didn't know I was pregnant—it wasn't anything like that. In fact, I don't know what it was like, because he didn't give me a reason. Only the day before, we'd been sharing a chocolate milkshake on the grassy lawn outside the student union building. He'd gone on and on about how much he loved my newest painting. It was evident he'd been studying art since we started going out so he could discuss it with me. Instead of the vague compliments I usually received on my paintings, he used words like *texture* and *tone*. He spoke of the way the muted colors and lost edges had a calming effect on him, like a lullaby. He joked that one day, when we lived together, we'd surround ourselves with my paintings and that it would be impossible to feel anything but peace and contentment.

I'd soaked up the praise, tracing circles and letters over his freckled arms until I saw that his pale skin was already roasting in the midday sun. When I got up, he brushed the grass off my jean shorts before taking my hand.

We were in love, together every day, making plans to get married after graduation. Then, out of the blue, he told me it was over.

It clearly pained him as much as it pained me, so I begged him to talk to me. To tell me what I'd done wrong. I called a dozen times, but he never answered.

The next day, he was dead.

I never told anyone he'd broken up with me. Apparently, he never told anyone either. Everyone treated me like the grieving girlfriend. And later, when they found out I was pregnant with his child, they treated me like the grieving widow, left pregnant and alone to care for a child that was meant to be part of a happy, loving family.

The truth was, Jake didn't want me anymore. There never was to be a happy family, a happy union of any sort. No traveling the world as a family of three. Once I realized no one knew the truth, I kept it to myself. Jake had died of a drug overdose, and yet, he'd never taken drugs in his life. Not that anyone knew of, at least. The circumstances of his death were mysterious enough that police looked into it briefly.

When questioned, I lied about the status of our relationship and the reason for my many calls, praying no one knew the truth about those last days. How would it look? I'd gone from the grieving partner to the scorned ex. The boy I loved rejected me, and then he just happened to end up dead?

Not long after, the police ruled that it had, in fact, been an accidental drug overdose. To cope with a difficult university course load, Jake had taken pills that weren't prescribed to him, that he'd never used before. He'd mixed them with alcohol, and the consequences were deadly. Jake Elliott became a cautionary tale among the students at our university.

I remember how upset he'd been the day he told me it was over. There was a darkness I'd never seen in him. Over time, I started to believe that whatever he was going through in that moment caused him to overdose.

I only wish I knew why he'd broken up with me before he did it.

When Jocelyn joins us up in the bedroom, she doesn't look happy. "Phylip said he was already on a job today. He might be able to bring us back this evening, but he can't take us to Conwy. Luckily, Uncle Paul offered."

"That's nice of him," I say.

"Yeah, I want to feel bad, but Paul and Helen are the ones who bought this place out in the middle of nowhere. You'd think someone would've advised against purchasing a property so far from all the sights."

"Some people go searching for places like this," Cady says. "The solitude, being one with nature, that type of thing."

"People like *you*, maybe," Jocelyn says, and Cady reddens.

"You did say you wanted a quiet week away from it all," I say.

"My aunt and uncle more than delivered. Too bad we need more than one meal a day." She checks her makeup in the bathroom mirror and emerges again, tripping over a boot that I discarded in the middle of the room. "Dammit, Rowan, can't you pick up after yourself?"

"Sorry," I say, hurrying to store the boots in the closet.

"Not sure how you manage to take care of a small human being when you live like a wild animal."

My jaw clenches. "I said I was sorry." I'm almost wishing I'd kept that boot. Just so I could use it to whack her in the head.

Jocelyn makes a big deal of rubbing her foot before she straightens. "Paul's waiting downstairs, if you two are ready."

◆ ◆ ◆

The car is quiet at first, Jocelyn and Paul apparently having caught up on all of life's events earlier.

"So," I ask, finding the silence suffocating, "will you and Helen ever move back to the States?"

Paul laughs. "At our age? I hope not. It would mean things took a drastic change for the worse. We've loved every moment of our lives here."

"That's wonderful. I hope to bring Molly one day. Though she'd probably enjoy watching the sheep more than touring the castles."

"Well, make sure to come stay with us. We'd love to see little Molly."

"You've made friends here?" I ask, winding a curl around my finger.

"Oh, sure. It's easier for me, though, with all the errands. Helen's been stuck at the inn. She holds down the fort while I go out with some of the guys from town." He glances back momentarily to smile at us. "She's so happy to have you three here this week. She's missed the company. We're hoping to hire someone else, eventually. Then Helen can get out more, have a social life. She works much too hard for someone her age, up at four or five a.m. to prep breakfast and ready the empty rooms. She does have a friend from Conwy who comes by every week or so. Becca. They're like two peas in a pod. Becca lost a sister too. I mean . . . sorry, I meant—not that Helen *lost* Teresa, but with the move."

"They lost *each other* when you moved," Jocelyn says, the words tinged with acid.

"Right." Paul clears his throat. "Anyway, Becca's been instrumental in getting Helen acclimated. It can be hard here in the north, not knowing the customs, not speaking Welsh. Sometimes, you feel like you can't ever truly belong."

"That must be difficult," I say.

I would know. It's the way I've felt around my two best friends ever since Molly was born.

Once Paul drops us off in the small seaside town, we let Cady take the lead. It's cloudy but dry, so we begin by walking the ruins of the town walls. Conwy is something out of a fairy tale: a castle by the sea, rolling green hills meeting the bay. Even Jocelyn seems truly in awe, though she maintains a sour disposition by complaining about the number of pigeons.

Jocelyn asks a couple of tourists to take a photo of the three of us, and it strikes me that these photos might be the only ones since college. We've seen each other over the years, brought together by Jocelyn for a girls' night out here or a birthday dinner there. But this is the first time I can recall it being just the three of us. Despite everything, it fills a void in my heart. In the years to come, when we look back on my smile in this photo, it will be genuine for once.

I've seen Jocelyn more than I've seen Cady, not because we're particularly close; I see her more because we're connected now, family. Molly is an Elliott, which means we get invited to all the family functions. Mr. Elliott has a trust fund set up for Molly. Joss and I are sisters, in a way. She's Molly's aunt, even if she doesn't act like it. Hell, she never even remembers my kid's birthday.

I know I can't change Jocelyn. She's the girl I befriended freshman year of high school; I chose her. And I'd choose her again. Despite her many flaws, she was a true friend when we were kids. But I do wish—if I could change one thing—I wish she'd have been the kind of aunt that doted on Molly. That losing her brother would've ignited a deep, unshakable love for my daughter, rather than having the opposite effect.

Next up on Cadence's itinerary is the castle. She attempts to pay for the tickets, but Jocelyn shoots her down. There are a dozen more photo ops from its many well-preserved passages and towers. For most of it, we end up separating, wandering the stairwells, standing upon the battlements and gazing down at the gray sea in silence.

When we meet up again, Jocelyn pats Cady on the back. "Good choice, Cades. Would give it five contemplative stars on Yelp. Now, where's lunch?"

It turns out that Cady does, in fact, have lunch plans at a quaint sandwich shop on the main street. The place is bustling—every shop is packed due to the vacation week—but the waitress finds us a table at the back.

"So, what's after this, Cady?" Jocelyn asks as we peruse the menus.

"Shopping, if you want. We've pretty much seen the town."

Jocelyn looks up at her. "The whole thing?"

"Well, remember the walls we walked? They border the entire town. So, other than the shops on this strip, there isn't much else. I read about a whiskey-tasting place, though."

"Count me in," I say.

"There you go, Ro," Jocelyn says. "No kid, so you're free to live a little."

"Because having a kid means you stop living," I say, unable to keep my resentment to myself.

Jocelyn makes a wide-eyed look at Cadence. "God, Rowan. Sorry. You know that's not what I meant."

I let out a breath through my teeth, wishing the overworked waitress would remember to bring us some water. "No, I'm sorry. I just miss her." It's always this way for parents, isn't it? As much as you love them, parenting is exhausting and relentless. You can't wait for a day to let loose and live a little, and when that day finally arrives, all you want to do is be with your child. Because, when it all comes down to it, that's what *living* has become now. So how can you *live a little* without them?

But you do have to, sometimes. Even when your child has been the only constant in your life for the past eight years. And this week, I do intend to live.

"We know, Ro." Jocelyn reaches over to squeeze my hand. "You should call her while we're in town and have reception. You know, just in case the Wi-Fi is still out at the B&B."

"Good idea. Will you call Landon?"

"We've been texting. As soon as we got out of the sticks, my phone basically exploded."

Beside me, Cady pushes her chair back. "I'm going to use the bathroom. If the waitress comes back, order me the bacon and brie." She stands, navigates through the closely packed tables, and turns down a small corridor.

"Is she okay?" I ask.

Jocelyn rolls her eyes. "She still can't stand Landon. You know that."

"Even after all these years?"

She puts the menu down. "It's jealousy. Cady doesn't like to share me."

It doesn't sound like Cady. Sure, she's never had a ton of friends, but she's not a particularly needy person. She can be on her own just fine.

"I think the engagement has really exacerbated whatever feelings were there in the first place, you know? It's real now. Landon isn't ever going away."

"Or maybe she wishes *she* were the one getting married," I offer, immediately feeling bad for falling into Jocelyn's gossip trap. "It's tough when someone close to you finds the love of their life, and you have no one."

Jocelyn's head pulls back. "Is that how you feel, Rowan? About me?"

My chest starts to tighten, the panic blaring through my skull. I can't talk about this—not with her. The waitress finally returns to take our orders, saving me.

By the time Cady sits back down, the food is already here.

"Everything okay?" I ask her.

She blushes. "Uh, yeah. Just decided to call my mom while I had service."

"Isn't it like five a.m. back home?" Jocelyn asks.

"That's when she wakes up," Cadence says, turning redder yet. "Always has."

Cady's mother is sweet but also fiercely protective of her daughter. It was one of the reasons we didn't go out much in high school and the main reason Cady didn't get invited anywhere. Mrs. Fletcher didn't approve of her daughter partying, and Cady's never been much of a rebel. Cady's belief system in a nutshell: if her mother didn't think it was safe or wise, then it probably wasn't.

Things only got worse when Mrs. Fletcher was diagnosed with breast cancer our freshman year of college. Cady spent whatever time she wasn't studying at her mother's side. Their roles seemingly flip-flopped, with Cady constantly on her mother's case to take care of herself. Then her worry transferred to her own health. She was no longer simply worried about the odd germ infecting her, but also that she'd have the breast cancer gene or that whatever caused the disease in her mother would soon find her too. She spent so much time researching foods, habits, and chemicals that can give you cancer. In the end, she tested negative for the BRCA gene, Mrs. Fletcher went into remission, and Cady eased up—as much as someone like Cady ever eases up.

"Thanks for ordering for me." Cady drags the plate closer and picks at the bread. I turn to my own turkey sandwich. It looks delicious, but after the enormous breakfast Helen fed us, I have little appetite. "So, what do we think of our neighbors?"

I shrug. "They're friendly. Thanks to them, we had a working toilet last night."

"Right." She takes a small bite, her gaze perched on something between us. "But the way she mysteriously had my phone in her pocket last night? And didn't you think it was weird that Magnus was listening in on our conversation through the wall?"

"It wasn't his fault," Jocelyn says, popping a fry into her mouth. "The walls are thin. We were drunk and loud."

"Well, that's the thing," Cady says. "So were they."

"So were they *what*?" I ask.

"Magnus and Valentina were drunk too. At least, they had as much to drink as we did. But they were just sitting there in the room, not talking?" She shakes her head. "I don't know. It's just odd. If they could hear us so clearly, why didn't we hear anything they said?"

"Maybe they were tired," I offer.

"I just got the strange feeling that they were . . . eavesdropping. On purpose." The chatter in the place seems to ebb and flow, and right now, it's gone uncannily quiet.

"Like with their ears pressed against the wall?" Jocelyn laughs. "You're a crack-up, Cades. Such an imagination. That's why we love you."

Only Cady doesn't laugh with her.

"I think that while they aren't around to *eavesdrop* this time," Jocelyn says, wiping her lips with a napkin, "we should revisit our theories as to what's going on between them. I mean, he was totally hitting on me this morning."

"Of course he was," Cady says, focused on pulling apart the layers in her sandwich.

"What is that supposed to mean?"

"Nothing," Cady snaps. "Just that everyone hits on you."

Jocelyn's head draws back. She looks my way, but I avert my eyes; I'm not getting in the middle of this. "What are you—where is this coming from?"

"Nowhere. It's coming from nowhere. I just . . . I thought maybe you'd been right, that he'd been interested in me last night in the pub. But then he started to flirt with you not twenty-four hours later." She bites her lip, like she's trying not to cry. "It stung, that's all. He obviously didn't really like me."

"Cady." Jocelyn frowns and throws her arms around her. "You said you didn't like him, remember? If I'd known, I never would've talked to him."

"I *don't* like him, so don't be sorry about that. I'm not the reason you shouldn't have talked to him. You're engaged, Joss."

Jocelyn's lips part and she pulls away. "So now it's a crime to be friendly?"

"Forget it. None of my business."

"Well, you've made it your business, haven't you?"

"I'm apparently the only person who cares about you enough to tell you when you're completely out of line," Cady says, her voice raised.

"Hey," I try, glancing around the restaurant and catching eyes on us. Sweat breaks out on my forehead.

"Oh, you care." Jocelyn laughs. "You cared so much about me that you told Valentina I can't hold down a job and that I get all my money from my daddy."

"I did not!"

"Okay, okay," I say, waving a hand in between them. "We are on a perfectly nice girls' trip, and we're not letting it get spoiled by a guy that none of us actually care about." I say the words, but they don't seem to hear me.

The tension is palpable. Like a living, crawling thing, it moves from the table up to my hand. I try to clear my mind, to banish the feeling, but it burrows beneath my skin and wriggles its way up my arm, making a sharp turn toward my chest.

Once the feeling is planted there, it expands to fill my lungs, making my entire chest tight. It hurts to breathe. "I've got to check my email," I choke out, getting up from the table and pushing outside into the cold air.

But of course, I don't check my email. I can't read in this state. Every shape and line in front of my eyes bleeds together.

There's only one thing to do when I get like this. I walk down the street, doing my best not to stagger as my lungs take slow and deliberate gulps of air. I'm already hot, but I pull my hood up to cover my head. I spot a toy shop up ahead on the left and duck inside it.

The woman at the counter is immersed in a conversation in Welsh, but she pauses to say "Hello."

I nod, keeping my face concealed as I head deeper inside. The shop is tiny and packed with displays. Customers meander the aisles, examining stuffed dragons and dollhouses. This was a poor choice. There are people everywhere, and I can't check for cameras without giving away my face.

But the feeling presses harder on my chest. If I don't make my move, it will consume me. I may even black out here in the toy shop. I turn around as if to leave, spotting a display of figurines near the door. I pause in front of it, blocking the shelves from the view of the counter. Taking a small red dragon, I drop it into my open pocket. I pretend to admire the colorful puppets in the display window and push open the door.

Immediately, the colors outside look brighter. The lines on the buildings sharpen. Air makes its way into my lungs with ease. Home free, I dig my hand into the pocket and examine my new treasure. Molly will like it. She isn't the reason I took it; I rarely take things based on a need or a desire for the item itself. I take things to help with the feelings.

When I look up, trying to gather my bearings so I can get back to the coffee shop, I see them.

Magnus and Valentina. They're standing outside the ice cream shop, watching me.

CHAPTER 8
CADENCE

Neither of us acknowledged Rowan when she got up from the table. Jocelyn is still fired up, unwilling to let this go. "I suppose Valentina just made it all up out of thin air, then." Her green eyes narrow as she leans in.

"She just asked me what you did for a living, and I told her that you'd finally found—"

"See? *Finally.*" She slaps the tabletop, causing my plate to bounce. "Because I've just been sitting on my ass, leaching off my father like some sort of trust-fund baby."

"Well, I didn't say that, but your parents do—"

"*Parent*, singular. It's not like my mother is out there working for a living."

Guilt gushes through me for the slipup. Mrs. Elliott used to be one of those hyper-involved mothers who managed to attend all of their children's school events while also holding down a full-time job and looking like a movie star. But she was never the same after Jake's death. Now, she sits around all day in her pajamas watching talk shows, her hair uncombed and gray, having gone without her monthly visits to the salon all these years. "I know, Joss."

"Hope you're enjoying the trip that Daddy's money paid for."

Resentment froths in my chest. "I did try to pay for the tickets today," I say, even though I should just keep my mouth shut.

"And I saw right through your act. You were just trying to make a point. You're such a bit—"

"Excuse me?" comes a shrill voice from behind me.

I turn around to find a woman sitting at a table with two small children. She widens her eyes and flicks her head toward the smaller of the two. "If you don't mind keeping your voices down," she pleads in an English accent. "You're scaring him."

My neck heats. "We're so sorry." Figures. The loud Americans, living up to their reputation. I turn back around, unable to look Jocelyn in the eye. "I really didn't mean anything by it, Joss. She asked me a question, and I answered it. I didn't realize the company's struggles were a secret."

She sighs. "I mean, they're not, really. I just—things are a bit stressful right now, that's all. I may have overreacted."

"It's fine. That's why we're here, isn't it? To get your mind off all that for a little while."

◆ ◆ ◆

We've finished eating when Rowan returns, looking somewhat lost.

"How was work?" I ask.

"Work?" She glances back at the glass window.

"You said you had an email."

"Oh, it turned out to be nothing." She sits down without touching her sandwich.

"Are you going to finish eating?" I ask. "That waitress keeps looking over here like she wants our table." And I'd like nothing better than to hide my face after the scene we caused in here.

"Let her look," Jocelyn says, crossing her arms and leaning back. "Rowan is going to eat the food that we paid for and take her precious time doing it."

"Actually, I might not," Rowan says. "I'm not very hungry." She looks at the window again. "They're here in town."

Jocelyn's brows knit together. "Who?"

"Magnus and Valentina. They said they were heading out to see those stones, but they're *here*, and I . . . I think they were following me just now."

With a shiver, I remember the way Valentina stared at me last night as I chatted with Magnus.

"Oh my god," Jocelyn says, rolling her eyes. "Not you too." She leans forward, taking one of my fries, but holds it up in the air before eating it. "What's with the fries, Cades? Aren't you worried about the acrymites anymore?"

"*Acrylamides*," I say. "As you've told me millions of times, the fried food–cancer correlation may have been a bit paranoid. I am still trying to cut down. But stop changing the subject. First our neighbors are listening to us. Now they're following us!"

Jocelyn puts up a hand. "What do you mean by *following you*, Rowan?"

"I mean I turned around out there, and both of them were standing on the sidewalk, watching me. Like they had nothing else to do in life."

"They probably needed lunch after their hike," Jocelyn says.

"The walk to Druid's Circle takes three and a half hours," I say. "Plus, there's the drive. They couldn't have done it."

"Are you sure it was even them out there?" Jocelyn asks Rowan. "Everyone looks the same with their puffy coats and hoods."

"I'm sure," Rowan says. "The strangest part was that our eyes met—they saw me and I saw them—and they didn't say anything. It was . . . creepy."

"Thank you," I mutter, popping one last fry into my mouth and pushing the plate away. Finally, someone gets it.

"I know what we need." Jocelyn waves the waitress over. "Some shopping. Let's go buy a couple of Welsh . . ."—she throws her hands up—"I don't know. Cady, what's a Welsh souvenir?"

"Guess we could find out," I say.

"Exactly." Jocelyn motions to the waitress. "Check please."

Out on the street, Rowan nudges me. "They were there. By the ice cream shop."

I glance over to where she points, but Magnus and Valentina aren't there on the sidewalk now. We walk by the shop, peering in through the windows. It's too jam-packed with customers to make out anyone with clarity. "You'd think it would be too cold for ice cream," I say, glancing up at the sky filled with swooping seagulls. All traces of blue from this morning have been covered by gray clouds. "Any idea why they didn't say hi?"

"No," she says, fidgeting with her jacket pocket. "I'm certain they saw me. Like I said, we made eye contact."

"Oh, look." I point to a toy shop up on the left. "Rowan, you could get something for Molly."

"Uh, already did," she says, moving right past the place.

"Oh? When?"

"When I was checking my email. I wandered over here and decided to pop inside. I got this." She pulls out a dragon figurine and then stuffs it back inside her pocket.

"Didn't realize Molly was into dragons," Jocelyn says.

"Her tastes change all the time. One day it's dolls, and the next it's robots or jungle animals. If I give her a dragon, it'll be dragons. If you bothered to spend any ti—"

She cuts off, leaving Jocelyn with her mouth open. The rest of Rowan's thought is unspoken yet suspended in our consciences, just as permanent as if she'd spray-painted the words on the sidewalk. *If you'd bothered to spend any time with Molly, you'd know all of this.*

"I think it's a great souvenir," I say after a moment, breaking the tension.

Jocelyn puts on a somewhat forced smile. "Not as good as a bottle of whiskey, though, is it?" She points to a wine shop across the street.

Rowan arches a brow. "For my eight-year-old?"

Jocelyn laughs. "Maybe not for her. But it will be the perfect souvenir for us. Except the part where we don't actually take it home because we drink it all tonight."

"Whiskey back in the B&B sounds perfect," Rowan says. "Maybe some cheese too?"

"There's this cute little fireside room off the reception area," I say. "Let's hit the boutique first."

"And the chocolatier," Rowan adds.

"Yesss." Jocelyn throws her arms around each of our shoulders as we cross the street. "This is exactly what I had in mind."

The sky above us begins to groan, and a moment later, lightning flickers.

"Let's hurry," Rowan says, glancing upward. "We still have to find a driver willing to take us all the way back to the B&B."

Our shopping spree takes us well into late afternoon, but we end up with matching cream-colored wool scarfs and a box of fancy chocolate truffles to show for ourselves. Despite our intentions to beat the rain, Jocelyn lets the clerk talk us into a whiskey tasting. When we finally pay for our two bottles and a charcuterie plate, it's pouring outside, the street a collage of umbrellas and hoods.

Rowan and I continue perusing the aisles as Jocelyn dials Phylip. "It just keeps ringing," she says, glancing toward the fogged-up glass and then to the clerk. "Miriam, what's a girl got to do to get a car around here?" Jocelyn has hit that perfect state of tipsy, the one where she's still steady on her feet and overly friendly to everyone, including strangers. Give her a couple more drinks, though, and it's a whole different story.

"There's a taxi stand around the corner," Miriam says. "You'll find one there."

Thanking her, we head out into the downpour, squeezing beneath Jocelyn's umbrella. I spot a taxi coming toward us, and try to flag it down. But it drives by, spraying my boots with water.

When we reach the corner, I hear my name called. "Did we forget some—"

But it's Valentina, waving at me from across the street. "Come on! We're headed to the car!"

We stay where we are, huddled beneath the umbrella. "What do we do?" I ask, my teeth chattering.

"We take the ride and get out of the rain." Jocelyn makes to turn without waiting for a consensus.

"I thought we were going to distance ourselves," I say, pulling on her sleeve.

"We could tell them we still have plans in town," Rowan says. "Then find a taxi."

"I'm freezing," Jocelyn whines. "Besides, we've already seen everything in town. I don't want to stay."

"Okay, but—"

"Come on." Jocelyn tugs us along by the crooks of our arms. "You two are being paranoid. They obviously changed their minds about that hike when they realized how boring it sounded." We cross the street, meeting the couple beneath a restaurant overhang, and follow them to the parking lot down the road.

Inside the car, we peel off our wet jackets and Magnus gets the heater running. "I guess we ran into each other at the right time," he says with a laugh.

I exchange a look with Rowan. "How was the hike?" I ask. "Were you able to see the Druid's Circle?"

"Oh yes. It was quite an experience."

"I bet you're tired. Doesn't the hike take a few hours, round trip?"

He shrugs. "We're experienced hikers." He grabs his phone from the center console, messes with it, and passes it back. "Have a look."

I flip through his photos, the others peering over my shoulders at images of stones like the ones from this morning. These are much larger, though. Magnus and Valentina pose in front of one for a selfie, and the stone comes up to Valentina's shoulder. They were definitely at the Druid's Circle today.

"The last few are from Circle 275," he adds.

"Amazing." I pass the phone back. "So, you finished up in Pembrokeshire, and then came to Conwy."

"It's less than a ten-minute drive," Valentina says. "We were sort of hoping we'd run into you for lunch, but didn't spot you until just now."

Until just now? "Oh, Rowan thought she saw you earlier. Right, Rowan?"

"Yeah." She focuses on removing her mittens. "You must've been looking at something else."

Rowan doesn't believe that, though. I can hear it in her voice. She thinks Valentina is lying.

When we park at the B&B, the rain lets up to a slight drizzle. We gather our things and make a dash up the cobblestone path, but a man wearing a yellow rain slicker kneels in the middle of it, blocking the way to the porch. "Excuse us," I say as he continues packing sand into a muddy patch just to the left of the walkway.

"The groundskeeper," Valentina tells us. "Hello," she says louder, waving her umbrella in an attempt to get the man's attention. He doesn't acknowledge her either, and I notice the earbuds.

"Let's just go," Jocelyn says, stepping onto the flower bed off to the right.

The others follow, boots sinking in the mud as they attempt to navigate around the flowers. I go last, the caboose in our train car that steers around this oblivious groundskeeper. I'm about to reach the porch when something clamps onto my wrist.

Startled, I let out a yelp and look back to find the groundskeeper's gloved hand gripping my wrist.

He's standing now, glaring at me with pale blue eyes, his thick brows angled beneath the rain slicker hood. Sharp bones jut out from his cheeks, the paper-thin, wrinkled skin barely seeming to cover them. "Stay off the landscaping," he snaps, rough leather gloves twisting over my bare skin.

"Hey!" Magnus shouts, and I turn to see him barrel down the steps.

The man releases me before Magnus's large strides reach us, and he backs away, head lowered. One of his earbuds dangles loose by the cord now. "You shouldn't walk on the flowers."

"That's no reason to lay your hands on a woman. She's a guest here."

"Sorry, sir."

"Apologize to *her*, not me."

The man clears his throat. "I apologize, miss."

"It's all right," I say, though it isn't. My wrist is sore where his fingers pressed down.

"Completely unacceptable," Jocelyn says, marching back to put a hand on my shoulder. She pauses to stare the man down. "I'm telling my aunt about this. You'd know her as Helen. Your boss."

The man's eyes widen. "S-sorry again," he stutters before retreating across the lawn.

Jocelyn guides me up the steps where Magnus is waiting. "Are you all right?"

I glance at my wrist, now imprinted with an angry red mark. "Yeah, I just—he frightened me, is all. Thank you for stepping in."

"Of course." He reaches out to take my wrist, inspecting the mark. "He had no right to touch you." His eyes brim with concern as he releases my hand. "Let's get you inside."

Despite my feelings for Landon—despite everything I said about Magnus earlier today—a flutter goes through me.

In the reception area, Helen is at the desk.

"Just the person I was looking for," Jocelyn says, passing her umbrella off to Rowan and marching over to the desk.

Magnus laughs. "Sounds like someone is in big trouble."

"That guy definitely messed with the wrong group," Rowan says, wincing. "You two don't have to stick around for this."

Magnus smiles at me. "Have a good evening, Cadence. You as well, Rowan."

"You too," I say, my face feeling hot.

Once we're alone and Jocelyn is busy filing a complaint with her aunt, Rowan tugs me over to the corner. "It's all too weird, right?"

"That a stranger just grabbed me?"

"No, Magnus's nice guy routine. Why would they follow us around town and then act like they never saw us?"

"They have been acting rather desperate, considering . . ."

"They look like models. Yeah, it's confusing."

Gently, I inspect my throbbing wrist. "He did help me out just now."

Rowan tilts her head. "Like you actually needed help with Jocelyn Elliott standing three feet away."

I laugh, my gaze veering to the desk where Jocelyn is failing to keep her voice down and gesturing animatedly. Helen nods, patient as Jocelyn continues her tirade: "Like, maybe you shouldn't block the path if you don't want people stepping outside your bullshit boundaries, you know?"

"Okay," I whisper. "Then he saved Jocelyn from ending up in Welsh prison."

"That I can't argue with." Rowan walks the wet umbrella over to the rack by the door, then lifts the bag from the wine shop, waggling it by the handle. "Hey, Joss. Remember this?"

I raise the one from the chocolatier, flashing a hopeful smile.

Jocelyn takes a deep breath. "Right. Uh . . ." She turns to Helen. "Can we use the fireside room tonight for a little girl time?"

"Of course." Helen claps her hands together, clearly relieved to be done talking about the groundskeeper incident. "It's there for the guests."

"Great. Thank you. Oh, and were you able to get the Wi-Fi running again?"

"Sure did. Everything is good to go."

The sound of a text message from my coat pocket sends a bolt of nervous excitement through me. I'm dying to reach down and read it, but instead I wait. I'll savor it later, in private.

◆ ◆ ◆

Once we've changed out of our wet clothes and had our downtime in the bedroom, we gather our supplies. "Ready?" asks Jocelyn, reaching for the doorknob.

I start to follow, but something beyond the partially drawn curtain catches my eye. A light.

No, not just any light. This is firelight.

"Hello," Jocelyn draws out, tapping her foot.

Instead of answering, I press my face closer to the glass. There it is again, bobbing among the trees. Fires don't move—they grow and they die. They do not get up and start walking. It looks like someone is carrying a torch. It weaves through the trees, and for a second, the flames lap over the long fabric of whoever's holding it.

"What is it?" Rowan asks, moving to my side.

"I thought I saw—" I point, but all I see is the thick blanket of darkness. Even the wood balcony blends into the night. I fiddle with the lock. When it clicks, I pull on the door until it slides open and head onto the platform.

"What are you doing?" Jocelyn drops her things onto the bed and follows me.

It's cold and windy; we aren't dressed to be out here. I move to the railing, leaning over it and staring into the starless night. "I saw a flame, like a torch or something, there in the trees."

"A torch?" Rowan asks, joining us. She's holding the flashlight that was stored in the dresser drawer.

"Well, there isn't anything now," Jocelyn says, shivering. "Let's get back inside. Maybe it's that creepy gardener. He lives back there."

"Yeah," I say, gaze still fastened to the trees. "But I thought I saw . . . never mind."

"Thought you saw what?" Rowan asks, aiming her light down below.

"In the firelight, it looked like the person holding it was dressed in some sort of . . . *cloak*."

For a moment, none of us move or even breathe.

Then Jocelyn snorts. "Jeez, Cady," she says, rolling her eyes. "It's your damned active imagination again." She heads back inside. My teeth chatter in my ear so loudly that I don't hear Rowan call to me, but I feel her touch on my shoulder. Begrudgingly, I return to the room, sliding the door shut and locking it behind us.

Jocelyn grabs the whiskey and heads to the door. "That gardener had a rain slicker, remember? With a hood."

"Yeah," I say, taking one last look out the glass before drawing the curtains.

Out in the hall, we tiptoe past Magnus and Valentina's room. Maybe they are nice enough, but we're on this trip to spend quality time together. That can't happen with those two constantly in the picture.

On the stairs, we pass the Welsh couple from room three. They must've been out, judging by their boots and damp coats. "Hi," Rowan says.

The woman returns the greeting with an uncomfortable smile. The man, however, keeps his head down and barrels up the staircase as if we don't exist. Rowan exchanges a look with Jocelyn, who giggles. The back of my neck heats; nothing embarrasses Joss.

Downstairs, Helen is behind the desk. "Let me know if you need anything," she says, waving us on toward the fireside room. Inside, the windowless space contains a few lounge chairs, a suede couch, and a crackling fire. A built-in bookcase that's only half-filled spans the length of one wall, and everything else is cherrywood paneling. On the coffee table, Helen has left a tray full of plates, cutlery, a pitcher of water, and some glasses.

"Thoughtful of her," Rowan says, already working on opening the bottle.

"It is." Jocelyn gets settled on one of the lounge chairs.

I begin unwrapping the charcuterie plate. "It's perfect. Reminds me of the cabin trip freshman year." For our first winter vacation in college, Jocelyn's parents rented us a cabin in Big Bear for two nights.

"Oh my god, you're right," Jocelyn says. "Except that place was tacky as hell. Remember the antlers? And the fish on the wall that sang a song?"

"I just remember the couch was covered in a lot more than its floral print," Rowan says, cringing as she sits down on this one.

"Yuck." Jocelyn laughs. "And remember how we were convinced that Jake had come up in the middle of the night and that—" She cuts off, her gaze drifting to the fireplace.

That trip was before Landon. Jocelyn's parents had a *no boys allowed* rule, which she always broke. Since she didn't have a boyfriend that winter, though, she chose to adhere to it in the staunchest manner. It was a *girls only* trip, even in broad daylight. Before heading up, the twins got into it about the rule, as much as those two ever got into it. Jocelyn couldn't handle having her brother mad at her; Jake could never stand up to his sister. They would always take the same side, even when, deep down, they disagreed.

I asked Jocelyn once why they never fought, and she had to think about this for a minute. "It's like fighting yourself," she finally said. "You don't want to stay mad at yourself forever, so you just give in. Move on."

When the three of us set off for the mountains, Jake and Rowan were still upset about having to be apart all weekend. Rowan sulked through our movies and trips to downtown. At one point, Joss and I were convinced that Jake had shown up and that Rowan had snuck out of the cabin to meet him; we could never prove said theory, however, and Rowan denied all allegations.

Now, Rowan starts pouring the whiskey, a wicked grin on her lips. "You guys were totally right."

Jocelyn's mouth opens wide. "You bitch!" She shakes her head, but her expression is one of admiration. "See, Cady? We knew it."

"We did." I loved the attention that weekend, being Jocelyn's sole listening ear as she and Rowan were at odds. Now, I accept my whiskey and take a swig, coughing as it burns my throat.

"Hey, hey," Rowan says. "Remember what Miriam said. This whiskey is meant to be sipped and savored."

"Oh, right."

"Knock, knock," comes a low voice at the door.

Jocelyn leans forward to mouth, *Magnus.*

"Can we come in?" A second voice, higher and muffled.

Jocelyn rubs her eyes with her free hand, bringing the whiskey to her mouth with the other. "Why not?"

I stare at her in shock. After all her talk about a girls' night, she's giving in, just like that? "I can tell them we prefer to be alone," I whisper.

Across from me, Rowan nods, like she feels it too. It isn't just about the peculiarities our neighbors have shown. Our stories, the ones shared between the three of us—even the ones that sting a little on the replay—this is what we came for. To relive them, to create new memories together. Once that door opens, the chance to be what we were eight years ago will slip away.

But Jocelyn mutters, "They did give us a ride today." Before either Rowan or I can argue, she calls out, "Come on in!"

Valentina enters first, wearing an unzipped hoodie over a tight, cream-colored crop top. Black yoga pants show off her curvy hips. "Helen told us you were in here," she says, sliding down onto the rug, using the legs of Rowan's chair as a backrest.

Thanks so much, Helen. I sip my whiskey, caramel notes dancing on my tongue, followed by that slight burn on the way down.

"Mind if we join you?" Magnus asks, eyes on mine.

"Of course not," Jocelyn coos. "Though we don't have any more glasses."

"Here, I don't need mine," I say, thrusting it toward Magnus. I never was much of a drinker.

"Don't be silly," he says, slipping back out the door. Two minutes later, he returns with a pair of glasses that match ours. Jocelyn pours the whiskey, and we sit staring at the fire in silence, the laughs and chatter from minutes ago obliterated.

Finally, Magnus stirs. He scoots closer to my chair from his seat on the rug. "You said you might see Caernarfon Castle tomorrow, right?"

"That was the plan." Though, at this point, we may need a decoy plan if we're ever going to spend a day on our own. "Depends on Joss."

Jocelyn looks over, eyes narrowed. "What is that supposed to mean?"

"Nothing," I say, trying to de-escalate the situation. "Just that it's your bachelorette trip, so you get the final say."

The corner of her mouth curls. "You make it sound like I'm the trip tyrant or something. Didn't we do everything you wanted to do today?"

"Yes, I just—"

"So if you want to go to another castle tomorrow, isn't that what we'll do?"

I try to send her a *shut up* signal with my eyes the way we used to do in class years ago, but she isn't paying attention. Instead, she pours herself more whiskey. "Joss, maybe you've had enough."

She turns to glare at me. "Nothing's changed since high school, has it? I'm a grown woman, fully capable of making my own decisions. But you're still Little Miss Perfect, Little Miss *Don't you think we should?* Little Miss *Aren't you worried that?* Where's your badge, Cady? Didn't the alcohol police give you one when you got through the academy?"

It hurts. She gets like this when she's drunk, but she doesn't often dig this deep. I can't help but think she's not quite over our fight from earlier. One thing is clear, though: I never should've let her finish off all my tastings on top of hers back at the wine shop.

Rowan leans forward, extending her hand for Jocelyn's glass. "Come on, Joss. You can tell you've had too much to drink by how bad that joke was."

Jocelyn doesn't laugh or give her the glass. Instead, she continues to glare at me as she downs the rest of her whiskey. Standing, she slams the glass down on the coffee table, tosses her hair back, and heads out of the room.

"Where are you going?" I call after her, but the door swings shut. When I set my glass on the table and start to get up, Magnus places a hand on my knee.

I stiffen at his touch, and he smiles softly. "Let me go," he offers.

She's *my* best friend. That's what I want to say out loud. I want to say that it's weird for a stranger to go after her instead of me. But I find myself nodding at this beautiful man, who's already shown up to save me twice today. I probably should simply sit here and let him fix my problems.

He exits and I look at Rowan, who's biting her lower lip. Then, I catch the look on Valentina's face. Her dark, narrowed eyes spark with as much heat as the fire as she watches the door. Her pink lips are pressed so tightly together they're blanched of color. It's just like in the pub last night. If I didn't know that she and Magnus had only just met, I would call that look *jealousy*.

But then she sighs, smiling, and I wonder if I imagined that look.

"You two fight like sisters," she says, nibbling on a slice of cheese. "Trust me, I have four of them."

"We've known each other forever," I say. "Neither of us have siblings." At least, not anymore. "So in a way, we've become like sisters."

"Once my older sister made me so angry, I punched her in the mouth." Valentina laughs and reaches for her glass. "Then she tack—tacked me? Sorry, what's the word in English?"

"Tackled you," Rowan says. "Wow. I don't have any sisters. That sounds brutal."

"We laugh about it now, about how swollen her lip was, thanks to me. At the time, though, we hated each other. No one can hurt you the way a sister can."

"What did she do to you?" I ask.

Valentina lifts her brows. "She stole my favorite dress and then spilled red wine all over the front of it."

"That doesn't seem so bad," Rowan says.

"Except when I asked what happened to my dress, she told me I was too fat to wear it anyway." She shrugs. "I was overweight. It was my biggest"—she screws her lips, coming up with the word—"*insecurity* back then, and she used it against me like a weapon."

"That's cruel," I say. "She deserved getting punched in the mouth."

"And it was thanks to my weight that, in the end, I was able to overpower her and pin her to the ground." Valentina winks.

"Impresionante," Rowan says shyly. "Did I say it right?"

Valentina blinks and then smiles. "Si, muy bien, Rowan. Hablas español?"

"Oh." Rowan reddens. "Not really. My mother does. She's—we're Puerto Rican. She spoke to me in Spanish, but I was too lazy and resistant to pick it up. I think every word I learned was from high school Spanish."

"Ah, well. There's always time to learn."

I try to focus on their conversation, but my gaze drifts back to the closed door. "I should check on Joss." Magnus obviously isn't having any success. I have to get her away from him so I can explain that I was merely using her as an excuse to be vague about tomorrow's plans. Then we can put this entire spat to bed.

"She's a big girl," Valentina says. "She said something curious about *you* this morning. I meant to ask you about it."

"She did?" What could Jocelyn have possibly told Valentina about me?

"Just that you'd had some trouble with your career."

My spine tenses. "My career?"

"I think she mentioned that it wasn't everything you'd hoped for. And that you knew a lot about failure." She says it like a question, as if I'll simply nod and elaborate upon how everything in my life went downhill.

"I'm very happy with my career," I practically cough out. "I teach middle schoolers. I help enrich the lives of the next generation." My tone is sharper than I intended. It isn't Valentina's fault that Jocelyn decided to go around spouting off my greatest insecurities to a stranger.

"Oh, I'm sorry," Valentina says, appearing flustered. "I didn't mean to—"

"I'm going to check on Joss," I say, standing up. And by *check on her*, I mean call her out on her crap. She had no right to talk about my job like that. I'm the one with a *real* career, the one who doesn't rely on my parents to walk them through life. And she has the nerve to talk about me like *I'm* the failure?

I head out to the reception area, finding the desk empty. When I make for the stairs, a noise off to the left snags my attention. It's a low voice, coming from the breakfast room.

Curious, I tiptoe closer, pressing my ear against the door. But the sounds are muted. I push the door open a crack and peek through, realizing with a guilty rush that I'm likely spying on Helen and Paul discussing tomorrow's breakfast plans.

I start to back away when I see them.

My body goes hot, palms slick against the knob. It isn't Helen and Paul.

It's Magnus and Jocelyn, only they aren't talking. She's on one of the tables, her arms looped around the back of his neck as he kisses her.

My brain says *flee*, but my body is frozen, my eyes compelled to watch the scene. A red sweep of fury rises in me. Why are guys only into me until she comes along? There's more to a girl than a pretty face. They never see it, though.

Jocelyn is a cheater. She promised to love Landon forever. Yet they haven't even made it to the altar, and she's already been unfaithful. She doesn't deserve him.

I should tell him. I've got the perfect view of the pair of them going at it. Stealthily, I slide my hand into my sweatshirt pocket. But my phone isn't there.

Rage runs like a tremor through my jaw. I must've left it in the bedroom after texting Landon back. I'd been so thrilled to get his message: Hey Cadybug. Miss you. It put a stop to those worries that being apart had stirred up all over again. After all, he'd tried to end things between us, due to the engagement.

Of course, it only took a couple of weeks of trying and failing to be content with Jocelyn for him to come running back. He always comes back.

We finally had a chance to talk today, though I had to sneak into the bathroom in order to conceal it. I had to make it seem like I was speaking to my mother. As much as I miss him and long to talk to him or stare at photos of the two of us—the way Jocelyn can whenever she wants—I have to be careful. *We* have to be careful, at all times. No matter the challenges, though, Landon always makes time for me. He and I are the ones who are truly meant to be together.

I only need to make him see that.

Easing the door shut, I slip away and head back to the fireside room.

CHAPTER 9
JOCELYN

Okay, so I lied when I said I'd never cheated on Landon before. There have been times over the years. I'd meant for my behavior to end once he'd placed the ring on my finger.

Obviously, I was unsuccessful last night. I didn't mean for the kiss to happen. I just missed Landon, and Magnus was there, warm and real and so near that his breath tickled my face. He was looking at me again, the way Landon used to. Like nothing else outside the room existed. Like no matter how many hours we had together, it would never be enough. No matter how close our bodies pressed together, it would never be close enough.

It was a momentary lapse in judgment. But no one will ever find out. Magnus lives in Norway, and he doesn't have my phone number or even know my last name. Once he and Valentina—whoever she is to him—leave on that ferry to Ireland tomorrow, I'll never see him again.

Last night, when Magnus and I finally pulled apart, I reminded him of my fiancé back home. I suppose I reminded myself, too. We smoothed down our hair, straightened our clothes, and tiptoed back to the fireside room.

When we returned, Cady was alone, looking flushed. She was obviously still upset that I'd taken offense to her comment. I sat for a while, working up the nerve to apologize.

Valentina stumbled her way back inside then, laughing about having gotten lost on the way to the bathroom. Rowan soon followed, making it a packed house.

I didn't need the audience; I was redder than Cady after what had happened in the breakfast room. "Cades, would you mind?" I asked, gesturing for her to join me outside.

She wobbled a little on her way to the door, and I realized she was tipsy as well as upset. That was my fault.

Out in the reception area, I threw my arms around her. "I'm sorry I got mad."

"You are?" She frowned. "Good, because I was only trying to keep the others from following us again."

"I know. I see that now. I'm an idiot. Forgive me?"

"Of course, Joss. I do think we should make it clear that we'd prefer to be on our own for the rest of our trip. I spent most of the evening learning about Valentina's entire life story. I barely got to talk to you or Rowan."

"We'll ditch them tomorrow," I assured her. "Whatever their plans are, we'll make sure to do something else."

That's why today, we aren't following Cady's original Tuesday itinerary. Magnus and Valentina were all too quick to copy us, to hijack our plan to tour Caernarfon Castle; instead, we'll stay close to the B&B. Maybe another small hike around the woods. Though I loathe hikes, I know this plan makes Cady and Rowan feel better.

"You guys ready?" Rowan's foot is tapping in the doorway. "I've got to eat something."

"You can go ahead," Cady says, kneeling on the floor by her suitcase. "Eat. That'll help."

Rowan has a headache, and we're all a little grumpy, thanks to our late night and finishing off that bottle of whiskey. I'm hurting too, but not in a physical way. Now that the alcohol has left my system, my mind is clear and my conscience racked with guilt. I felt this way last time, so horrible that I swore I'd never do it again—that part wasn't a lie. I truly believed I would never do this to Landon. Not again. Not now that we're engaged.

Yet here I am with a diamond ring wrapped around my finger and guilt, like barbed wire, wound around my stomach.

"What are you looking for?" I ask, searching my own bag for socks.

"My phone," Cady says, dumping everything out. "I couldn't find it last night, and I was too tired to look."

"Obviously." I smile at the memory of perfect Cady going to bed without washing her face or brushing her teeth. "What would your mother say about this, Cadence Fletcher?" I'd teased. "And don't your teeth fall right out of your head if you miss a brushing?" But Cady had only mumbled and pushed me into the bed frame on her way to the bed.

"I figured it was somewhere in the room."

"I'll help you look for it after breakfast," Rowan says. "But I need water and something to eat. Preferably not seaweed."

"Yeah, Cady, let's find it later," I say, motioning her along. "It's got to be buried underneath all of Rowan's shit."

"I resent that," Rowan says from the doorway.

"You live like a frat boy." I turn back to Cady. "When was the last time you had it?"

She frowns, using the bed to pull herself up. "Here in the room, I think."

"It's got to be here, then. I'll call it." I rustle my phone from my jacket pocket and dial her number. But there's no ring. "Was it on silent?"

"No." Her eyes fall shut. "But it was low on battery. It must be dead."

I sigh. "We'll find it later. I can tell your mom to text my phone if she needs anything."

Cady casts one look back at the room before following Rowan into the hall. "My mom will be fine. I just . . . don't like not having it. Maybe I'll check the fireside room."

"Good idea," Rowan says.

Downstairs, Cady goes off in search of her phone while Rowan and I manage to snag the table with the best view and get through breakfast on our own. No sign of our neighbors.

As relieved as I am not to run into Magnus, part of me wonders what he's thinking. Am I the girl he hooked up with late at night, one he's trying to avoid in broad daylight? Or is he going to be hard to shake, the way boys back in school used to be? Did that tiny taste, that vaguest hint, leave him wanting more?

God, I hope not. That's not my life. I'm marrying Landon, the man I love. All I want is for us to finally become husband and wife. Settled and secure. We'll end up like those elderly couples on anniversary cards, wrinkled and smiling in the glow of the sunset. That's all anyone really wants, isn't it? I don't know why my eyes keep drifting toward the door, checking to see if Magnus will turn up.

"Did you see Magnus and Valentina this morning?" I ask Helen when she comes to clear our plates.

"I did." She pauses, fiddling with the ruffles on her blouse. "They got an early start. Headed to Caernarfon, I think."

Rowan's eyes widen as they meet mine. "Looks like we dodged a bullet."

"How do you mean?" Helen asks.

I shrug. "They've been a bit clingy. They showed up at our girls' night in."

"Oh." Helen winces. "That was my fault. I thought you were all getting along so well."

"Don't worry about it," Rowan says, helping to stack the plates.

"But if they ask where we are again," I say, "maybe don't tell them."

"My lips are sealed." Helen makes a zipping motion over her lips with her free hand. "If you want to take it easy today, I can put together a picnic. The views by the river are lovely this time of year—*Oh.*" She checks over her shoulder before leaning in. "I wanted you girls to know. I put the groundskeeper, Mr. Kemble, on leave for his behavior. You don't have to worry about him while you're here."

We thank her as she lifts her tray and scuttles off toward the kitchen.

A picnic is just what we decide to do. In her vast research, Cady read on some travel blog that the view of the river and the woods from a nearby mountain peak is even better than the one Helen suggested. So, after spending a quiet morning lounging around the B&B, we're hiking again, Cady at the lead and Rowan taking up the rear. After all the rain, the path is sloshy but hikeable. Our phones stopped connecting to the B&B's Wi-Fi ages ago, so we're following the signage along the trail rather than Google Maps.

We divvied up the picnic among our backpacks and brought plenty of water, at Cady's behest. My aunt let us borrow a blanket.

"So, I'm curious," Cady says, hopping a puddle. "What did Magnus say to convince you to come back last night?"

"Last night?" I ask as though my memory is hazy. Why does Cady want to rehash our argument? It's in the past, everything forgiven and forgotten. "Just that . . ." I think back to what Magnus really did say last night: "I just wanted to make sure you were all right." He'd followed me into the breakfast room, finding me sitting at one of the tables. The moonlight streamed in through the large window, but his face was cast in shadows as he approached me, cautiously. Because of the whiskey and because I was angry with Cady, I spat, "She's jealous of me, you know."

"And who wouldn't be jealous of you?" Magnus asked, stepping closer.

"She has a crush on you," I added.

"Oh? So, the jealousy—it isn't over the fact that you're getting married? Or that you're always going to be the most gorgeous girl in the room?"

I narrowed my eyes at him, tilting my head back slightly, exposing my throat. "What about Valentina?"

"What about her?" he asked, coming closer yet.

He looked at me with those deep-blue eyes, his arms half outstretched, muscles practically pulsing. I stood and stepped closer to him, to see what he'd do. Valentina's face danced at the edge of my consciousness. Who was she really to him? And would any of that matter, now that the two of us were in this dimly lit room together? Whiskey swam in my veins, blurring my thoughts and propelling me toward him.

That self-assured smile crept onto his lips as he waited for me to make a move. For an eternal moment, we stood there, the space between us lit with tension and pounding pulses. When I slid my fingers up one of his forearms, he finally swept me up, lifting me onto the table.

Now, lost in the memory and flushing, I nearly run face-first into a pine branch stretched over the trail. Swatting it out of my way, I hurry after Cady. "He just asked if I was all right." *There.* A morsel of truth for a change. "And I realized that I'd been stupid to run out. Of course you'd only been looking out for the three of us."

Cady stops suddenly, and my breath hitches. I've been caught in another lie.

But she squints at the trail and then looks back at Rowan. "The path's a swamp up ahead. We'll have to go around."

"What? I'm sure we can . . ." Rowan brushes past me to check it out. "Hmm," she says, craning her neck for a way around it. "You're right. Too slippery to risk it."

I see what she means. The trees up on the mountain keep this narrow stretch of the trail covered in shade. It's nothing but a sliver of slick mud that drops off to the right.

"Should we head back and try the river?" Rowan asks.

"Aren't we almost there?" I peer down the drop. "I'm hungry."

Cady glances up at the trail again. "I saw another little path leading down into the woods a stretch back. We can find a place to sit and eat."

"Great." I allow her to pass, and we descend until the drop converts into a shallow slope. Rocks stack the side, and Cady scouts out a way down, encouraging us to follow.

It's slippery, but we find our way to the forest floor. We wander through the trees in search of a fallen log or a sunny spot to lay our blanket down. The trees are packed so tightly together, the only thing to do is keep moving. I follow Cady, my out-of-shape muscles screaming. When my boot catches on a tree root, I nearly wipe out, backpack and all. I wait for Rowan to laugh.

Only she doesn't. In fact, she's not walking or even paying attention. She staring at something in her hand.

"Hold up, Cady!" I call out. "Rowan, what's going on?"

She glances up at me with a shrug. "Nothing. Just a weird pamphlet thing." She hurries to catch up, still clutching what looks like a piece of trash.

When we reach a small clearing, we head toward it, noting a couple of rocks large enough to sit on. But as we get closer, the full picture comes into focus.

It isn't a couple of large rocks at all; it's a circle. In the middle of it lies a flat stone, approximately two meters long and one meter wide.

"Another stone formation," Rowan says, wandering through the center of it. "I wonder if Magnus knows about this one."

"Let's not tell him," I say. "We don't want to walk him all the way up here later."

"No," Cady says. "We wouldn't want to spend more time with Magnus. That could get us into trouble." Her gaze moves from the stones to veer my way, sending a shiver through me.

"What do you mean?" She can't possibly know about last night, can she?

"Nothing." Shrugging, she sets her backpack down on one of the stones. "Just what we discussed. He's getting in the way of our time. And after what Rowan said happened in town, I don't trust the guy. Or Valentina, for that matter."

My shoulders relax. "Right." I unzip my own pack, removing the rolled-up blanket and searching for a place to lay it down. Like the stones we saw yesterday, these are tall, sharp in places, and jutting out at odd angles. But the flat one in the middle looks perfect for picnicking. I wander toward it, backpack slung over a shoulder, and begin to unfurl the blanket.

I spread it over the lichen-covered stone and ease onto it. Cady removes the bag of sandwiches from her pack and doles them out.

Together we eat, listening to the soundtrack of the birds, the critters moving through the undergrowth, and our chewing. It's cold here in the forest, but the sun filters through the boughs overhead to beat against my face. I shut my eyes, taking it all in, until the crumple of a sandwich bag finally kills the moment.

"Helen's sandwiches are as good as her breakfast," Rowan says.

I nod, popping the last bite into my mouth and helping the others gather the trash.

"Should we head back?" Cady stands and zips up her pack.

"I need to sit a bit longer," I say. "My legs are cramping up."

"Drink something," Cady says without sitting back down. The moment Rowan gets up, Cady tugs on the blanket beneath me.

"Thanks." I hop down before she manages to swipe the thing clean out from under me. I grab my water bottle and tip it back, but only a single drop touches my tongue. "It's empty. Fantastic."

"You drank it all on the way up?" Cady furrows her brows, like I'm one of her students in need of chastisement.

"You can have some of mine," Rowan offers, pushing her bottle toward me.

As I reach for it, something catches my eye. Among the yellow and green lichen is a spot that stands out: a dark-red splotch with like-colored spatter marks over the surface of the rock. The spot twists and turns down the face of the stone, and my stomach takes a similar path. My hand drops. "Guys? I don't like this place."

"Well, we'd be on our way back if it weren't for you," Cady says, her tone bordering on irritated as she folds the blanket.

"Would you just look at this?"

Cady huffs, but Rowan inches closer, peering at the rock alongside me. "Is that . . . *blood*?"

The leaves behind us rustle, and we spin on our heels to look. "Just the wind," Cady says.

"I don't care what it was." I wrench the blanket from her and drape it over my shoulders. "I want out of here."

Rowan paces around the stone, examining it. "If it's authentic, it could be blood. Remember how Magnus said these circles might've been places of sacrifice?" She takes her phone out and snaps a few photos.

"Thanks, Rowan. That's really helpful." I point at the splotch. "Except that this blood is fresh. Red. Not centuries-old brown stuff."

"Yeah." She frowns. "You're right. This is weird. Maybe I should . . ." She bites her bottom lip, then digs something out of her jacket pocket. "I found this back there," she says, handing over a soggy, filthy religious tract of some sort, its cover missing.

"What the hell?" I try to flip through the pages, but they're all stuck together, ruined by the elements. A few torn pages later, I pry it open, making out what looks to be a subheading titled "The ritual of fire." I decipher a few words here and there—something about "the god of old, Beltane," but the rains have muddled the ink on the rest of the page. "It's some sort of pagan cult shit."

"Wow," Cady says, taking the pamphlet from me. "It seems to detail all the various rituals performed at the stones. Magnus mentioned that modern pagans use the stones for worship." She gestures to the circle. "This could be, like . . . their church."

"But who even comes out this way?" Rowan asks. "I doubt these formations are listed in the pagan-pilgrimage guides."

"Someone obviously knows." Cady glances up from the stones suddenly. "The fire last night. The cloak. I told you two, I saw someone. Maybe whoever I saw was here, in this *sanctuary*. Can I borrow your phone?" she asks me. "To take a photo."

"Yeah," I say, handing it over, "but what about the blood?"

"It could've been animals, right?" Rowan says. "We are in the woods."

"Yes." I nod. "Animals often kill their prey over an altar. Checks out."

Rowan gives a nervous laugh. "People could live out here."

"Yeah, pagan psychos or the Welsh version of *Deliverance*. Either way, time to go." I pitch a thumb over my shoulder. As I retreat, the snap of my boot over a twig makes me jump. "Seriously, I'm not dying on my bachelorette trip."

"No," Cady says, "you're having too much fun on this trip to die."

I turn to squint at her. These little comments—they're too sardonic, too barbed for my friend. "Do you have something you want to say, Cady?"

She stands, shoulders square to me this time. Her jaw is clenched, fingernails digging into her palms. "You don't deserve him."

The words are jarring enough that I flinch. "What—*who* are you talking about?" This is about Magnus. It has to be. She must've seen us last night.

"Nothing. Let's just go back to the B&B."

"We're not going back until you tell me what's up with all these snide little remarks."

"Okay," Rowan says, pressing in between us. "We're just tired."

"And thirsty too. Right, Joss?" Cady tosses her water bottle at me, but I'm not ready. It hits me in the chest and tumbles into a puddle of mud.

"What the hell is wrong with you, Cady?"

"Here's what's wrong!" she growls. "You telling Valentina that I know a lot about failure!"

I freeze, a deer caught in headlights.

Cady lets out a bitter laugh and shakes her head. "So, she wasn't lying. I told you yesterday at lunch that I didn't trust either one of them and you still managed to take her aside and whisper your true feelings about me into her ear."

"Look, Cady. I'll admit I reacted poorly to what you told her about me. I said something I didn't mean."

"You meant it." She bulls past me, heading back to the rocky slope that leads to the trail.

"Wait a minute."

"He deserves someone better than you. Someone honest."

"Wait—is this about *Landon*?" So Cady did see me with Magnus. I chase after her, scrambling for a foothold on the first rock. "I thought you hated—" But the fury rises, drowning out reason. "What would you know about relationships?" I ask, and she spins around so fast she loses her footing.

A rush of pebbles and dust spray down in a torrent as she slides down the rocks. Her body smacks the sharp edges along the way, and she lets out a grunt. "Cady!" I scream, a vision flashing through my head: her body slipping off the rocks to soar through the air for one brief moment before landing on the ground, limbs contorted and blood seeping into the dirt.

But she manages to grab hold of a shrub that grows between the crevices of the rocks. She dangles there for a moment, breathing loud enough for me to hear. Rowan clambers up alongside me, finding her own way up to Cady before my paralyzed limbs can restart. "Are you okay?" she asks, pulling Cady to safety.

Cady shifts so that her back is against the rocks, her knees pulled into her chest. "I think so," she says, wiping at a cut on her forehead. Her hand comes away bloody. "Thank you," she says to Rowan—and Rowan alone.

It stings, this slight. But any desire to continue our argument from a minute ago vanishes, replaced by overwhelming relief; Cady is okay. The vision I saw never came to fulfillment.

Feeling finally returns to my hands and feet, and I climb up to the next rock. Cady's cradling her elbow, so I offer to take her pack.

When we're all safe at the top, I look her over, noting the tear in her jeans and the dirt and moss covering the face of her jacket. "I'm sorry," I say, brushing the hair off her scraped forehead before hugging her delicately. "I was a bitch."

"No, I was," she says, leaning her head on my shoulder. "I don't know why I said those things. I guess in all the excitement for your wedding, I got jealous."

"I get it. I've been so self-involved. I never thought about how all the wedding stuff has been affecting you. We just have to stop talking to that meddling bloodsucker, Valentina, and everything will be fine."

Rowan scrounges up a water bottle for Cady. We wait for her dizziness to pass and help her to her feet.

When we get to the end of the trail, my phone dings in my jacket pocket. "Finally, a signal." I hurry through the trees to the place where the B&B comes into view.

"We should check if those stones are on Google Maps," Rowan says, fishing for her own phone.

"Ask Google if it knows anything about animals ritualistically sac-rificing other animals." I pull up my text messages, and my insides go cold and hollow.

The text is from Landon: Do you want to explain this?

Attached to the message is a photograph of Magnus and me, our bodies entwined. My fingers are tangled in his hair, and his mouth is on my neck.

NOW

The crime scene unit works through the night, long after the detective takes us back to the B&B. I get in bed, but I don't sleep at all. Not even a wink. When the sun's rays slant through the crack between the curtains Thursday morning, my head is pounding from exhaustion and dehydration. The pain becomes an audible sound, and I realize—after burying my head beneath the pillow—that the sound is actually a knock on the door.

I force myself out of bed at the same time my friend does, and the two of us stumble to the door together. Helen is there, worry lines drawn on her face. "DI Collins is downstairs. She needs to interview you both."

"Again?" my friend asks.

"Apparently so," she says. "I'll tell her you'll be down in a minute."

I nod and shut the door. I go to the bathroom to wash my face and brush my teeth. I don't know exactly how hard to try at this. Does looking too put-together signify a lack of feeling? Does appearing disheveled give the wrong impression, or impose an unnecessary bias? The word I cannot allow to cross anyone's mind is the one that continues to repeat like the tick of a metronome in my head. *Guilty, guilty, guilty, guilty . . .*

Downstairs, DI Collins asks to speak with me first, while my friend waits in the reception area.

I walk into the fireside room, finding the detective inspector sitting on one of the lounge chairs, pen and pad in hand.

"Did you find him?" I ask before she can get a word in. "Magnus?"

The detective inspector frowns, motioning for me to take the chair beside her. "Unfortunately, no. We haven't been able to track him down yet." She taps the pen against the pad—tap, tap, tap. "There's another matter I wanted to discuss with you, though."

"Oh?" The knot in my stomach tightens, but I try to appear calm. I focus on my breathing. *In, steady. Out, steady.*

"I spoke to your other neighbors, Dr. and Mrs. Pearce. They mentioned the three of you weren't getting along. They claim to have overheard a fight that broke out in front of the bed-and-breakfast, just the day before the deceased was found."

The slow, even breaths catch in my throat. They don't believe me. They think I'm *guilty, guilty, guilty.* "Well, yes, there was a fight. But friends fight. That wasn't even—it's Magnus you need to question. He was stalking us, messing with us. *He* did this!"

But the words ring out pathetic and hollow, and I can see in her eyes that she doesn't trust me.

CHAPTER 10
JOCELYN

My hand trembles so violently I drop the phone, which tumbles in the dirt. Turning on Cady, I let out a strangled scream. "What did you do?"

"What are you talking about?" Cady asks, still cradling her bruised elbow.

I pick the phone up out of the dirt and glance down at the screen again, the image and its accompanying messages turning my stomach. I reread the texts.

> Cadence sent me this photo
>
> Is this you???

More texts begin to pop up before my eyes, each ding hitting me like gunfire.

> What the hell Joss??
>
> It really looks like you

"You sent this photo to Landon!" I scream. "Oh my god, what am I going to do?" My shoulders hunch. My teeth are bared. I imagine myself rushing at her and sinking my incisors deep into her neck. Tearing into her delicate flesh, letting the blood spurt freely.

Instead, I thrust the phone at Cady and grab at the back of my neck, my dirty fingernails scraping the skin.

Cady looks at the screen, and her eyes widen. "No," she says, shaking her head. "I didn't—I wouldn't. You know that."

"*You* sent it to him, Cady! That's what he says!" Her words from the hike ricochet through my mind: *He deserves someone better than you. Someone honest.* She knew about Magnus. She saw us together, and instead of walking away, she took a photo of us and sent it to my fiancé. But why?

Suddenly, it hits me like an electric volt. The years of grumpiness whenever I spoke of Landon. The way she always stared down at her feet in his presence. The way she would always invent an excuse to avoid hanging out with us.

The way she always checks her phone when I mention getting a text or call from him. A habit, an instinct. A tell.

I can't catch my breath as the thought sits there in my throat, clogging my airways.

Cady never hated Landon.

"You're in love with him," I choke out.

Her face pales, and it's as if she's handed over a signed confession.

CHAPTER 11
ROWAN

I rush over to take the phone from her, squinting at the screen. The lighting in the image is so poor that it takes me a second to make out Magnus's tall frame and blond hair. Beneath him is a woman who definitely isn't Valentina. Her face is turned away from the camera, a sweep of auburn hair over one shoulder. The man appears to be kissing her neck. "Is this you?" I ask, my stomach turning.

"It doesn't matter if it's me," Jocelyn snaps, taking the phone back. "How am I going to convince Landon that it isn't?"

"I don't have my phone," Cady says gently. "Remember, Joss? I haven't seen it since yesterday."

"Yeah, when it conveniently went missing, right around the time this photo was taken."

"I don't understand," I say. "You cheated on Landon . . . with *Magnus*?" Getting my head around this is like trying to lasso a swarm of bees. Jocelyn and Landon have been the perfect couple since we were nineteen. How could she do this to him?

Then I remember. Last night, during Jocelyn's drunken fit, Magnus chased after her. Apparently, he did a lot more than coax her into returning.

The blow feels strangely personal. For all her faults, *loyalty* was once a word I ascribed to Jocelyn. My view of her faltered for a while, when she refused to be a part of Molly's life, and mine as a result. But then she invited me here, on a trip that seemed an olive branch. This chance to work on our friendship—one that's gone through ups and downs over the years—proved that our bond is one she's never fully relinquished. A minute ago, that meant something to me.

Now, Jocelyn has just taken the word "loyal" and contorted it into the shape of a hammer fit to smash Landon's heart to pieces.

"It was just a kiss," Jocelyn says, still glaring at Cady. "I was right though, wasn't I? That's why you did it? You're in *love* with my fiancé, so you—so you what? Spied on me to try and dig up some dirt?"

"I didn't take the photo, Joss! I certainly didn't send it to Landon. I didn't even have my phone!"

"Right. Wow." Shaking her head, Jocelyn turns to push through the last line of trees.

Cady chases after her. "And all that stuff about hanging out with Magnus to help your single friends? I suppose that's all it was? Jocelyn Elliott, world class philanthropist. Always doing her part to help a friend in need!"

Jocelyn stops on the grass in front of the cabin, auburn hair softly billowing in the breeze as she half-turns. Anger becomes her, painting a rosy glow onto her cheeks.

"You have the greatest—" Cady's voice breaks off. "You have *everything*, and you treat it like nothing." She steps onto the grass, clothes shredded and muddy, dark-blond strands matted against her bloodied forehead; the antithesis of Jocelyn. "I didn't send that photo. But I meant what I said back in the woods. You don't deserve him."

Jocelyn's jaw is clenched, fists balled at her side. I inch closer because she looks ready to take a swing at Cady. Part of me would like to see that fight.

"Let's just talk about this," I say. Even as a heavy weight presses in on my muscles from the tension, part of me relishes this moment. Ever since Molly's birth, it's been those two on the same side. The ever-united front. When Jocelyn wanted to go to dinner in LA and I wanted to stay closer to the suburbs so I'd be near Molly, Cady was the final vote. And guess who was suddenly craving the sushi on Sawtelle?

But we're in Wales, on Jocelyn's bachelorette trip. Right now, I'm the only person who can fix this. "Cady says she didn't do it." I'm not sure if I believe this. While it doesn't sound like something Cadence would do, it also seems highly unlikely that anyone else would take her phone and send that photo to Jocelyn's fiancé. "Let's hear her out."

"I've got things to take care of," Jocelyn spits, looking at Cady with eyes full of rage. She marches up the porch steps and disappears inside the B&B.

It's sick, the sense of satisfaction I feel at her storming off, leaving her other half. For years and years, though, I dreamed of this. Of it being back to me and Jocelyn again, with Cadence trailing after *us*.

Now, oddly, I'm left with Cady, tears streaming down her face, mingling with the dirt from her fall to create a muddy mask. I've never quite been able to put my finger on the reason she and I were never closer. If there were ever a competition for best friend, on paper, Cady's the clear winner. She's certainly never said the kinds of things that Jocelyn's said—things that left scars that lasted years. In fact, Cady has talked me out of some of my darkest times. She always seems to be there with a compassionate word or a motivating pep talk.

Jocelyn's friendship is one that defies logic. It's not a cookie-cutter definition of a friend; from most angles, it looks plain bad. But something I felt way back in high school, I still feel at times—that when you're the one at her side, you don't have to worry about anything. You're safe.

Sure, there have been times over the years when Cady and I ended up together, just the two of us. But it felt like we were two parts of a story missing their middle—the crux, the glue, the piece that held them together and created any semblance of coherence.

Or maybe it felt like we were doing something wrong, hanging out without Jocelyn. Betraying her trust, somehow. Maybe Cady and I could be closer, if we really gave ourselves the chance.

"I didn't do this, Rowan." Cady sniffles, then leans forward with her hands on her knees.

"I know," I say, even though I don't. After what I just learned about Jocelyn, anything's possible.

A familiar groan sounds in the vicinity, and it takes me a moment to place it: the sliding balcony door. Stepping back, I glance up to find all three balconies empty now. Whoever it was certainly got a show.

"Let's sit down," I say, helping Cady to a wooden bench on the front porch, beneath the overhang.

"I just wish I knew where my phone was," she says, wiping her eyes with the back of her hand. "Someone must have it—whoever sent that photo."

"When exactly did you see it last?"

"I don't know." She twists her lips. "I thought I had it in the bedroom, but it could've been with me in the fireside room last night. When I went to check on—" She reddens. "Well, I couldn't find Joss, so I thought I'd call her. But my phone wasn't in my jacket pocket."

The pieces fall into place. "You saw them," I say. "That's what the jab about Joss not deserving Landon meant."

Cady latches on to my hands with her dirt-caked ones. "Yes, but I swear to you, I *did not* take a photo of them. I was shocked, obviously. So I went back to the fireside room. And that was when . . ." Her eyes widen and she draws back, releasing my hands. "You and Valentina weren't there anymore." It's like she's talking to herself, rather than to me. "I searched for my phone on the chair and on the floor, but it wasn't anywhere. I sat alone in that room, waiting for everyone to return." She stares at her lap now. "Where did you go, Rowan?"

My heart thumps at the implication.

I didn't steal Cady's phone, but I did steal *something* when I left the room.

Valentina said she needed to use the bathroom, so she went upstairs. Alone in the fireside room, I started to get bored. My thoughts were treading water at first, simply fixating on how much I missed Molly.

How I hoped she missed me, too, but not so bad that she cried herself to sleep at night.

Then, no thanks to the alcohol, my thoughts swam out past the current, too far out to return safely. Molly had her first ballet class, and I hadn't even bothered to ask how it went. I was a terrible mother, and my parents knew it. They were probably talking about it at that very moment. Maybe even making plans to take custody away from me.

They'd talked about it before, hadn't they? When Molly was born and they thought I was too young, with too much of a future to throw it all away and raise a baby. *My* baby.

I didn't want or need anything from Helen's fireside room, but the pressure started up. The colors began to bleed together. A whispering voice told me to go to the bookcase.

The books are for guests; there's nothing wrong with borrowing one. Only I didn't take a book. I took a small porcelain figurine of a corgi. It meant nothing to me, but possibly a great deal to Helen. I stole it anyway.

"We drank too much whiskey and had to go upstairs to use the bathrooms," I say now to Cady. The truth was that I went upstairs to hide the corgi in my suitcase, as it created an obvious bulge in my sweatshirt pocket.

"So then . . ." Her eyes narrow, their focus on mine so intense that I'm positive she thinks I'm lying. "Valentina must've taken my phone."

My head pulls back unbidden. "Wha—oh. Well, I don't know. You think she's like . . . a *klepto* or whatever?"

"No." Cadence's gaze veers off to the trees. "I think she was trying to mess with us. I saw how upset she got when Magnus chased after Joss. Just imagine how she must've felt if she caught them together. She's probably punishing all of us for what Jocelyn did." She picks at her dirty fingernails. "I told you it was bizarre the way she ended up with my phone after the pub the other night. She pretends to be friendly, only to siphon information out of us that she uses to pit us against each other. She's a little devil whispering lies into our ears. Think about it. If

Valentina had simply stumbled upon Magnus in the act, she could've stormed in there and called him out. Instead, she takes my phone to snap a pic of them and sends it to Jocelyn's fiancé." She dips her head once for emphasis. "Now we're all screwed."

"What about your passcode?"

Cady shakes her head. "With the way they're always hovering over us, she probably watched me unlock it when I wasn't paying attention. I never should've ignored my instincts about her. I had this strange feeling she'd been through my phone that first night in the pub. Maybe the passcode was the reason she'd had to give the phone back. And then, when she'd spied on me enough to unlock it herself, she stole it again."

I frown, searching Cady's wide, light-brown eyes, scrutinizing the strain in her voice. "Sounds pretty devious, Cady."

"And it's what happened. We don't know anything about Valentina. Apart from you, she was the only one with access to my phone. She did this. Unless . . ." Cady does that thing again, where she chews on the inside of her cheek, refusing to look at me.

"Unless what?" I snap, unable to keep the resentment from my voice. She's not going to pin this on me. I didn't leave my daughter back home to be dragged into her drama and accused of something I didn't do.

"Nothing." She shakes her head and rubs a fresh track of dirt across her face. "I'm sorry. I just—Joss has never been this upset with me before. I don't know what to do. How can I prove that this was Valentina and not me?"

I study her, trying to decide whether or not I can believe her. She's never lied to me before. Has she?

"We'll figure out a way," I say, helping her onto her feet. I turn toward the front door when something in the tree line across the lawn catches my eye. Something that stands out among the greenery.

As soon as his eyes meet mine, the man emerges, leaving the cover of the trees. Branches rustle in his wake. My heart starts to thump out of my chest. "Oh my god," I hiss under my breath.

"Yeah." Cadence's fingers clamp onto my arm.

Magnus was standing there in the woods, watching us.

Listening to every word we said.

CHAPTER 12
CADENCE

"Good afternoon," Magnus says, waving at us. He has the nerve to act casually friendly, as though we didn't catch him spying on us. A black, woven beanie covers his blond hair, and he tugs it off for a moment to remove a pine needle embedded in the brim.

As he places it back on his head, nearing us, his eyes narrow. He extends his fingers toward my face. "What happened?"

I wrench back, my hand darting to the cut on my forehead. "Nothing. I slipped and fell on our hike. But I'm fine." I don't have time for this. I need to talk to Landon, to let him know I didn't send that photo. I have to find my phone.

"You look like you need a first aid kit. I've got one in my room."

He makes to skirt past us, but Rowan waves him off. "We do too. I've got an eight-year-old. I doctor up cuts and scrapes all the time."

I clear my throat to dislodge the nerves, making a mental note to hug Rowan later. "Helen said you'd gone to Caernarfon."

He nods. "Well, that was the plan. But then Valentina changed her mind."

"Oh?" Rowan says.

"She decided to go back to Argentina." He shrugs. "I knew our travels couldn't last forever. Something happened with her job, and she had to return home."

Liar. Valentina went back home to get away from him. She found her lover—or whoever Magnus is to her—in a *compromising* position with another woman. "But I thought she worked remotely," I say.

"Yes, but this 'desastre'—her word—required some in-person meetings, and she would've had to be on a computer all day. She couldn't sustain the job from here anymore."

"That's too bad," Rowan says, and I wish with everything in me I could read her thoughts. Is she actually falling for this *work* excuse? Or does she now believe that Valentina witnessed what happened between Magnus and Jocelyn, and it caused her to take off?

Magnus lowers his voice. "Hey, sorry, but I overheard something about a missing phone. You think Valentina stole it?"

My stomach flips. Before I can respond, Rowan says, "Cady probably misplaced it."

"We may never know," I say, "now that Valentina's gone."

"Hmm," Magnus says, scratching at his beanie. "I wish I could say for sure she didn't do it. But I have to admit, I didn't know her very well."

And we don't know you, Mr. Always Around, Always Watching. "I guess we never know anyone as well as we think, do we?"

Magnus nods in agreement, but I catch Rowan's sideways, inquisitive glance.

I believe I know Rowan, I do. Loving mother, good friend. Somewhat desperate for Jocelyn's attention. I'm surprised she stayed back with me out here in the yard at all. I'd expected her to chase after Joss, eager to fill that best friend–sized space she'd carved out—the one I'd occupied only minutes ago.

I want to hate Jocelyn for believing I could do this, but I am partially to blame. I'm the one who let my true thoughts about her relationship with Landon slip, after all these years of holding them in.

Sure, I'd tried to sabotage them before. In small, discrete ways, always making him seem like the bad guy. Like the time I was left alone in his bed and heard his phone ping on the bedside table. It was a message from Jocelyn, telling him where to meet her for dinner. I deleted it. Then, later that night when she was furious with him, I became her listening ear. "I can't believe he would stand you up like that," I said while filling her wineglass. "He doesn't deserve you, Joss."

Today was the first time I've ever switched the message around. I guess the pressure of their impending nuptials did me in.

I constantly want to hate my best friend. But the truth is, I never do. That's the strange thing about our friendship; it's the perpetual conundrum where Joss is concerned. Even though she's engaged to the man I'm in love with—even though I believe he's the one thing missing from my life—if it came down to winning him at the cost of losing her, I'm not sure I could go through with it.

It's a choice I've never actually had to make.

Maybe now, I'll finally have to make it. Landon isn't going to stand for this. He'll have to break up with her and cancel the wedding, won't he? He'll finally realize that he made the wrong choice all those years ago.

And we can finally be together.

Of course, if we're together, it means Jocelyn and I are over. I've never been without her before. Going a day without her friendship would be like trying to knit a scarf without a needle. She's always been there for me. In high school, she stuck up for me when my classmates called me a "goody-goody" or a prude. Especially sophomore year, when a group of boys thought it would be fun to change things up and use only ironic vocabulary words they learned from our Shakespeare lessons. "Wanton, unchaste, and lascivious" were whispered in the halls whenever I passed through, followed by billowing laughter. Joss would stare them down or call them all pathetic virgins until they shut up and skulked off. I only survived those formative years because of her.

Great. Now I have to go fix this when it wasn't even my fault. Jocelyn made her own bed. She threw away her own relationship and blamed me for it.

Magnus shifts his boots over the wood porch. "Well, I'm heading to Caernarfon now, if you want to join me." He dangles his car keys in front of us. "We could get dinner at this inn I read about on Tripadvisor."

"Sorry," I say. "I'm not feeling much up to it, but thanks for the offer."

Rowan mumbles an apology and heads into the B&B. I start to follow when Magnus leans forward, whispering into my hair. "I wonder just how well Jocelyn knows you, Cady."

A wave of terror crashes down my spine. My eyes snap back to his, then down to that hint of a smirk on his lips. "What do you mean?"

"Just that a woman like you has a lot of . . . *depth* to her. Secret parts of her that not even a good friend could possibly unlock."

"You don't know anything about me." But he does. *He knows about Landon. That bastard has my phone.* I whip around, leaving Magnus on the porch, and quicken my steps to catch up with Rowan in the reception area. Valentina couldn't have acted alone. It all rings too much like a setup. All that talk about the castle last night, Magnus getting so close to me in the fireside room—what if *he* was the one who snatched my phone? He couldn't have taken the photo himself, but he could've passed the phone off to Valentina. Or maybe Valentina really was shocked and upset to find Magnus and Joss together. Maybe she took that photo, and then, when she confronted Magnus, things went haywire.

They fought, she left. In his anger, he went through my phone and sent the photo to Landon.

Or am I making too much of that one little comment back there? Maybe I'm being paranoid. It wouldn't be the first time. Jocelyn loves to remind me of my tendency to worry too much.

If it's not a case of paranoia, though—if Magnus knows about Landon and me, and he's hell-bent on screwing with us this week—he'd only have to let it slip to Joss.

Heart thumping, I rush past Rowan up the stairs. Even from down the hall, Jocelyn's crying is audible. I open the room door, one arm in a defensive position in case she throws something at me. Only she's sprawled out on the bed, face in her pillow, sobbing. I glance out into the hall at Rowan. "Can you give us a couple minutes?"

"Of course." She offers a sympathetic wince. "I'll be down in the fireside room."

I shut the door, tiptoeing straight past Jocelyn. After ducking into the bathroom to clean up a bit, I sit on the edge of our bed. "Joss." When she ignores me, I tentatively reach out to rub my hand over her back. "Joss, it's going to be okay."

"No, it isn't," she blubbers into the pillow, voice half-muffled. "He was my whole life, my future, and I wrecked everything. I'm such an idiot. I—please forgive me, Cady." She still isn't looking at me, almost as if she can't bear to watch me reject her. It's the most vulnerable I've seen her.

"I know you didn't send the photo," she says. "This is my mess. I did this. Now he's gone, and I-I just can't lose you too." It's a rare moment, Jocelyn with her defenses down, allowing me to see this insecurity, this desperation.

"You're never going to lose me." I refuse to let that psycho Magnus ruin everything she and I have spent fifteen years building. "And I'm sure Landon's not *gone*."

She fumbles for the phone beside her and unlocks it, handing it to me. I read the text from Landon: It's over, Joss.

A delirious sort of bliss comes over me at the words. It's everything I've ever wanted. I've won.

And yet, I find myself saying, "I'm going to call him."

"What?" She wrenches her body upright to gape at me, her nose red, expertly lined eyes dripping black.

"I'll tell him it's not you in the photo." I shrug, as if the task will be simple. "It's too dark and blurry to make anything out. I'll tell him it was a prank. That I saw this girl who looked like you, so I took the photo to mess with him."

"But why would you play a joke on Landon? You two aren't even friends."

No, *friends* probably isn't the word for us.

I'll admit, the story is a bit weak. It would make sense to Landon, though, for me to try to mess with their relationship. After all the times I begged him to leave Jocelyn. He'd believe I sent a fake photo, and I'd look horribly pathetic. The only person he'd be done with would be me.

"Because I despise him, remember? I don't want the two of you to end up together." Saying this aloud is like walking the highest tightrope, holding my breath and hoping to make it to the other side.

She scratches at the back of her neck. "I guess anything is worth a try."

I relax, relief flooding through me. The feeling only lasts a moment. I still have to go through with it.

When I call, Landon doesn't answer. It's Cadence I text, keeping it formal because Jocelyn is peering over my shoulder, reading everything I type. Please pick up.

The next time I dial, he answers. "Cady? Why are you calling on Joc—"

"I wanted to apologize for the confusion," I cut in. "That photo last night was a joke—albeit a mean-spirited one. I never intended for it to get so out of hand. It wasn't Jocelyn in the photo. It was some strangers I came across on our trip, and from the back, the woman's hair looked a bit like Jocelyn's. Again, I'm really sorry. Please don't be mad at her."

"Wait, I don't—"

I hand the phone over to Joss, who's frantically wiping at her under eyes as if Landon can see her, and pat her on the arm. "I'm going to join Rowan in the fireside room." I give her a half smile, and she mouths *Thank you*, looking as though she's about to cry all over again.

It's up to her to salvage things now. Jocelyn is no stranger to lies.

Though this one might be different. This isn't a little white lie here and there. This is the kind of deception that can suck you dry. I know what it's like to be hiding something in a relationship for years; I've done it with Jocelyn every day since Landon and I started things back up again—while he was still dating her. It's a constant drain on your soul. It's a black shadow over all the good times. And when things get rough, it's the thought that makes you want to throw it all away. That's what Jocelyn is committing to if she doesn't fess up to her sin.

Downstairs, I find Helen with Rowan in the fireside room. True to its name, a blaze is going in the fireplace. A sweet scent mingles with smoke, and I look to find a tray on the coffee table holding a teapot and a plate full of cookies.

"Cadence." Helen sets her mug down and gets to her feet. "Do you need a doctor?"

I must not have done a particularly thorough job cleaning up my scrapes. I laugh and wave her off. Is there even such a thing out here? "Please, sit down. I'm fine."

She smiles, but keeps walking past me to the door. "I only stopped by to bring Rowan some tea. She seemed lonely in here, all by herself."

"Well, I'm here now." I force a smile, though my face is fighting it.

Helen gestures toward the tray. "There's an extra mug. Have a good afternoon, girls. And, Cadence," she says in a motherly tone, "make sure you disinfect that wound."

"I will. Thanks, Helen."

The door closes and I grab a cookie.

"Tea?" Rowan asks, reaching for the pot.

"Yeah." I hover near one of the wingback chairs without sitting. The crackling of the fire should be soothing, but I can't relax—can't even sit down.

"Everything okay with Joss?"

"Mm-hmm. I think it will be. She knows I didn't send the photo, at least." And if she managed to make up with him, I wonder what that means for Landon and me. Will he be upset with me for the *joke*? Will he want things between us to continue? I'll never know as long as someone else has my phone.

My mind's a blur. Unable to focus or process anything until I know the truth about Magnus, I step past Rowan in the direction of the door. "You know what? I'll be right back." I head back into the reception area and peer out the front window. Magnus's car is still outside.

When I return, Rowan's brows are hoisted, teapot still in hand. "What's going on, Cady?"

"Have you seen Magnus? He hasn't left yet."

"You and I both know he's not really going anywhere." She pours the tea and hands me the mug. "If we stay, so does he."

"Yeah." I start to pace behind the couch. "I think he has my phone."

"Magnus? That doesn't even make sense. He couldn't have taken the photo himself."

"I know. I can't explain it." Actually, I can, but not without incriminating myself. Magnus practically admitted to having the phone, but only by hinting at the top-quality dirt he has on *me*. "I think he and Valentina orchestrated that whole thing last night with Jocelyn to try to destroy our friendship."

"Why would they do that?"

"I don't know." I blow on the tea, my mind spinning. "For entertainment, maybe. They're weird, you said it yourself."

Rowan's lips twist. "That sounds more than weird, Cady. It sounds—"

"Psychotic, I know." I take a sip of tea, wincing as it scalds the tip of my tongue. "But Valentina took my phone from the pub our first night. She's been stirring up drama between Jocelyn and me since we got here. And Magnus just said something to me out there, something that gave me a really bad feeling. I want to check his room for my phone."

"What?" Her mug clanks down onto the tray. "As in break into his room?"

I shrug. "I want my phone back, Rowan. And I'm almost positive he has it." Without that phone, Magnus could never prove my relationship with Landon.

"What if Valentina has it, and it's on its way to Argentina?"

Then I can sleep easier, knowing that Magnus's comment earlier meant nothing. "The only way to find out for sure is to check his room."

"How do you propose we do that?"

I shrug. "We'd either have to pick the lock or steal his room key."

Rowan is silent for far too long, gazing into the fire, mug hovering over her lap. "I have another idea. But we'll need Jocelyn's help."

CHAPTER 13
JOCELYN

"You want me to *what?*" I ask, eyes still blurred by tears.

They'd been tears of desperation at first, soon morphing into tears of joy when Landon apologized for ever having fallen for that "prank." Once our phone call ended, I saw Rowan's text asking me to join her and Cady in the fireside room. I came down, my chest lighter.

Then I heard what they were asking of me.

"Why does it have to be me?"

"He trusts you, Joss." Cady whispers the words. "Please." Her eyes keep darting to the walls of the fireside room, as if Magnus is watching us from some camera hidden between the boards.

"So, first it was this shameful act of indiscretion, and now it's some sort of advantage we have over him. Have I got it right?"

"Keep your voice down," Cady hisses. "He's always listening in on our conversations."

"Look," Rowan says, leaning forward onto her thighs. Her curls are piled into a high bun, and a few spirals hang loose in a haphazardly angelic way. "Cady and I will head to the river. All we want you to do is go up to Magnus's room and knock on the door. Act panicked. Tell him we were all at the river, and Cady passed out. Her head wound must've been worse than we thought. A concussion. Tell him to grab that first aid kit he was bragging about and go down, that you're right behind him, but you need to grab water first. Hopefully, he buys it and forgets to lock up."

"And then I'm just supposed to snoop around in his room?"

"Pretty much," Cady says. "Rowan will text you if something goes wrong and we return to the B&B. But it's a small room. Shouldn't take too long to find my phone."

"Why the hell do you need your phone so bad, Cady?"

"Because it's mine," she hisses. "Because my mom has probably called me one thousand times, and all of my emergency numbers that I've stored if something happens to her are on there." The words come out quiet, but fast and jumbled, like her mouth can't keep up with her brain. "And I'm scared that if I—"

"I told you, you can use my phone to call your mom."

"It's the only way to prove it to you," she says, suddenly somber. "Once and for all. I know you said you believe me, and I'm grateful for that. But I want to show you."

"You don't have to do that, Cades."

"I know, but I want to."

I inhale slowly, as if I'm the one out of breath after Cady's rambling. I play with a snagged thread on my sweater, not ready to buy that Magnus's intentions with me last night were malicious. Though if I believe that Cady didn't do it, then someone really was trying to hurt us. "And what are you going to do when he realizes you're fine?"

"Pretend like I just woke up, I guess. Convince him not to call emergency services." Cady quiets for a moment, looking more anxious than usual, even for her. "He was watching us, Joss. Rowan and me. He was watching us from the woods, and if she hadn't spotted him, he never would've revealed himself."

"And there's no chance of Valentina showing up while I'm snooping?"

Rowan shakes her head. "She went back to Argentina, probably because . . . well, you know."

"Right." As much as I'd like to avoid Magnus for the rest of our trip, I owe my friends. My actions got us all into this mess in the first place. If I'm going to fix things, I'll have to participate in their little plan. "Well, I should probably head out that way with you, just in case he's spying from the window or something."

The girls exchange a glance. "That's a good point, actually," Rowan says.

◆　◆　◆

We slink through the reception and out the front door. The sky above is full of shifting gray clouds, and the wind has picked up since our hike. Rowan lets her curls down, stuffing a beanie over them. I zip my coat all the way up to my throat. The moment we reach the tree line, the roar of the river hits us, and we follow the sound until the blue-gray water comes into view. The river is rushing, white froth forming as it crashes over rocks. Overhead, an egret leaves a nearby treetop to dive down to the bank.

"Enjoy the view, I guess." I wish I could stay and actually do that with them. Instead, I turn and head back into the trees.

"Thank you, Joss," Cady calls out after me.

I trudge on through the pines without a reply. With each step, resentment toward those two builds. I feel it in my muscles, the tension and soreness, like lactic acid needing to be purged. Or maybe it's all the hiking we did this morning. I don't know. I learned all of that science stuff from my private trainer, back before I decided that the gym wasn't really for me. The trainer, however—tall, dark, and muscles for days—wasn't quite as easy to kick.

But he was the last one—well, before Magnus.

I should want to do this. Cady's right. Finding her phone in Magnus's room would eliminate any shred of doubt I've had about her.

Still, I can't help thinking that she and Rowan are making too big a deal of Magnus. It's a small B&B. Conwy's a tiny town. He's bound to show up everywhere. And it's not *his* fault the walls are thin. What if Cady's only trying to exonerate herself by shifting the blame onto him?

I guess we'll find out. I approach his room, messing up my hair and pinching my cheeks to make it look like I've been running. When I knock, the thud of his footsteps sends a spike of nerves through me. He opens the door with a grin and leans an elbow against the doorjamb. "Hi, Jocelyn." His low voice alights my nerves. Every feeling from last night—desire, guilt, pleasure, fear—floods back. He gestures inside his room, a space identical to ours. The two beds have been made. All of Magnus's belongings are apparently stored in the wardrobe or tucked within his enormous pack—one of those backpacker's types. "Come on in." He must assume I regret pulling away from him last night. That I'm here to pick up where we left off.

"No, I-I just came to"—I huff and fold over onto my knees—"get help for Cady. She's down by the river. We think she has a concussion. She wasn't making any sense, and then, it was like she blacked out."

Magnus straightens, helping me over to the bed. "Here, sit. Let me just . . ." He grabs his boots by the door and shoves his feet into them. "Did you call anyone?"

I shake my head. "I figured it would take forever. Rowan mentioned you have a first aid kit."

He nods. "Sounds like she needs medical attention, though." He frowns down at me. "Maybe you should catch your breath. Where are they, exactly?"

I take another dramatic, wheezing breath. "Just through the trees, on the riverbank."

He marches over to his backpack and wrangles the first aid bag from it. Grabbing his coat from the foot of the bed, he starts toward the door. For a moment, I think he's going to leave me in his room, but he stops in the doorway, turning back. "I'll make sure she's okay, Jocelyn. Let me help you to your room."

"Thanks," I force out as he offers me his arm.

A disturbing thought squirms at the back of my mind. He doesn't want to leave me alone in his room. Not even for an emergency.

"I'm actually fine," I say, testing him. "You should go find Cady."

He hesitates, his gaze darting to the back of the room. I fight the urge to follow it. His eyes narrow at me—with concern? Or something else entirely? Maybe the others were right after all. "Please hurry," I add. "I'm so worried about her." Time to push things even further. "I'll just get some water from your tap and be right behind you."

It would be extremely suspicious to force me out of here now, wouldn't it, Mr. Gallant? Mr. Norwegian Savior?

He smiles. "Of course." With that, he shrugs on his coat. Quick-tapping his hand on the doorjamb twice, he takes off down the hall, first aid kit slung over one shoulder.

I listen to the sound of his footsteps trailing off down the hall, then move to the window. When his tall figure emerges into view, barreling across the lawn toward the river, I scan the room. His pack is on one of the beds, but my gaze darts to the back of the room. There's a tall wardrobe, its oak doors shut. I race over, flinging them open. I'm staring at an empty space.

This can't be right. It's nothing but a bunch of bare shelves and hangers. There's a high shelf I can't quite see to the back of, so I climb up on the bed nearest me to get a better view. I shine my phone's light over the wood, but it's empty. No phone.

Did I have it wrong?

I hurry to the bedside table, yanking open the drawer and rifling through it. Nothing but a brochure about Snowdonia, a pocket-size Bible, a blank pad of paper, and a blue pen. There are a few crumpled, loose papers and ticket stubs, including one to Leeds Castle dated last week. I stick my hand inside the drawer and fish for something at the back. But it's bare, hiding only the dust that now coats my fingers. I jostle and lift the objects. I feel for something beneath them and, in my hurry, manage to flick the pen out of the drawer and onto the floor.

It bounces and rolls beneath the bed. Giving a growl, I drop down and reach for it. Immediately, I wrench my hand back. I touched something, but it wasn't a pen.

It was much, much bigger.

I swing my head down lower and shine my light at whatever's there. It's another bag, though this one's been flattened to fit beneath the bed. I reach for it, pulling it toward me by a nylon strap. When I free it, my heart speeds up as my brain registers the object.

It's another pack. A purple one. I unzip the main compartment, pushing aside some toiletries and a Swiss Army knife. Then my stomach turns. I've found a phone, only it isn't Cady's.

It's Valentina's. I recognize its glittery gold case from the pub. In fact, the entire bag is hers, by the look of it. Digging deeper, I tug a few items of clothing free, including the cashmere sweater she wore the night we met her and the black yoga pants she had on last night in the fireside room. Even her navy-blue coat is stuffed inside here.

It's as if she never left.

My phone pings in my hand, startling me. Rowan: Almost back.

Adrenaline pumps through me as I zip up the bag and shove it back underneath the bed. Checking that the room is exactly as Magnus left it, I exit. I stop by our room to grab Cady's water bottle and tuck it beneath my arm before heading through the hall and down the stairs.

On the ground floor, I sprint out the door and toward the trees. I have to make up the distance I should've covered while searching Magnus's room. But I don't get far before spotting them—Magnus helping a wobbly Cady over the rock-strewn path, and Rowan carrying the first aid kit.

"Oh, thank god she's okay." I make a show of brushing the hair and sweat off my forehead as I near them.

"You can also thank Magnus," Cady says, smiling shyly. She takes the bottle from me.

The back of my neck prickles, and I scratch at it. "Of course. Thank you, Magnus. I'm not sure what we would've done without you." I avoid his eyes, afraid he knows what I've been up to. Afraid of what he's capable of doing.

He claims Valentina went home to Argentina, but her things are still in his room.

Buried in his room. Like a dirty secret.

What if Valentina didn't go home at all?

"Well, I can take it from here." I attempt to shoulder my way between him and Cady.

He sidesteps me, though, tugging Cady along with him like a rag doll. "It's really no trouble. We're all going the same way."

They brush past me on the path, and I stand there, helpless. His arm is looped around her waist, and as I watch, I can barely believe what I'm seeing.

Magnus pulls Cady tighter into his body. His hand starts to inch lower, until it's clutching her hip. He glances back at me over her head, like he knows I'm watching.

Inside the B&B, Helen is back at the desk. "Oh," she cries, hand darting to her mouth. "What happened?"

"Nothing, Helen," Cady mumbles. "Guess I should've taken it easy, after all."

"I'll call the paramedics." She picks up the desk phone from its cradle.

Rowan's eyes flood with panic as they meet mine. "No, Helen," she blurts. "That's not necessary. Cady is fine. Magnus checked her pupils and all that. She just needs some R and R."

"Thanks again, Magnus," I add, dismissing him.

"Sure you don't need me to help her up the stairs?" he asks.

"Nope, we've got it." I fake a smile and turn to my aunt. "I thought now might be a good time to chat about wedding stuff—oh, and Rowan never showed you those photos of Molly, did she?"

Helen takes the bait, clapping her hands together. "I'll make a pot of coffee. Girls, get Cady settled." She points to the fireside room and hustles off through the door to the breakfast room. We usher Cady along, leaving Magnus standing at the base of the stairs.

Once inside, Rowan looks at me. "So, did you—"

"Shh." I press my back against the door and put an index finger to my lips. A moment later, I open the door a sliver and peek out to find the reception area clear. "I didn't find the phone. But I did find Valentina's things."

Cady squints. "What sort of things?"

"Her entire pack. Her phone, clothes . . . I didn't have time to look through everything, but I definitely recognized her phone case and her blue coat."

Rowan removes her beanie and fluffs her curls. "So, she came back?"

"Or she never left." Cady's gaze is on the fire. When she finally looks at us, her face is pale.

"Cades, are you okay?" I ask, nearing her. "You might've been faking back there, but you really did take quite a spill earlier."

"I'm fine."

"Good," I say, still unconvinced. "Because there's more. Magnus said he came from the east, right? That he'd wanted to see London, but since they were already in North East Wales, they decided to head this way. But in his drawer, I saw a ticket to Leeds Castle, dated last Friday. Two days before we all arrived here. Leeds Castle is in England, not Wales."

"Wait," Rowan says, finding a seat on the sofa, "so you're saying he lied?"

I shrug. "I mean, unless he just happened to have someone else's ticket to Leeds Castle in his drawer."

Cady's back stiffens. "I know that name, Leeds. Can I use your phone?"

I unlock it and pass it over, and she starts navigating through Google. "That's where I saw it. I looked up Chilham—the place where that girl went missing—on a map. Leeds Castle is right next to it." She licks her lips and passes the phone back. "That means Magnus was there when the girl—"

"Lisa Granger," I cut in, recalling my conversation with Magnus. "He was there when she was abducted. He told me it turned out she was a runaway."

Rowan gets on her phone, no doubt googling the incident.

"But what if she wasn't?" Cady licks her lips and lowers onto the sofa. "What if something terrible happened to Lisa? And now the same thing has happened to Valentina? Magnus claims she headed home to Argentina and he never saw her again. If Joss hadn't found her stuff, no one would ever suspect anything different."

"I don't know," Rowan says, still focused on her screen. "The countryside where Lisa was last seen is only a couple hours from London. That isn't good news, obviously. But Magnus wasn't lying about the runaway thing. According to Lisa's friend Jaquelyn, Lisa talked about disappearing for good. Homelife was rough, so she often spoke of getting out of the country and never returning."

"Sounds like the perfect victim," I say.

Cady nods. "And Valentina. Her company might not really be expecting her soon at all. Magnus could've made that up. What if it's weeks until they report her missing?"

"The stones," Rowan says suddenly. "We got distracted from researching the stones, but we saw blood out there."

"And Magnus is obsessed with those stones," I say.

"It could be some sort of sick murder ritual," Cady says, sending a shock of cold through me. "Like, his signature."

There's a knock on the door, and I open it to find Aunt Helen holding a new tray full of mugs, this time with a coffeepot. Her chipper demeanor is in stark contrast to our somber expressions. "What happened?"

I look at the others, communicating the question with my eyes, as she sits down on the blue-and-white-striped wingback chair and pours herself a cup of coffee. They nod. We have to tell her.

As she stirs in a sugar cube, we proceed to fill her in, our tones hushed. Afterward, she takes a silent moment to absorb it all. She finally leans forward, her coffee still untouched.

"So, what do you think, Helen? Should we be worried?"

She inhales, and the wrinkles around her eyes deepen. "It is odd that she would leave without her bag. Did you happen to see if her passport was in it?"

I shake my head. "I didn't see it. But I didn't have much time to search the bag."

"I'll put a call in to the local police. It could be nothing, but we need to confirm Valentina got on that plane." Her gaze veers over to the fire, her slate-blue eyes reflecting the lapping flames. "Of course, she could've gone somewhere else. If she didn't want Magnus to know where she was headed, that would make the most sense."

"But why would she go without her stuff?" Rowan asks.

Helen frowns. "I don't know. Did you hear anything suspicious? From their room? It's possible she left in a hurry."

"No, nothing," I say. "We never saw them argue once."

"That doesn't mean they never did," Cady says. "Magnus is leaving tomorrow, isn't he? He told me they were leaving on Wednesday."

Helen lets out a sigh, and the mug shakes in her unsteady grip. "I'm so sorry, girls. I—yesterday, Magnus asked if he could rent the room for another three nights. It wasn't booked, so I said yes."

"I knew it," Cady says, right foot jouncing. "This is about *us*. His travel plans revolve around the three of us and what we do."

"I can tell him I made a mistake with the booking," Helen offers.

"No, you don't have to do that." Rowan gets up and starts pacing. "We don't want to let on that we're suspicious. Just in case we're right. We have each other. We'll be fine. Let us know what the cops say, though."

"Of course. Stick together, girls. And stay in tonight. I'll fix you up something to eat in the breakfast room." With a last sip of her coffee and a reassuring squeeze of my hand, Helen heads back out to the reception area.

"She's right," Cady says. "We have to stick together. Magnus's goal seems to be turning us against each other to isolate one of us. We can't fall for it."

With a shudder, I remember the way he glanced back at me, eyes unreadable, as his hand moved possessively down Cady's hip. Or did I imagine it? I've been through a lot today. Maybe my mind was as tired as my eyes. "I don't know," I say, going over today's events in my head, one by one. I'm the one who found the bag; maybe there is a perfectly reasonable explanation for it. "He seemed pretty helpful today, didn't he?"

"Joss," Rowan says, and my heart squeezes at the desperation in her face. Maybe because it reminds me of another time she looked desperate—much more than this.

It was the day before Jake's death, when he broke up with her. Rowan lay in our dorm room for hours, likely racking her brain for a possible reason. She couldn't fathom why he would've done it. She kept fiddling with her phone, staring at the screen. Waiting for something that never came. She refused to speak to me about why she was so upset. She didn't want to talk about it. To this day, she must still believe that no one knows that she and Jake weren't a couple the day he died.

But I know. And I know the reason he broke up with her.

In fact, I invented it.

I told a lie about Rowan, and Jake, my ever-faithful twin, believed me.

NOW

"I'd really like to talk more about the fight that broke out the day before the victim's death," DI Collins presses. "Tuesday."

"Has anyone bothered to find out if Valentina got on that plane?" I ask, the flames from the fireplace lashing at my cheeks.

"We did check, though nothing's come up so far."

"That's because he killed her! Just like he killed Lisa Granger! Just like . . ." The thought begins to strangle me, so I suck in a deep breath. It only leaves me dizzy and slightly nauseated. "Just like he killed our friend. Don't you see?"

"Do you think it's possible that Valentina didn't go back to Argentina after all?" DI Collins's lips twist as if she's examining the merit of her question; really, she's examining me.

"Absolutely. I think it's highly improbable that she went back to Argentina, actually. Because she's dead."

DI Collins allows one corner of her mouth to curl. "We can't exactly look for her without any leads. Did she or Magnus ever talk about where exactly in Ireland they were headed?"

I shake my head. "They only mentioned the ferry ride over."

"Was there ever a reason, that you could see, for Magnus to be angry with any of you?"

I shake my head again. But this time, it's a lie. There was a reason.

Only none of us knew about it until it was too late.

CHAPTER 14
ROWAN

The three of us hustle past Magnus's door. I unlock ours, stopping as soon as I push it open.

There's a note on the floor. No envelope, just a white, folded piece of paper with jagged edges, like something ripped from a notepad in a hurry. "What is that?" Jocelyn asks.

Shrugging, I kneel down to unfold it, and an uneasy feeling weaves its way beneath my skin.

The note is handwritten in big blue letters.

Cady,

We need to talk. Please have dinner with me.

Sincerely,
Magnus

"What's wrong?" Cady asks, reaching for the note. She reads, her face going ashen as she collapses onto the nearest bed.

Jocelyn snatches the note out of her limp hand. She reads it, then motions for us to follow her into the bathroom. We squeeze inside, my hip pressed against the wall, Cady sitting on the countertop, and Joss with her back to the door.

"He won't go away," Jocelyn whispers. "He gave up on getting me alone again, so now he's after Cady."

She crumples up the note, making to toss it in the trash.

"Wait." I take it from her and slip it in my pocket. "Could be evidence, you know. If the cops ask for proof that he's stalking us."

Jocelyn nods. "Good thinking."

I run a fingertip over the bumpy wall spackle. "Wonder what he meant by 'We need to talk.'"

"No idea," Cady says, her hands fidgety in her lap. "Joss is probably right. He's trying to isolate one of us, like he tried with the phone scam. He'll probably tell me something terrible about one of you—a lie—to make me turn on you. That way he can be the hero."

"Too bad we're done falling for his act," Jocelyn says.

"What are we going to do?" I ask.

"Leave, of course." She takes a step toward the counter to shove her loose cosmetics inside their bag. "We don't have to stay here. Cady, can you check the train schedules?" She hands her phone over to Cady.

"Do you think Helen will be okay?" I ask, feeling like I'm glued to this wall.

"Magnus targets young women," Jocelyn says. "He's after us, not my aunt and uncle. Plus, the police will be looking into this soon. They'll handle him. Are we all in agreement?" She glances at Cady first, who nods before continuing to search the train schedules. Then her eyes lock onto mine.

I nod too. "We can't stay here."

"No, we sure as hell can't."

"Bad news," Cady says, pursing her lips. "No trains until midday tomorrow."

"What?" Jocelyn digs her fingernails into the back of her neck. "How?"

"You've seen the size of the stations around here," Cady says, still typing. "Trains come through like twice a day. Best we can do is tomorrow at eleven forty-five, Conwy Station to Edinburgh."

"Scotland?" I ask, panic and awe clashing within me. "What will we do until then?"

"I'll have Helen call around and find us a place for tonight," Jocelyn says. "Maybe Uncle Paul can drive us somewhere." She opens the bathroom door and hurries across the room to grab her suitcase. She lifts the sweater slung over the chairback and stuffs it inside. "Well, what are you waiting for?"

Cady jumps into motion now, the color returning to her cheeks. She removes a lone jacket from a wardrobe hanger and gathers the rest of her clothes from the shelf she claimed on day one.

When we're finished packing, we leave the suitcases in the room and head out to speak with Helen. I lead the way, reaching the stairs just as a door creaks in the hall behind us.

"Cadence?" The deep voice stops my heart. I turn to find Jocelyn standing protectively in front of Cady and Magnus slouched against his doorjamb. "Did you get my note?" His voice sounds pleasant, but his intense blue eyes scream danger.

Cady is visibly trembling.

We forced Jocelyn to deal with Magnus last time. I'm supposed to be the brave one in the group. It's my turn to step up. "I'll handle this," I whisper, pushing past the others. "Go ahead to dinner."

"Yeah right," Jocelyn says, refusing to budge.

My resolve buoys. It's just like being back at the lake house all those years ago. Like having my own personal guard dog—snarling, poised, and ready to leap. I'm protected.

Then a thought stops me in my tracks. I've been telling myself that I changed, that Molly forced me to abandon my former reckless ways and live a more cautious life. But maybe I was never brave. Maybe I only felt as though I could do anything because Jocelyn was beside me. Without her the past eight years, I've become my true self: a coward.

I shake off the revelation. The chance to disprove it is standing right in front of me. I'm going to do this on my own.

"Stay here." Leaving the others by the stairs, I press down the hall to where he's waiting. "Hey, Magnus." I smile. "Thanks again for your help with Cady earlier. But we really did come on this trip for some quality friend time. We've only got a couple more nights, and—"

"Cady can speak for herself," he cuts in.

"No, it's just—"

His gaze slowly skims my chest and remains there. "How's the coat working out for you, Rowan?"

It's like an icy draft has blown straight through the puffy coat and every layer of my clothing. Past my skin and deep into my bones. "What?" I ask, too frozen to glance down to where his gaze roams.

The coat.

"Not quite your size, is it?"

I try to ask what he means again, but I'm numb from the shock. I've been wearing this oversized black sack of polyester since day one, believing I got away with stealing it. Believing no one would ever know the truth because I swiped it back in Manchester, England, and we're here in the middle of nowhere, Wales.

But Jocelyn found a ticket to Leeds Castle, dated last week. We know Magnus didn't really come on a train from North East Wales. He came from somewhere in the vicinity of London, and he lied about it. It means he could've had something to do with Lisa Granger's disappearance.

And that isn't all it means.

If Magnus was near London until Sunday, he could've easily passed through Manchester on his way here at the same time we did.

I stole his coat, along with his ticket to *somewhere* in Wales and his money. And he ended up staying at the same B&B as me, in the room next door.

He never randomly targeted our group. He chose us because of *me*.

Because this time, I stole from the wrong person.

My breathing gets shallow, the borders around my vision blackening. They push in, until only a sliver of the man in front of me remains. Just those hauntingly blue eyes, twinkling with amusement above pink, sneering lips. "Cost me nearly five hundred pounds, you know." His voice is low now, barely a purr. Too soft for the others to hear. "Not just to get a new train ticket that didn't leave for another six hours, or because of the cash. But to replace the coat too." He tugs on the zipper of the slate-gray puffer jacket he's wearing now. "Had to buy this one at a fancy airport shop. I don't like it nearly as much."

Sensing the others stirring behind me, I force myself to snap out of it. "I'm sorry, but I don't know what you're talking about."

"Don't you?" He smiles, taking a few slow steps toward me. I hold my ground, even as he leans in, his warm breath hitting my face. The pressure keeps building, cutting off my air supply and impeding my vision. I could be inches away from the man who killed Lisa Granger and Valentina. "Do they know?" He flicks his head in the direction of the others. "*About your little problem?*"

I wheeze in a breath and spit out, "The only person with a problem here is *you*. What do you want with Cady?"

He shrugs. "Just to have dinner, like I said."

"Leave her alone. In fact, leave all of us alone." Everything is black and fuzzy. I can't take a full breath. I'm too unsteady to make it down the stairs. There's only one way to fix this. One thing that ever helps to ease this horrible, suffocating sensation.

But Jocelyn hurries to me, followed by Cady. "It's okay," I try to tell them. "I've got this." I can't let them hear this. But Jocelyn takes my arm, and I inhale. When the air hits my lungs, I take my fill.

"What's going on here?" Jocelyn demands. She grips my shoulder so hard that her fingernails dig through the coat, into my skin. It's the way Molly used to hold on to her stuffed bear—no one's taking me away. On my other side, Cady slips her arm around me. Just like that, it's the three of us again.

Magnus's gaze sharpens and he steps closer. *Too* close. "I'm glad you managed to work everything out with—what was his name? That's right, Landon. It's a shame I've got another photo, and in this one, there's no denying it's your pretty little face."

Jocelyn's defiant look falls. "That's what this is? You're blackmailing us?"

"I think you all know I'm not afraid to send it. Actually"—he tilts his head in thought—"I could just call this poor guy and tell him I'm the man who kissed his fiancé."

"You want money?" she grits out. "Is that it?"

Instead, Magnus sneers, his gaze flicking to me. It's all over. This is when he tells the girls about how I stole from him, and it's only right that we pay him back. "I think ten thousand dollars should about cover it."

"You're insane." Jocelyn's glare could cut glass. "Show us this photo."

Magnus merely stares back, still looking smug.

"He doesn't have one," Jocelyn says, rolling her eyes. "This is bullshit. I'll just tell Landon that if some creep calls, ignore him because he's been stalking us since we got here."

"Maybe I don't have a photo," Magnus says glibly. "Or maybe I've got a photo of you"—his eyes dart to me, then to Cady—"and a whole lot more."

My heart lurches, and I feel Cady's grip on my arm go slack.

Jocelyn studies the man another moment. Then, with an ambivalent look to match his, she shrugs. "I guess we'll just see about that," she says, tugging me and Cady along.

Magnus doesn't say a word, just stands there in the hall as we push past him. Somehow, it's even more unsettling than if he'd made a move to block our path.

"We're getting out of here," Jocelyn whispers as we descend the staircase.

At the bottom, Helen's forehead crinkles, seeing us. "Is everything okay?"

"We need to talk to you in private," Jocelyn says.

Helen nods, but the creases in her brow remain. "Of course. Your dinner is ready." Once we're inside the breakfast room, she locks the door behind us. Savory smells dance around us. They should be enticing; instead, they turn my stomach. "What's going on?" Helen motions for us to sit at the table at the back, where our plates are loaded with roasted chicken, leafy greens, and crispy potatoes.

"Did you get a hold of the cops?" Jocelyn asks.

She shakes her head. "I haven't heard anything since I called this afternoon. They said they were looking into it. Though"—she frowns—"I'll admit the man on the phone didn't sound too concerned. He said something like, 'Well, if she was supposed to get on a plane, chances are, she got on a plane.' He said they'd continue to look into it, but that without a passport number or even a full name, these things take time."

"Dammit," Jocelyn says. "I wish I'd found that passport. We're going to need to stay somewhere else tonight. Magnus isn't letting up."

"Helen," I say, my mind still spinning. "How far in advance did Magnus and Valentina book their room?"

Her lips twist for a moment. "They were a same-day booking. They called on Sunday, looking for a room, and I happened to have one available."

Nausea pushes from deep in my stomach up to my throat. I knew it. They followed us here from the train station.

Helen and the others are looking at me, as if for an explanation. When I don't elaborate, Jocelyn tells her aunt, "Magnus just got in Rowan's face. I'm talking *menacing*. And he sent Cady this bizarre note. Aunt Helen, we think he's dangerous and that he's targeting us."

Helen nods, worry lines deepening around her mouth. "It's high season and Conwy's busy this week, but I'm friends with the owner of an inn. Go ahead and eat. I'll talk to her."

She leaves, the lock clicking behind her again. "At least we know he can't get in," Cady says, her shoulders tucked in close to her body. "But maybe we should just pay him, Joss. Maybe he'd go away."

"I'm not handing over ten thousand dollars to this parasite."

"But he might've killed a girl, Joss," I say, surprised to be on Cady's side for once. "And aren't you at all worried about Landon?"

"You heard Helen. Let's eat." Jocelyn lifts her fork and knife. "We've already given this man too much power. There are three of us. We're going to be fine, no matter what." She takes a bite, and tentatively, Cady follows suit.

"Eat, Rowan," Jocelyn says, her mouth half-full of potatoes.

"I'm not very hungry," I say, taking up the knife anyway.

"What was all of that about back there?" she asks. "Why was he going on about a coat?"

"Because he's a psycho." I place a sliver of chicken into my mouth.

"Obviously." She stops chewing to study me. The chicken sits on my tongue, slowly becoming heavy, soggy. I can't swallow it with her eyes on me. "But what did he whisper? When it was just the two of you."

My fork falls to the table with a clank. Taking my napkin, I spit the chicken into it. I can't do this. Jocelyn's right. Magnus has too much power over us. Over me.

If I tell them the truth about why he's targeting us, at least he won't have that anymore. Jocelyn had my back upstairs; she'll have it now. "I have to be honest with you guys about something." As soon as I say it, I'm not sure I can go through with it. It's a secret I've kept since high school. The most shameful secret I've ever kept.

"Okay?" Jocelyn drags the word out as she watches me. It's as though her gaze radiates heat. On my other side, Cadence is staring just as intently.

"Sometimes," I start, my throat dry and scratchy. I take a sip of water, and Jocelyn's impatience becomes a fourth presence at the table. When she goes from squirming in her seat to throwing a hand up, the words finally burst free. "Sometimes I take things. Things that aren't mine."

Jocelyn lifts one brow. "So, like, a candy bar from the gas station?" She laughs, turning to Cady.

"Yes, like that. But other things too. Like, yesterday in the fireside room, when everyone else left, I took a little dog figurine from Helen's bookcase."

"Why would you do that?" Jocelyn asks, the smile completely wiped from her face. "After everything my aunt has done for us?"

"That's what I'm—"

"You're unbelievable, Rowan."

Cadence reaches out to touch Jocelyn's arm lightly. "Let her talk, okay?"

"What I'm trying to explain is that I don't do it to hurt people. I don't even do it because I need whatever it is I'm taking. It's just this . . . *impulse* I get. Sometimes, the impulse itself becomes overwhelming and suffocating if I don't give in. Other times, it's stress from life or"—I wave a hand—"whatever. The only thing that calms it down is taking something."

Jocelyn frowns. "That's pretty messed up. You should probably get help."

It stings. This is why I never told her in the first place. It's all turning out the exact way that I feared. I never should've opened my mouth.

"Did it start when Jake passed away?" Cadence asks, her eyes bleeding sympathy.

I wish with all my heart I could tell her *yes*, that I'm only this way because the love of my life was wrenched away from me. The truth is that I've been this way since I can remember.

I shake my head. "I've always done it."

"Oh my god." Jocelyn claps a hand over her mouth. "Is this why you work at a bank? To steal money whenever these . . . *impulses* come on?" She makes a face like she's taken a rotten bite of food.

"No, of course not. I've never taken anything from my work."

"Well, have you taken things from me?" Jocelyn asks, examining herself. Like maybe I swiped the gold chain right off her throat at some point today.

I nod, a tear dripping down my cheek. Too many times to count. "Nothing important, though." Nothing she ever missed either.

Oftentimes, Jocelyn was the best and the worst target. The worst because of how I felt afterward; she was my closest friend. The best because she had so damn much, she never found me out.

"What about me?" Cadence asks quietly.

The tears come down harder now. "I'm sorry," I answer, the words breaking. The truth is that I only stole from Cady once.

But the thing I took was everything to her.

CHAPTER 15
CADENCE

"Why are you telling us this now?" Jocelyn asks, impeding my follow-up question. "We're in the middle of a crisis, not some confession circle."

"Because I stole Magnus's coat," Rowan mumbles, and even Jocelyn sits in stunned silence for a moment. "That's what he was going on about back there. This coat"—she tugs on the front pocket—"is his. And the pockets were full of money and an unused train ticket."

"Why the hell would you steal from *him?*" Jocelyn finally asks.

"I didn't know it was his," Rowan says, her voice rising. "I stole it back at the train station in Manchester. I never imagined I'd see its owner again."

"I don't understand," I say. "How did we end up at the same B&B as the man you stole from?" It's too big of a coincidence.

"The travel wallet," Rowan says, her head dropping into her hands. "They obviously saw me steal the coat. They must've followed us to try to get it back."

"And when Jocelyn dropped her travel wallet—" *The B&B address was missing.* I meet Rowan's eyes, which widen in horror.

"One of them took it," she breathes. "They called and booked the last room while we were on that train. They followed us here."

"Great," Jocelyn huffs, leaning back in her chair with her arms crossed. "Just great. Rowan antagonizes the wrong damned psychopath, and now we're his next victims."

"I'm sorry," Rowan says, teary now. "I told you, I can't help it."

"Why didn't you just give the coat back?" I ask. "When you realized it was his?"

"I didn't know it was his until just now in the hallway," she says, voice choked with emotion. "I thought I had to play stupid, so he'd believe he'd made a mistake. So that you two wouldn't . . ."

"So we wouldn't find out," Jocelyn spits.

I should want to reach out and console Rowan. That's what friends do. But I can't get my mind off that question that was left unanswered. It's still buzzing like a fly in my head. "What did you take from me?"

Rowan flinches. She picks up a napkin off the table and wipes her nose and her eyes. A stalling tactic that only makes the buzzing grow louder. "Please, Cady. I don't think—"

"Just tell me. I'll forgive you. I will. I want to support you, but you need to tell me."

"You won't." She shakes her head, and her mouth contorts as she cries. "You'll never forgive me if I tell you."

"Shit, Rowan." Jocelyn sits up straighter now. "What the hell did you do?"

But nausea surges in my stomach. I know what she did. Because at one point in my life, it was the only thing I thought about: Who could've done this? Who *would've* done this?

My eleventh-grade English teacher, Mr. Pruit, wouldn't believe that I'd written the paper and placed it in my folder the previous night. When I swore someone must've taken it from my folder, he smiled condescendingly at me. He never really liked me. He'd been waiting for just such an opportunity to cut me down a notch.

With a zero on the paper—the biggest assignment of the semester—my grade in the class dropped down to a B-minus. It was my only B, but it lowered my entire GPA. It was the reason I missed being valedictorian. The reason I didn't get in to UCLA, on which I'd set my sights. Instead, I tagged along after Jocelyn and Rowan.

This entire time, I'd been right about everything. The culprit had been standing by my side, pretending to be shocked. Pretending to be my friend. She'd even joined Jocelyn over the years in "playfully" calling me Valedictorian, despite knowing how much the nickname stung.

"You're right," I say calmly, despite the fire brewing within me. "I won't forgive you."

Rowan wipes at her eyes. Reaching over the table, she grasps at my sleeve, my hand. "Please, Cady. I'm so sorry. I never meant to take it forever. I forgot to write my paper, and then the stress got so bad I almost blacked out. I just meant to look at it, so I could write my own, and then I was going to put it back."

I inhale, trying to force some calm into my body, to cool that fire. "But you didn't put it back."

"I know. It was horrible."

On my other side, Jocelyn leans an elbow onto the table and starts scratching at the base of her hairline.

"It's not just about the valedictorian thing," I say. "Maybe it was for a long time." Two dreams shattered in the wake of one missing term paper. "But it certainly isn't now." It didn't matter in the larger scheme of things. If I'd wanted to, I still could've achieved my goal of becoming a college English professor, even without the title or the degree from UCLA. "You never came forward, not even when Mr. Pruit laughed at me in front of the entire class. You let everyone call me a liar. You let me question my own memory, over and over, for . . ." For far too long.

"And it was the worst thing I've ever done."

"A thing you've *done* is something that happened once, Rowan. This was a choice you made repeatedly, every time I brought it up. Every time you overheard someone call me Miss *Practically* Perfect or Shady Cady."

My accusation echoes loudly in my own ear. I'm not so oblivious as to miss it. Every moment I've shared with Landon over the years was a moment stolen from Jocelyn. Our kisses weren't really ours—they were taken. It doesn't stop me from saying, "You're absolutely right. I don't forgive you. I never will."

"Okay," Jocelyn says, scooting her chair closer to mine and laying a hand on my arm. "Look, this is . . . a lot right now. But we have to stay focused. You said it yourself, Cady. We can't fall into Magnus's trap. That is exactly what he wants."

"Magnus had nothing to do with this," I snap. "Do you think *Magnus* knew that Rowan screwed up my entire life back in eleventh grade?"

"No, but—"

"*She's* the one who took his coat. We should let her deal with him."

Jocelyn is the most patient I've ever seen her as she brushes a wild strand of my hair back behind my ear. "You just need a moment to cool off. We're not sacrificing Rowan to this maniac. No matter how screwed up she might be."

"Thanks, Joss," Rowan mutters through a sniffle.

"She changed the entire course of my life." And I believe it. If I'd gone to UCLA—if I'd kept on the track that was meant for me—I never would've met Landon first. Then I wouldn't be stuck where I am now, in love with my best friend's fiancé.

"Come on," Jocelyn says, frowning at me. "Your life is amazing. You have a loving family. You have me. You always wanted to be a teacher, and you are."

"You know damned well I wanted to be a college professor!"

"*You* changed your plan, not Rowan."

She's right. But somehow, it feels like Rowan is responsible. Before the incident with the term paper, I truly believed that I could achieve anything I set my mind to.

Afterward, life became a much more crooked path, full of moving obstacles. I realized that there are things—circumstances and people—outside of your control. Even if you do your absolute best, even if you *are* the absolute best, even if you deserve it more than anyone, something can get in the way.

It made me start to aim a little lower. There's nothing wrong with being a middle school teacher—I love it, I do. But achieving it took a little less time, a little less work, allowing for fewer outside forces to get in the way.

"Fine. But once we're safe at home, she and I are done."

"She needs help, that's all," Jocelyn says, suddenly forced into the peacemaker role.

"I'm really sorry," Rowan says. "So sorry. I hate that it's all my fault we're in this mess." She runs her fingers through her curls, creating a halo of frizz. "Maybe he'll let this go if we make amends. I could give him back the jacket and apologize."

"No," Jocelyn and I say at the same time.

I wonder if she's afraid for Rowan's life or if that quick response was due to the trouble Magnus could stir up for her and Landon.

I know my own fears are twofold. Even if he's not a murderer, every moment we're in this place with Magnus feels like a bomb could go off. The kind of bomb that rains down information about my hidden relationship with Jocelyn's fiancé.

"We have to remember that he could be dangerous," I say, hopefully extinguishing Jocelyn's line of thought. "Valentina is gone and he has her stuff. It screams of something criminal."

"And let's not forget Lisa Granger," Jocelyn says. "He lied about being near the area she went missing. People don't lie unless there's a good reason."

"You'd know about that," I mumble.

Jocelyn's lips part, ready to combat my snide remark. But there's a click, and Helen pushes open the door. Rowan quickly wipes beneath her eyes while Jocelyn sips her water nonchalantly. I stay slouched in my seat, arms crossed.

"My friend says she can fit you," Helen says, taking the remaining chair. "The room sleeps two, so you'll have to make do. Like I said, with high season, you'll have to take what you can get."

"Thank you so much, Helen," Jocelyn says.

Rowan, remembering her untouched meal, begins moving things around on her plate like a child.

"As soon as you finish up here, Paul will drive you."

"Thank you," Rowan says, her voice nasal.

"We'll need to leave in secret," Jocelyn says. "Our bags are packed. Have Paul meet us at his car in twenty minutes."

Helen smiles, but her eyes are dewy. "I wish you didn't have to go so soon. It's been so good having you all around here. We enjoy the solitude so much that we forget about how wonderful it is to have loved ones around."

"We wish we could stay too. But this guy is becoming more and more unpredictable. He has this strange vendetta against us." At this last part, Jocelyn's gaze drifts to Rowan, who sits with hunched shoulders, still pretending to pick at her plate. "Do you know if the cops are going to look into Valentina's disappearance?"

She nods. "I called back just now. They're looking at all the flight logs with Argentina as a destination."

"Well, maybe we should go talk to them in person," Jocelyn suggests. "So they can do something about Magnus. You can't just stay here with a potential murderer, Aunt Helen."

"He's done nothing to threaten me, Jossy. And your uncle plans to drive out to the station in the morning. We'll be fine. I promise." She reaches out to squeeze her niece's hand.

"I still think we should go to the cops *now*," Jocelyn says.

"I, uh," Rowan starts, her features twisted with worry. "It just might not be a good idea to get overly involved at this point. You know, considering . . ."

"Considering what?" Helen asks.

Rowan gnaws on her lower lip, completely useless. We can't even go to the cops because she's afraid he'll say something about that damned stolen coat full of money.

"It might antagonize Magnus, is what she means," Jocelyn says, rescuing Rowan yet again, even though she doesn't deserve it.

I can think of a few things Rowan deserves.

CHAPTER 16
JOCELYN

Twenty minutes later, we're outside in the dark with our luggage. "Ready?" Paul whispers, the engine of his blue Ford Fiesta already running. Quickly, we get in. I shut the door behind me as softly as possible, my eyes drawn to the top-right window. The curtains block the glass. No one's watching.

I want to breathe easy as Paul pulls away from the B&B. But I can't. There's another criminal among us, and she's in this car.

When we reach Conwy, the streets are lit but empty. Everything closes up early in Wales; the only establishments open past sundown are the restaurants and pubs. There aren't many of those here either; despite it being high season, it's mostly a ghost town. We park in a common lot around the corner from the inn and start to walk, Paul helping with our luggage.

But Rowan stops behind us, like an animal caught in a truck's high beams.

"What's wrong?" I ask, annoyance pinching behind my eyes.

"I thought I saw—" She tips her head toward the back of the lot. "That car back there. I could've sworn there was a shadow, like a person sitting in the front seat."

There are no streetlamps surrounding the lot, only the moonlight that comes and goes as the gray clouds drift overhead. I squint at the car, making out its vague shape and dark color. But there's no one in the driver's seat. No headlights. Nothing. "You're just on edge," I say. "Besides, that car was there before we parked."

"Let's get you inside." Paul's thick but fragile figure provides little comfort as he huffs along, my suitcase in his wake.

I glance back at the car again, apparently infected by Rowan's paranoia. But it's still sitting there, dark and empty. I turn and follow the others.

The Starboard Inn is a charming little brick house edged up against a wooded area and fringed by gardens. Music flows from the pub attached to its side. A long driveway curves up to the inn steps, and Paul sees us inside.

It's late—nearly nine when we arrive—and he rings the bell at the reception desk. A moment later, a woman emerges from a door behind the desk. She runs a hand through her silver, shoulder-length waves and checks the top button on her floral blouse before greeting us. "Paul, nice to see you again."

"Hi, Glynnis. Thanks for taking them in on such short notice. We, uh, had an issue with the toilet in their room."

Good lie, Uncle Paul. It's not even a lie, really. Not that Paul knows our toilet was actually broken. I'm glad Paul hasn't told this woman the truth about our change in accommodations, though. There's no need to alarm her.

"It's no trouble at all." Glynnis has kind brown eyes and round, rosy cheeks. Did we interrupt her from work or from her favorite TV show back there? Maybe the Welsh are as obsessed with *The Real Housewives* as I am. Maybe they have their own Welsh version. Clearly, my mind is a frazzled mess. "Just glad I had a room available. I actually had a cancellation just an hour or so ago. If you ladies want, you could even space out a little." She tilts her head. "I'd give you a discount on the second room."

Rowan nods at us, knowing how much we'd like to put that space between her and ourselves.

But I say, "No, thanks," ignoring the way Cady bristles at my side. "One room will be fine. Nice and cozy." I hand Glynnis my credit card. The goal is to get through the rest of the week as peacefully as possible. Further isolating Rowan will not achieve this. Besides, not even Rowan deserves to be left in a room alone after everything that happened back at the Water View B&B.

"Suit yourself," Glynnis says, running the card. After that's settled, she turns, her finger zigzagging over the key ring on the wall and landing on one with the number nineteen. She removes it and hands it to me.

"Thanks so much, Uncle Paul," I say, giving him a hug. Breathing in his scent of cigar smoke and orange peels takes me back to childhood. My eyes sting thinking about little Jake and me, running around in my uncle's yard on hot summer weekends while our parents sipped sangria on their back porch.

"Anything for you, Jossy." He smiles, cheeks flushed, gray wisps of hair windblown from the outside elements. "Call us if you need anything."

"We will." I tug on his sleeve before he pulls away. "If *you-know-who* asks about us, tell him we decided to head home early. And be careful, Uncle Paul."

Paul nods, wariness showing in the wrinkles around his eyes. "We'll be fine. I'm heading to the police station in the morning to have Magnus removed from the property. I've got to get back to Helen, but take care, you three."

We say our goodbyes and follow Glynnis down a hall with mint-green wallpaper, and then up a flight of stairs.

Our room is sparsely furnished, containing a wooden desk and chair situated against one wall and twin beds on the other. Immediately, Cady plops down on one of the beds.

"Someone has to sleep on the floor," I say, hoping this place doesn't have bugs. I squint at the carpet, already itchy at the thought.

"Yep," Cady says without offering to take it, the implication obvious.

"I will," Rowan says. "All of this is my fault."

"Damn right it is," Cady mutters, going through her suitcase. "You should've made her stay in that other room, Joss. She can pay for it."

"It's my trip," I say. "And I want us to be together." Over at the corner desk, Rowan gives me a somber but grateful smile.

She thinks that my standing up for her is some magnanimous act. But the truth is, after what I did to her before Jake's death, I owe her some grace.

When Rowan and my brother first got together, I found the idea weird, but not repulsive. It was funny, in a way. My best friend and my twin. They'd known each other for four years, but neither had ever hinted at liking the other. I got to tease both of them, and at first, the relationship was the perfect excuse for Jake to hang out with my friends and me more.

I never expected things between the two of them to turn so serious so quickly. Or to last. Before long, it wasn't the four of us hanging out together anymore; it was the two of them sneaking off to be alone. A night that was supposed to be Jake and his friends hanging out with the girls and me somehow morphed into Cady and me watching movies with Jake's friends. Jake and Rowan had disappeared. And it wouldn't be the last time.

I began to miss my friend *and* my twin. I missed my time with each of them, on our own. One night, the happy couple promised to meet Cady and me at a party. Only they never showed. On the way home, my car broke down, so I called Jake to come get us.

Normally, he would've dropped everything for me and been there in minutes. But that night, he never even picked up my calls. I left messages; he never checked them. We got a ride from a guy who was interested in me, though the feeling wasn't mutual.

Then came the gut punch. When Jake and I were five years old, we became obsessed with this show about two child adventurers that took place in Costa Rica. We begged our parents to take us there, but they preferred to vacation in Europe. We waited, deciding that one day, when we were old enough, we would travel there together.

So when Rowan told me that Jake wanted to take her—and *only* her—to Costa Rica for spring break our sophomore year of college, I reached my limit.

Rowan could not date my brother. My brother could not date my best friend.

I convinced Rowan to attend the next party sans Jake. For one evening, it was the three of us against the world, like old times. Except at the end of the night, when Rowan and Cady were tucked inside their beds, I snuck inside the boys' dormitory, crept into Jake's room, and woke him.

It was dark in the room, but he let out a half-growl, confused and a little irritated to be roused from a deep sleep. "What's going on, Joss?"

"I'm so sorry. I-I wasn't sure if I should tell you this."

He tried to prop himself up on an elbow and fumbled for the little reading lamp clamped onto the bed. "What is it?" The light clicked on, casting a faint glow about him.

I sniffled, like I'd been crying. "It's Rowan."

"Oh my god, is she okay?" He sat up then, tearing the sheet off his torso.

A spike of bitterness ran through me at his attentiveness to her. "Yes, she's fine. It's nothing like that. It's just . . . we were at this party. Her, me, and Cady. Everything was fine at first, but then we got separated from Rowan. And"—a sniffling pause for dramatic effect—"when I finally found her, she was full-on making out with this guy."

"What?" The word came out strangled, and I hated myself.

"I'm so sorry. I can't believe it either. I thought she loved you."

Jake didn't answer at first, just stared into the blackness of the room. "Are you sure about this?"

"I know what my best friend looks like."

"Who was the guy?"

I shook my head. "I'd never seen him before. He doesn't go to our school. Are you going to talk to her?"

"Oh, I'm going to talk to her," he said, lying down and turning over, his back to me. "But it won't be much of a discussion."

It was unfair on so many levels. The lie; the fact that I knew Rowan would never be able to refute it. Yes, he loved her. But he'd loved *me* since the womb. Rowan and Cady knew about my nasty habit. Jake was the only one who loved me so unconditionally that he never saw me for what I truly was.

A liar.

Maybe that's why—guilty as I've felt these past eight years—instead of taking the full weight of Jake's overdose upon myself, part of me has always blamed Rowan for what happened to him. Not because I truly envisioned Jake breaking up with Rowan and her retaliating. But because if she'd never come along and captured *my* brother's heart, none of it would've happened.

"I hate for us to go to bed angry," I say. "We're finally away from Magnus. Let's leave the drama back at the B&B with him. How about we head down to the pub and have a drink?"

"I'm tired." Cady removes a stack of folded clothes from her suitcase and places them on a closet shelf. She returns to the suitcase, shaking her pajamas free.

"Please, Cades. At least pretend to be civil and happy. It's my bachelorette trip."

"Well, when you put it that way." Cady's shoulders sink, and she tosses her cotton shorts back into the suitcase.

I hate that I have to use the trip and the money to manipulate her, but she really does need to get over this. We all make mistakes. We'll just have to keep closer eyes on our things around Rowan from here on out.

"Cady," Rowan says, looking torn between moving closer to her and staying where she is. "I'll do anything to make this up to you."

"You can do that by staying the hell away from me when this trip is over."

"That's not exactly the kind of civil I meant," I say, gathering up my coat and following Cady, whose hand is already on the doorknob. I glance back at Rowan.

She's sitting on the desk chair, head downcast, knees pulled in close. "I'm just going to stay here. You two go, have a drink. Have fun."

"Oh, come on." I motion her along. "You know Cady will get over it. She's horrible at this whole tough-and-grouchy act. It never lasts long."

"She'll cool down faster without my face there to rub it in."

I arch a brow. "You may be right about that."

She removes the elastic from her hair, shaking her curls free. "Seriously, I'll be fine. This place has *Wi-Fi*, can you imagine?"

I place a hand over my mouth, feigning shock.

"I have to call Molly today, anyway."

I study her another moment. "If you insist."

"And Joss?" she says as I reach the threshold. "Thanks for being there for me, despite how *screwed up* I might be."

At her choice of words—*my* words from dinner—a hot trickle of embarrassment courses through me. I give her a sheepish, one-eyed grin. "Heat of the moment, you know. But I am here for you, Ro. Always have been." *Lie.* "Always will be." *Hope it's not a lie.*

I stay where I am, the weight of my past sin against her keeping me glued in the doorway. I catch Rowan's eyes on my left boot, the way I keep jiggling the toe up and down. Over the years, the truth about her relationship with Jake has been this constant, nagging pain, like a thorn in my shoe. Rowan has always been the victim—the girl whose boyfriend died during her pregnancy. The single mom, left alone after tragedy.

Now, we're finally on a level playing field. She's the one in the wrong here. Maybe it's time to fess up. "Look," I say, my foot jouncing fiercely, "there's—"

"Are you coming?" Cady's voice calls from down the hall. "Because I'd rather just go to bed, anyway."

I take a deep breath, the words that danced on my tongue a moment ago traveling back down my throat to my gut, left down there to torment me a little longer. I share a knowing look with Rowan—*that girl, right?* Then I shut the door and chase after Cady.

There's no indoor access to the pub, so Cady and I brave the cold winds and the light rain the few meters it takes to get there. Inside, the pub is dimly lit by a trio of iron chandeliers dotted with electric-candle lights. The walls are limestone, and several dark, solid oak beams run from floor to ceiling, giving it a medieval vibe. The place is pretty packed. Three separate parties dot the circular tables—two filled with college-age kids and one with a family, including two children who should probably be in bed. The only people at the bar are a middle-aged man and woman deep in conversation.

Cady and I take the stools at the end of the bar nearest us. The bartender, a young woman with two black milkmaid braids and a silver nose ring, comes to take our orders right away. "Hiya. What can I get'cha?"

"Two gin and tonics, please."

"Anything to eat?"

I look at Cady, who shrugs. My stomach is a little rumbly. "Some fries to share, please." When the woman frowns, I amend my order. "*Chips*, sorry."

I tap my fingers nervously on the bar top as we wait. "For the record, I'm allowing you tonight to wallow. Tomorrow, you've got to go back to your chipper self."

She rolls her eyes, but I'm certain she'll concede. Cady's not a big drinker; it won't take much to smooth her out. She'll calm down about all of this after a gin and tonic or two.

The waitress places two coupe glasses of ice and gin in front of us, then pops the caps off two tonic bottles and shoves them across the bar.

"Cheers. Chips'll be right up." She gives us a flat-lipped smile, the kind I'm used to getting from other pretty girls, even young ones.

"Look, I'm not saying you have to just . . . pretend like it never happened. What she did was wrong, and it had consequences."

"Damn right it did."

"But cut her a little slack for being human. I know, I know, you can't imagine what that must be like since you're busy being perfect all the time. Being Little Miss—" I almost say *Valedictorian*, and Cady must catch it. Her eyes dart from her glass to mine, her fingers curling so tightly over the stem that her knuckles turn white.

I get a flash—a vision of the glass stem breaking in her grip, shards cutting into her skin, and blood spurting all over the shiny wooden bar top veneer. "Little Miss *Never forgot to take her vitamins once*," I say, not even remotely saving myself.

"She's always been more your friend than mine," Cady says, her voice distant, like it's drowning, coming from the bottom of a glass of bitterness. "I don't need her. I would've been better off if I'd never pretended to like her."

"You don't mean that," I say, but deep down, I know she does. I've always been the glue in this trio. For all my jealousy issues, I never once had to worry about the two of them. Sure, Cady goes over and visits, plays the dutiful aunt to Molly on my behalf. But their relationship has always been held together by that purple stick-glue they use in elementary school.

It only took one mistake to pull it all apart.

The fries come out, hot and greasy. I reach for one, determined to settle this hollow, nauseated feeling in my stomach. That's when I notice something that causes me to wrench my arm back. Someone at the opposite end of the bar who wasn't there when we arrived. My elbow knocks into the coupe, which hits the bar top, its contents spilling out.

"Shit." I pick it up, trying in vain to keep the liquid from dripping over the side and onto Cady's clothes.

The waitress comes over to check on us, and I apologize.

"Nothing to worry about," she says, wiping up the spill and taking away the glass. "I'll just bring you another."

"Thanks," I say, though I no longer want the drink. My entire body is shaking. Cady stares at me, completely abandoning her tough act as she hovers over me, checking that I'm okay.

But I'm far from it. Because the man is gone, having slipped out during the commotion.

I swear it was him, though. Magnus was sitting at the opposite end of the bar, a smug, malicious grin on his face as he raised a glass to us.

NOW

"So, then," DI Collins says, "you claim Magnus was stalking you—that he killed this Valentina person—and that you were afraid for your lives."

"Yes, exactly."

"Why didn't you ever call the police?"

My heart drums in my chest. *Ba-bum, ba-bum.* "Helen reported it, but no one did anything."

DI Collins pauses with her eyes on me for too long a moment. *Ba-bum, ba-bum.* "I see. And you weren't concerned enough to follow up on it?"

We couldn't, I think. But I can't tell her this.

Or can I? "Helen did, but no one took her seriously. Nothing moved quickly enough. We were scared. We thought getting away from him would be the quickest solution, after the authorities failed to handle things the first time around."

"So you think Magnus is some sort of . . . serial killer?" She gives me a skeptical look, one that stirs up angry thoughts and frustration. She isn't going to listen to me. I'm not from around here, and my words are as worthless as my American dollars. And then there's how it all looks.

"I don't know what he is," I snap. "He was strange from the beginning. That fascination with the stones. We—"

I remember the blood on the stones, suddenly. My friends and I meant to research them once we'd found a signal closer to the B&B, but then the drama with Landon started and everything exploded. "There was blood on the stones. In the woods. At the time, we believed Magnus when he said that Valentina had gone home to Argentina, but . . ." I lick my lips, the skin of which is cracked and tastes of copper. "Maybe he's into something really dark. Something that involves those stones."

DI Collins only stares at me, like I've lost my mind.

But I know what I saw. I know what he did.

"You have to find him," I plead. "Before he hurts someone else." She glances down at the folder on her lap, and I know I'm losing her.

I could tell her about the reason Magnus was after us. I couldn't tell anyone before, but none of that matters now.

I start to open my mouth, but the detective, eyes still on the folder, cuts me off. "I'd like to talk about that second fight. Your neighbors, the Pearces, claim to have heard another commotion. This time, it was the morning of the murder."

CHAPTER 17
ROWAN

My phone call with Molly ends, and I sit up on the bed. I wipe the tears from my eyes, the ones she'll never know I cried because I'm here and she's back home. I would give anything to hug her right now.

Her voice was nasal, like she was stuffed up, so when we were done chatting, I had her put Grandma on the line. "Why didn't you tell me Molly was sick?" I asked.

"It's nothing," my mother assured me. "No fever and the girl's got energy for days. Just a little cold. I didn't want to worry you over nothing."

I should appreciate her attempt at letting me enjoy my trip. Molly's on spring break, so it's not like she'll have to miss any school. What *does* a little sniffle matter? Still, my heart aches at not being there for her. If I were there, she'd be watching the same cartoons, but at least she'd be snuggled up next to her mommy. The guilt creeps in too, not just for Molly but for forcing my parents to care for a sick child. *My* sick child.

I never should've left.

I'm not sure how things went so incredibly wrong. Scratch that. I'm one hundred percent certain that I'm responsible for messing everything up. I should've gone with my gut and stayed home with Molly. In the beginning, becoming a young mother—one whose pregnancy was unplanned, one who failed to learn all the lessons about what *ruin* would come to my life if I wasn't careful—came with a metaphorical contract. I'd signed away my right to fun things. My new responsibility was a full-time job as well as an identity, and it would own me, twenty-four seven. Then, the baby was born. I fell into a routine and started to realize that it wasn't true. Not always. I'm not a prisoner; I enjoy being a mother most of the time.

But sometimes, when I find myself having a good time, I can't help that former way of thinking from trickling back in. This isn't part of it. I've breached the contract. At some point, there will be hell to pay for this moment.

That's how it feels now. I've breached the contract, and it's come to bite me. I should've stayed home with that sweet child and never taken her for granted.

There's a knock on the door, and I stiffen. The girls wouldn't knock; they have the key. I don't even remember them locking the door behind them when they left for the pub. Maybe it's Glynnis. Jocelyn probably forgot to sign something earlier at the desk. I've already changed into pajamas, so I reach into my suitcase for a sweater. "Who is it?" I call out, shrugging it on quickly.

"An old friend," answers a deep voice that sends a chill over the nape of my neck.

Magnus. He followed us.

The door isn't locked. All he has to do is twist that knob and give it a push.

"What do you want?" I ask, my voice ragged.

"Just to talk."

I can't let him in here, but the door only locks with a key—one I don't have. If I call to the desk down below, they'll never get the police here in time. Frantically, I look around for something to use as a weapon, spotting a vase full of flowers over on the desk.

I lower myself from the bed, which lets out a massive groan. I freeze, holding my breath, eyes on the door. But the knob remains still.

"Rowan?"

"We're sleeping," I say, even though the light is on and the last thing I want to do is turn it off. The carpet yields beneath my bare feet, nearly soundless as I cross the room, reaching for the vase.

"I know that isn't true, Rowan. I know you're all alone in there. I saw Jocelyn and Cadence down in the pub."

Oh my god. I tiptoe toward the bed to text Jocelyn, but the knob clicks behind me.

My heart lurches. I dump the water and flowers onto the carpet, waiting for him to rush through the door. But it stays cracked, showing only a sliver of darkness.

"I'd like for you to invite me in, Rowan. So we can talk about what you did and what that means for you now."

"I already told the others!" I blurt. "They know about the coat, so your mind games are pointless."

"You think I'm playing games?"

My legs begin to shake as a horrible thought grabs hold of me. Two hours ago, the worst-case scenario was the others finding out about me. Now, all alone in this room, I can think of a much, much worse outcome.

"You can have it back," I say weakly, picturing Valentina's lifeless body on the floor.

The door begins to open, swaying as if in slow motion. I should scream.

"I'm not here to get the coat back. I actually think it looks better on you. So would anything, for that matter." His voice is teasing, flirty. As if my very life isn't being threatened. "I know everyone probably talks about Jocelyn. *She* certainly thinks she's god's gift to the earth." He lets out an airy laugh. "In my eyes, you're the real beauty, Rowan."

At the words, nausea surges through me. This psycho can't actually think I'm going to buy the same act he used on Joss and then Cady? After he tried to blackmail us? "I just stopped by to let you know that I've booked the room next to yours," he says without stepping into the room. "Like old times."

He isn't moving, isn't coming any closer. If I screamed, *I* would look like the insane one. I have his stolen coat, for god's sake. His money is stuffed at the bottom of my suitcase. My breathing is so fast and fierce, it feels like it's shaking the room.

"Please go away," I say. "Please go away." The vase is heavy in my hands, but I raise it high, waiting.

My legs start to give way beneath me, my vision tunneling. When the door flings open, I wheeze in as much air as I can, cocking my elbow to try for one hard blow.

But instead of Magnus, I see a flurry of red hair as Jocelyn pushes through the door. "Oh my—" She rushes toward me. "Rowan!"

My arm lowers, the empty vase with it. My legs finally give way, and I crumple to the carpet.

"Are you okay?"

I nod, the words stuck in my throat.

"Just breathe." She wraps her arms around me tightly. "You're okay. We're here."

"Oh, Rowan." Cadence's voice. When I open my eyes, she's standing above us, lips pursed with concern. "We never should've left you alone."

"He was here," I finally gasp. "Magnus was here."

"We know," Jocelyn says. "He was down in the pub. I thought it was my imagination at first." Her gaze goes to the carpet. "You were about to whack him in the head with that vase, weren't you?" Her eyes gleam with admiration, and despite everything, my chest swells.

"I was going to try." Then I remember, my back arching. "He's staying in the room next to ours. The one Glynnis tried to offer us."

"Dammit." Jocelyn pounds a fist against the bedpost. "We'll have to call the cops."

"What about the jacket?" I ask, panic returning. "What if he tells the cops what I did?"

"Put the money back in the pocket, and we'll ditch it in the pub or something," Cady says, coming around behind me and putting her hands on my shoulders. Pressing down. Grounding and calming me the way you'd handle a child during a tantrum. "We have to get help, Rowan."

I nod, getting to my feet. "I'll make the call." The others will think it's because I'm the capable one, the girl who grabbed a vase to ward off a giant. In reality, it's because I don't have a choice. I can't allow anyone else to control what's said about our situation. I move to the room phone, lifting the receiver without bringing it to my ear. "Does anyone know how to call the cops in Wales?"

Jocelyn looks up the number for the local police, and a moment later, I'm speaking with the desk clerk. "Hi, I need you to send some officers out to the Starboard Inn. My friends and I are being stalked."

"There's only one officer here tonight, ma'am," the woman says. "It's close to midnight, you know."

"Yes, I know," I say, unable to keep the irritation out of my voice. "It's important."

"Hold on just one moment," she says, and before I can tell her I don't have much time, I hear a click, and the sound of smooth jazz starts playing in my ear.

I pace over to the desk, spotting a label on the phone's base with the number for emergency services—999. I'm about to have Jocelyn try it when a deep male voice comes on the line. "This is DC Sullivan."

I repeat what I told the desk clerk about Magnus.

"I see," the man says, sounding bored. "And have you filed a report?"

I clench my jaw. "There isn't time for all that. He followed us to the inn we're staying at. He was just outside our door. Can't you just . . . send someone?"

"Did this person threaten physical harm?"

"Yes! Well, I mean . . . not *exactly*."

He makes a strange clucking noise with his tongue. "I'm afraid there's not much we can do if he hasn't actually said anything or done anything to threaten you or your friends physically. But we'll go ahead and file the report, just to have a record in case things continue."

I shake my head, even though he can't see me. "By then it will be too late! I assure you, he's very threatening." I think of the way he hovered just outside the door like the Big Bad Wolf. But of course, he never explicitly said he wanted to hurt me. The opposite, in fact.

"And can you show us some sort of verifiable proof?"

"What's he saying?" Jocelyn asks, pushing her ear up near the phone.

"They can't do anything about Magnus. Not unless we can prove he threatened us."

Jocelyn snatches the phone from my hand. "Listen, we are in serious danger from this lunatic. He's stalking us. And we believe he's already killed a woman."

"Why do you believe that?" I hear the man ask, a hint of urgency to his voice now.

"Because he was traveling with a woman, and she completely vanished."

"I see. And have you filed a report?" he asks, and Jocelyn shakes the receiver in the air, letting the officer's voice spill into the room.

She brings the phone back down and says in a clipped tone, "Yes. A report was filed." I can't hear what the man is saying now, but I see the panicked expression on Jocelyn's face. "No, no, no, no! Dammit!" She shakes the receiver again. "He transferred me to missing persons."

"What?" Cady says. "But what about *us*? They're not sending someone?"

At that moment, my phone dings over on the desk. I cross the room to pick it up. When I see the photo texted to me from an unknown number, my stomach drops.

It's a photo of me in the Conwy toy shop. I'd pulled up my hood and turned away from the camera.

But I hadn't concealed my face from the *window*. It's through that window that this image was captured: me stuffing that damned dragon into my jacket pocket—Magnus's jacket pocket.

He has proof, not just that I robbed the toy shop, but that I was wearing his stolen jacket. "Hang up," I say.

But Jocelyn shakes me off, my voice nothing but an irritating buzz in her ear. "I'm on hold."

"I said hang up!"

Jocelyn's gaze snaps to mine. "What the hell, Rowan?"

I force a swallow and walk my phone over to her, my feet lead weights that barely lift off the carpet. I show her the image on the screen and watch as the snarl on her face quickly drops, replaced by a wide-eyed look of terror.

Cady hurries over to join us, her eyes narrowing at the screen. I can hear a man's garbled voice start to speak down in Jocelyn's hand, but she doesn't answer. Finally, Cady spins away, digging her fingernails into her hair. "Dammit, Rowan."

Jocelyn lifts the room phone to her ear. "Officer, I'm afraid I made a mistake. I don't need help anymore." She slams it down onto the base.

"I'm sorry," I say. "But we can't bring the cops out here, you guys. We don't know what it's like in Wales. The legal system. I could be stranded in some Welsh prison. I can't be apart from Molly—I *can't*." I start to hyperventilate, the breaths coming shorter and shallower.

"Calm down," Cady says. "We'll just . . ." She glances around before crossing the room to rifle through the drawer on the bedside table. Removing a pad of paper and a pen, she scribbles something down. Then she hurries back to drop the pad on the carpet between us.

We'll get on a plane. Tonight. We don't have to stay in Wales.

"She's right," Jocelyn whispers, dipping her face in front of mine, forcing me to make eye contact. "We're going to get away from him. You don't have to worry about being apart from Molly. We promise." She reaches for the pen and writes her own note:

I'll call a taxi to take us to the nearest airport. You two, get packed and ready to move.

We nod, and Jocelyn locks herself in the bathroom to make the call. I start some music on my phone to drown out the slightest trickle of conversation. Then I change back into my jeans. Cady, true to habit, organized half her things on the shelves the moment we arrived, so she gets to work packing. Once my boots are on and my suitcase zipped up, I sit down on the bed.

But I notice that Cady has stopped working. "What's wrong?" I ask. She's kneeling in front of her suitcase, merely staring at it.

"I think he took more than my phone," she says, the color drained from her face. "My passport is gone. Driver's license too. That son of a bitch took everything."

"No," I say, knowing the word isn't helpful but saying it anyway. "That can't be right. Maybe it's just . . . let me help you look." Together, we dump out her entire suitcase onto the floor and dig through its contents.

"I had a little travel organizer," Cadence says.

"The purple one. I remember it from the airport."

"But it's not in the pouch where I stored it when we got off the plane."

The bathroom door opens. "Good news. I—what are you doing?" Jocelyn looks ready to hurl her phone at my head.

"Cady's travel organizer is missing," I explain, still rummaging through the inner zip pockets while Cadence pieces through her clothing.

Jocelyn marches to the closet and opens the door. She runs her hands over the shelving before turning to us. "Maybe it fell out of your bag back at the B&B."

"I never took it out of its zipped-up pouch. How could it fall out?"

We search everywhere—the shelves, the drawers, beneath the bed. We turn Cady's bag inside out, ravaging her belongings. Ten minutes later, she's crumpled into a ball on the carpet, knees to chest. "We can't get away," she says. "We can't get home."

"Calm down, Cady," Jocelyn snaps. "We've got to keep it together. You're letting him win whatever psychological war games he's playing. Just let me think." She begins to pace. "We can't stay here. We can't get on a plane. There are no trains in the area until tomorrow. We can't go to the cops." Her steps halt. "There's got to be something we can do." She picks the pad and pen off the ground and taps it against her thigh repeatedly.

Another text message comes in on my phone. We gather around to read it.

Tell Cadybug we still have a small matter to discuss.

"Cadybug?" Jocelyn looks disgusted. "Now this sick freak's got a pet name for you?"

Beside me, Cady turns ashen. "Maybe we should just pay him."

"What?" Jocelyn asks. "Just pay the terrorist? He's lying about that photo of me. And Rowan stole a stupid *toy*! It's not like she robbed a . . ." She licks her lips, eyes honing in on Cady as if she's seeing her for the first time. "What does Magnus want to talk to you about, Cady?"

Cady's head draws back. "How the hell should I know?"

"What does he have on you?"

"Nothing! Haven't we already established that he's a psychopath?"

Jocelyn shakes her head, stepping closer to Cady. "Psychopath or not, his intel on Rowan and me was pretty damned accurate."

"If he had something on me, he'd prove it. You said it yourself when he wouldn't cough up another photo of you." Jocelyn drags her fingernails up and down the back of her neck. "But paying him might be the only way to get rid of him. Did you forget that he followed us here, and he probably killed a girl?"

"Hey," I say, trying to push my way in between them. "We're doing it again. Turning on each other." Jocelyn looks ready to press the issue, but Cady gets to her feet. She yanks the pad and pen away from Jocelyn and scribbles something down. When she thrusts it into my hands, adrenaline jolts through me like an electric charge at the words.

Cancel the taxi. Forget running, forget the money. I've got a better idea.

CHAPTER 18
CADENCE

Once we're shut inside the bathroom, Jocelyn turns on the shower and leans an elbow against its door, looking irked that I got the nerve to head up a plan. Rowan's music is playing out in the room to further mask our voices, some horrible pop tune from our adolescence. The humidity of the bathroom combined with my nerves makes my skin sticky. I wipe at it, my senses swiftly latching onto Rowan's anxious foot-tapping over by the toilet. It sounds like a jackhammer drilling into my skull. I need my stuff back. I'm handling this because he has my stuff, and I need it back. "He wanted to speak to me, right?"

"What the hell are you talking about, Cady?" Jocelyn asks, throwing her head back.

"I'll go over there and invite him down to the pub. Make him think we're giving in."

"No, absolutely—"

"Will you just hear me out?" I want to clamp my hand over her mouth. "I have some sleeping pills in my overnight case."

Jocelyn straightens. "I didn't know you had trouble sleeping," she says, as if we have time to talk about my sleeping habits.

"I don't. At least, not usually. My mom gave them to me for the jet lag. But I can spike Magnus's drink with them. That combined with the alcohol should make him too drowsy to follow us."

"Okay," Rowan says, her brows drawn together.

"That's only half of the plan," I say. "While I'm with him in the pub, you two are going to steal his car."

"Wha—" Jocelyn starts, but I lift a hand to silence her.

"Once he's down, I'll find you—Rowan, I can take your phone. Tomorrow, he'll wake up stranded, and we'll be long gone."

"How do you propose we steal his car?" Rowan asks wryly.

"You do your robbery bit. Hot-wire it or whatever. I'm assuming you know how to do that."

"My *robbery* bit? I have no clue how to hot-wire a car."

Jocelyn rubs at her temple. "Even if she did, we're seriously going to fix a problem caused by Rowan's theft by stealing a car?"

I let out an exasperated growl. "Then just mess with the engine. Keep it from running again. Is that so hard? We'll take a taxi to a train station—one with actual, running trains. I'll take back my stuff." I shrug. "His stuff too—phone, wallet, passport. He won't be able to pay for a way to find us. He won't be able to send any damned photos of us." They fix incredulous stares on me. "It's what he deserves, isn't it? If we pull this off, we'll be on a train before he ever finds us."

Rowan shakes her head. "Sounds impossible . . . and risky. He's a big guy. What if he doesn't get drowsy and just decides to take care of you the way he probably did those other girls?"

My mouth goes dry at the thought. "We have to try," I finally say. "You said it yourself, we can't stay here forever. He's made it his life's goal to screw with us. We can't go to the cops, so we've got to handle him ourselves. I think this could work."

"Fine, then I'm doing it," Rowan says. "He just . . . uh, told me that I'm a real beauty or some such bullshit."

"No," I say sharply. "It has to be me."

"Why?" Jocelyn asks, reminding me yet again why I rarely challenge her attempts to control things.

"Other than the fact that I slighted him earlier by rejecting his invitation to dinner, because I'm the innocent one. He'll never see it coming from me." This isn't quite true anymore. He obviously saw the text conversation between Landon and me; that's the only way he could know about *Cadybug*. Magnus knows one thing about the real me.

He doesn't know *everything*, though.

Then I remember the second bottle of whiskey we bought in town, and my plan gets a little better.

◆　◆　◆

A few minutes later, with Jocelyn's finishing touches on my face and hair, I'm knocking on Magnus's door.

He answers it, raising a brow as his too-blue gaze drifts from mine down to the black coat draped over my arm.

"I'm told this belongs to you," I say, pushing it toward him.

"And I told Rowan I didn't need it back." I smell the alcohol on his breath from whatever he was drinking down in the bar.

"What about the money in the pocket?"

He twists his lips. "Guess I could use that, yeah." He takes the coat, exposing the bottle of whiskey I'm gripping by the neck. "What's going on, *Cadybug*?"

"I'm trying to make amends on behalf of the group. I had no idea Rowan had stolen your coat. She fooled all of us, really."

"Mm-hmm. Sure it's not about more than that?"

There it is again. He's not going to let the Landon thing go until it tears my relationship with Jocelyn in two. "You said you wanted to talk. So, let's have a drink."

I lift the bottle.

He eyes me a moment, clearly unconvinced. But he swings a hand to gesture inside the room. "Fine. Let's have a drink."

I brush past him, finding myself inside a room similar to ours, only with one queen-size bed and the bathroom on the opposite wall. Two wine-glasses rest on the wooden desk alongside an unopened bottle of expensive, noncomplimentary wine. The room smells of his cologne, something spicy with a faint hint of citrus. It reminds me of an old-fashioned, Landon's favorite drink. Maybe, if it were Landon wearing this cologne, I'd find it sexy; knowing what I know about Magnus, the scent is sickening.

Magnus hangs the coat in the closet, and I move to the desk to uncork the whiskey. When I hear his footsteps moving toward me, I make a shivering motion. "Brr, it's freezing in here. Would you mind adjusting the thermostat?" I give a shy smile over my shoulder, watching him shrug and make his way to the other side of the room.

While his back is to me, I pour the bag with the crushed pills inside one of the glasses, letting the caramel-colored liquid slosh over the powder.

An unsettling click sounds from the thermostat behind me. "There." Magnus's footsteps pad over the carpet again, and my pulse accelerates. The powder hasn't dissolved yet. It sits thick and murky at the bottom of the glass.

Quickly, I add whiskey to the other glass, whipping around with it just as Magnus approaches. "Here you go—" The glass crashes into Magnus's brick wall of a chest, tipping, and I let the liquid splash all over his shirt. "Oh, no!" I say, patting his shirt. "I'm such a klutz. Can I—"

He waves me off. "It's fine. I'll just . . . clean up a bit." He heads into the bathroom. The second I hear the sound of the faucet, I turn back to the glasses. Grabbing the pen from the desk, I stir his glass a few times before adding more whiskey to mine.

Magnus exits the bathroom shirtless, and a flash of heat rolls through me. I avert my eyes as he rifles around in his bag for a new one. Once he's clothed, I hand him the drugged glass. He sits down on the bed, patting the space of the beige comforter beside him.

Already buzzed from the gin and tonic I had earlier, I comply and nurse my own whiskey. "So," I say, "you wanted to talk."

He grins and takes a sip. "I know that whole thing with the concussion was a show. I know that Jocelyn was in my room."

My heart freezes. He must be aware that we found Valentina's things. That we're onto his lie about her heading home. He may even know we found that ticket to Leeds Castle, too, uncovering yet another lie.

"Some theory." I pull my hair back off my forehead, exposing the swollen, crusty gash. "Does *this* look like a show to you?"

"I know Jocelyn found Val's bag, but I wanted to explain all that to you."

My palm starts to sweat, making the glass slippery in my hand. "Why me? Jocelyn was the one in your room, so you say."

"Because I think you and I understand each other." He shifts closer to me on the bed in a way that makes my skin crawl.

"I'm listening." I take a small sip of whiskey, feeling the burn as it courses down my throat. I have to get him out of this room. The pills aren't working fast enough for whatever he thinks is happening here. I won't be able to fend him off for long. Not to mention that getting him out means that the others can search for my stuff. Jocelyn didn't find it last time, but she'd been distracted by Valentina's bag. My things have to be here somewhere.

"I don't think she really left."

I choke on the whiskey, coughing. "What?"

"We got in an argument, and she threatened to leave. But I don't think she really left. I think she's just"—he shrugs—"around."

"Around?"

"Trying to punish me for . . ." He flushes. "Well, I think you're aware of what happened with Jocelyn. I heard you all arguing about it."

When he was spying on us from the trees. "What makes you think Valentina's still around?"

"The bag," he says as if it's obvious. "Because of the way she hid it under the bed, almost like she hoped I wouldn't find it. If she really left, she'd have taken the bag with her. And then there's what happened next."

He leans forward, black pupils dancing as he holds me in suspense. "The bag disappeared. It was there one minute, and gone the next. I would've thought it was you and your friends who took it, but I checked after your little charade with the concussion, and it was still there." He lifts a finger as if to punctuate the statement. "This happened later."

"Later when?"

"Not sure. The next time I checked, some hours later."

"So, you think she's still around," I say, trying to keep the skepticism from my voice. "And I suppose she's the one who took my phone?" I don't mention the other missing things. I'll give him a chance to slip up, to incriminate himself.

He tilts his head, eyes drooping like he's bored. "You're rooming with a pickpocket, and something went missing."

"But you called me . . ." I start, suddenly unable to say the nickname Landon gave me in front of this man.

"Sorry, what?" he asks tauntingly. "Don't you think maybe Rowan told me about your little nickname? To keep me quiet about what *she'd* done? She and I had a nice conversation while you and Jocelyn were down in the pub."

"Rowan wouldn't take my phone," I argue. As soon as the words are out, though, I'm no longer certain. Could Rowan have sent the photo in order to mess things up between Jocelyn and me? It doesn't seem like her. Then again, I never pegged her for a thief. She has always been a bit envious of my relationship with Jocelyn. And she was missing when I got back to the fireside room that night. Just like my phone.

No. He's doing it again. Slowly stealing my allegiance. Twisting things. Getting me to turn against my friends. He's done it before; I can't let him do it again. "Well, if you don't have my phone, then I guess you don't actually have jack shit."

He looks at me for a moment, expression cold yet inscrutable. I picture him reaching out that massive hand to wrap it around my throat. I'd be helpless, just like Valentina probably was. If I ran now, could I make it out the door? Maybe I should try my luck with the glass in my hand—he might be slower with the pills in his system. But his eyes are still on mine, sharp and lucid, as if he can read everything going on in my head.

Just when I'm about to lunge for the door, he says, "Wish you were here."

I flinch, about to ask what the hell he's talking about, but he cuts me off. "Wish I could hold you. Wish I could hear your voice." With that same stony look on his face, he puts on a softer, eerily feminine timber. "Sorry, haven't had a moment alone. I'll try to get away."

I go numb all over. Those words, they're the exact words of my text exchange with Landon before my phone went missing. My nearly full whiskey glass starts to slide from my grasp. I take it in both hands. "I'm just a schoolteacher," I force out through a dry throat. "I don't have money."

He shrugs, that horrible smile sliding back onto his lips before he takes another swig of whiskey. "We could arrange something else."

I tense.

"I mean your company," Magnus says with a laugh. "I'm in need of a new traveling companion, and like I said, you and I understand each other. Don't you want to travel the world?" He finishes his glass and pushes it toward me for a refill.

"We could see all the stone circles in Britain," I offer.

"Each and every one," he says with a sleepy smile.

"Where is Valentina, really?"

He laughs again, alcohol heavy on his breath. "Probably watching us."

My gaze veers to the closet door. I blink, pulling my thoughts back to the real monster in front of me.

By the time he's drained the next round, Magnus's eyelids are drooping and his body is much too close to mine. "You know what?" I say, gripping the bottle by the neck. "Let's take this party to the woods. I want to show you something."

"Why can't you show me here?" he asks, words slurring.

I laugh. "Not like that. I was doing some more research on those stone circles, and there's supposed to be something—a tomb or an altar—back behind this place."

He reaches out, and I force myself not to flinch as he runs a rough index finger down my cheek. "Why don't we go in the morning?"

"Because wandering a creepy, ancient burial ground at night sounds thrilling," I say, channeling Rowan. "I think it's still sprinkling. You could keep me warm." Add a dash of Jocelyn.

The corner of his mouth lifts at this. He glances toward the window, though the curtains are drawn. "Won't your friends worry?"

"I don't care. I hope I never see Rowan again. You're right about her. She probably did take my phone. It wouldn't be the first time she's stolen from me."

"Oh?"

I nod, the sting in my eyes real even as I act my part. "And Jocelyn only cares about herself." I expect him to say something about Landon, a dig—anything.

But he merely watches me with fascination. He takes my hand in his, squeezing lightly. "I'll need my coat." Swaying on his feet, he wanders back to the closet, retrieving the coat I just returned.

After shrugging it on, he gathers the glasses and abandons them on the desk. He grabs the whiskey bottle and guzzles directly from the lip. Then, bottle swinging at his side, he slips an arm around my waist and guides me to the door.

But the moment we step into the hall, he stops. Pulling away, he blinks like the light is too strong. "Sorry, let me just . . ." He digs the room key from the pocket of his jeans and fumbles it. When it falls to the floor, he lets out a laugh, tipping his head backward.

"Here, let me help you." I take the key and insert it into the lock. Only instead of turning it once and removing it, I turn the key once to the left and once to the right, effectively unlocking it again. "There."

I slip back beneath the crook of his arm. I'm dying to text the girls that the room is unlocked and unoccupied, but Magnus knows

I lost my phone. Having Rowan's on me could spark suspicion, especially as we're meant to be in a fight. Instead, I leave it on silent in my jacket pocket, hoping the girls hear our footsteps and try the door on their own.

We amble down the stairs, Magnus rocking and stumbling along. I help to steady him as much as a small woman like me can help a giant like him.

Once we're outside, I completely detest myself for the idea. It is indeed still sprinkling, and the damp night air chills me to the bone. But it seems to have given Magnus a second wind. "So, where is it?" he asks, ducking a pine branch as we search in vain for a trail where there is none.

"Hold on a minute," I say, scanning the area. A thick layer of fog weaves through the bases of the trees, leaving only the tops visible. "There should be a—ah, there it is." I clap my hands together in victory. "Those two pines that sort of cross. That's where this blogger said to start."

Magnus frowns. "I don't see a cross." His accent is stronger now, the drugs and alcohol bringing it out.

"Of course you do." I reach for his hand, finding it warmer than mine, and interlock our fingers. "Come on."

After a few minutes, I'm shivering, and Magnus is stumbling over every rock and branch in our path. "Are you sure this is the way?" Even his words knock into one another. "Maybe we should try again tomorrow. I could really lie down." Without waiting for a response, he slumps down against a tree trunk.

"Whoa, Magnus. Are you all right?" I kneel down in front of him. Without warning, he pulls me in close to him.

"Just give me a moment," he mumbles, shutting his eyes, one massive arm wrapped around my torso.

It almost feels nice, being nestled into the warmth of his chest. I wrangle Rowan's phone from my pocket and send off a text to Jocelyn: Door's unlocked. Find my stuff

They'll need a few minutes. Instead of getting up right away, I allow myself to remain a few moments, lowering until my cheek is pressed against the beating of his heart. Listening to his breathing. Imagining that it's Landon here with me, protecting me from the elements.

Once Magnus is out, I turn him enough to remove his phone, wallet, and room key from his pockets.

When it's all taken care of, I get a text from Jocelyn. It's not here, Cady. We searched everywhere.

Biting back my frustration, I place an icy hand on Magnus's cheek. "We should get back," I whisper into his ear. "I'll tuck you in."

Trembling from the cold, I tug the cord of my hood to keep it from blowing back. It's too frigid to stay out here any longer. I heft him up, and he wobbles a bit. Then I text Jocelyn: Fine. We're headed back.

CHAPTER 19
JOCELYN

"I've got his car keys." Cady dangles them in front of me as I let her into the room. She moves to the bed, casting her spoils onto it.

"We're not stealing his car," Rowan says, eyeing the mud that Cady has tracked all over the carpet.

"Says the thief." Cady grabs her suitcase and begins shoving Magnus's things inside it. "I still don't get how you didn't find my stuff."

"Sorry," I say. "We turned the place inside out. What did you take?"

She shrugs. "Anything that seemed important."

"But again," Rowan says, sitting down at the desk chair, "we're not taking his car."

"No, we just have to take his keys, so he can't follow us. Or . . ." Cady tips her head, power-drunk over her part in this mission. "We could drive it to the station."

"No," I say. "Cady, you don't have a passport, which means we can't leave the country right away. We can't get caught stealing a car in the meantime. They don't give passports to women who visit their country, drug people, and steal their cars."

"I think the whole *worried for our lives* part cancels all that out, but fine. We'll take the keys and hide them somewhere."

"What happened to you?" I ask, indicating her muddy boots and the filthy hem of her coat.

"Magnus and I went for a little hike."

Rowan's fingers fidget over the handle of her suitcase. "We should go."

"You're sure he's out?" I ask, glancing at the wall we share with Magnus.

"I gave him two of those things. He could barely make it back to the room and was snoring again by the time I shut the door." Cady's suitcase is stuffed to the brim now with Magnus's things. "He's not going anywhere."

We leave our room key at the desk and head outside, dragging our suitcases behind us. The walk to the taxi stand is long beneath the dark-gray sky. A few lamps light the way, but the thick fog smothers their glow. We sit on the bench, rain drizzling over the glass shelter, waiting for a taxi.

We wait for two delirious hours, huddled together for warmth. Rowan searches for a train station with something running late in the night. It doesn't matter where we go, as long as it's far away from here. The fog rolls back to reveal the sun's rays as they peek over the horizon. Just as a car pulls up, my phone buzzes in my pocket.

The driver is a stern-looking man with a black unibrow. "Where are you headed?" he asks, helping us to stow the luggage in the trunk.

"Llandudno Station, please," Rowan says.

"Actually," I say, showing the others the text message, "we're headed to 55 Riverton."

Cady stares at the screen, looking more baffled than relieved. The text is from Helen.

Found Cady's stuff just now while cleaning the room! Should I have Paul deliver it?

I make sure the driver can take us out there for a quick pickup before shuttling us to the airport. Then I text Helen back. We'll come get it now.

The driver starts the car. We sit in silence, exhaustion setting in.

"I checked the room," Cady whispers finally. "I know I checked everywhere."

"I did too," Rowan says. "He could've put it all back. We didn't lock the door on our way out. Maybe he snuck in and returned everything."

"Unless . . ." Cady starts, but then shakes her head.

"What is it?" I peer back through the rear windshield. There's only a haze, no headlights chasing us.

"Never mind," she says with a headshake. "That has to be it. Magnus put it back there to make us feel crazy."

"Or to keep us here for longer than necessary," I say, the words chilling me through. "Cady, tell me you're sure he can't come after us."

"I'm sure." She lays a cold hand on mine. "Remember, if my passport is there, we can leave the country."

"Yeah." I want to believe her, but I crane my neck to check the windshield again. "We'll just grab your things and leave."

By the time we reach the B&B, the rain clouds have gone, making way for a sunny blue sky. The taxi driver waits for us on the dirt road.

Cady races ahead of us, likely nervous that this is all some fluke. I start to follow her up the path when something snags my gaze over by the hedge.

The groundskeeper. He's in his work clothes, wearing garden gloves and holding a shovel. He speaks in hushed tones to the man staying in the room next to ours, the plastic surgeon. The doctor raises his voice now. I can't make out the words, but there's a sharpness to it. Maybe the groundskeeper grabbed him too.

Noting our presence, both men halt their conversation, the doctor cutting us a haughty, irritated glance. But the groundskeeper's stare looks to be one of pure malice. His bony, hollowed cheeks and dead eyes would give small children nightmares.

Training my focus back on the front door, I keep walking. I guess his suspension was only a formality meant to appease the three of us. The moment we left, Helen allowed that creep back onto the property.

Inside, Cady lets out an audible sigh as my aunt pushes her phone across the desk, along with her purple travel organizer. "Oh my god," she says, ensuring that the passport and driver's license are inside. "Thank goodness."

"Sorry, but you girls look awful," Helen says, wincing. "How about some breakfast?"

"We can't, Helen—"

"Maybe a quick bite." Rowan looks at me pleadingly. "I'm starving."

I remember that she didn't eat Helen's dinner before we set out for the Starboard Inn. My resolve crumples. "Go tell the driver it'll be a few minutes and he'll be compensated."

Rowan nods and heads out the door.

"And if it's not too much trouble, Helen, can I use the restroom?" Cady asks.

"Of course. Use the one in your old room." Cady takes the key, and my attention diverts to the desk. Her phone is flashing blue.

It's on silent, so the others don't notice. But I see the twelve missed calls as well as the name of the caller before she snatches it up and pockets it.

At the name on the screen, my heart plunges into my gut.

NOW

The door to the fireside room opens, and my friend walks out from her interview looking dazed. She spots me at the table in the reception area, and the way she eyes me sends shivers dancing up my arms. "Your turn," she says quietly.

I get up and brush past her. Inside the fireside room, DI Collins has set up a folding table and some chairs, converting her temporary base into a proper interrogation room. "Did you find him yet?" I ask, taking a seat.

DI Collins still holds a pen, her pad of paper on the table beside that same folder she had the last time she interviewed me. "I'd like to talk about that second fight. The one that happened yesterday morning, before the murder." She is the picture of patience and grace.

I am anything but patient. And grace? Well, any last ounce of that drained away the moment I started fearing for my life.

"Let me speak to someone else," I say, the volume of my voice climbing. "You aren't hearing me. Magnus was after us. I told you, he followed us to the inn in Conwy. He booked a room right next to ours!" I pound on the table, but the detective doesn't flinch.

Instead, calmly, she lays the pen down and folds her hands together. "Magnus is no longer a person of interest in this investigation."

I sit back in my chair, stunned. "Wha—this is incredible. Have you listened to a single word I've said?"

"Magnus Larsen is no longer a person of interest in this investigation," she repeats, slower this time, "because he is now a victim."

I try to make sense of the words, but they bend and break, failing to form a cohesive whole.

"I'm afraid his body was discovered in the woods behind the Starboard Inn in Conwy," she says.

"No, but that's . . ." Magnus—handsome charmer, towering brute, menace incarnate—cannot be dead.

"I'm going to need both of your phones," DI Collins says.

"Do you have a warrant?" I object, remembering the movies again.

Her subtle smile twists my insides. "We don't need a warrant to seize a phone in the UK."

My palm is slick as I hand mine over.

When I follow the detective into the lobby, my friend is sitting in my spot. I don't join her, despite the tempting oatmeal cookies and carafe of hot coffee.

Instead, I look at her.

She looks at me.

CHAPTER 20
ROWAN

Jocelyn and I are at the breakfast table when Cady returns. She sits down and unfolds her napkin, placing it in her lap.

"Cady, unlock your phone for me," Jocelyn says, reaching an open palm across the table nonchalantly.

Cady frowns, and her elbows lower as if to guard her pockets. "Why?"

"I want to see if there's any clue on there as to who took it. The culprit could've made other calls or texts that will point us in the right direction."

"I'll check it out when we're on our way to the airport," she says, easing forward again to take up some eggs with her fork.

"Cady, give me your phone."

Cady glances up, irritation creasing her brow. "Joss, what the hell is going on?"

"Why was Landon calling you?" Jocelyn leans over her plate now, placing both palms on the table.

"What? How did you—he was probably checking up on *you*. When was the last time you called him?"

"You hate him. And yet, he's called you twelve—no—thirteen times, if you count that call yesterday. Thirteen calls from *my* fiancé while we've been here. It's not to check up on me. I've had my phone this entire time. Give me yours." Though there's something undeniably beautiful about her in her anger, Jocelyn looks feral, her hair unkempt for once, spittle forming in one corner of her mouth. She looks ready to lean over the table and bite or claw at Cady.

"You're acting crazy," Cady says, setting her fork down.

"If I'm crazy, prove it." Jocelyn pounds a fist on the table. "Show me your phone!"

I reach out to keep my water glass from falling over. Then I look from one girl to the other. "Joss, no. You're just tired after last night. Whatever you're thinking . . ."

"Then why won't she just show me her phone?" She turns on me now, and I flinch.

"Because it's private," I say, to which Cady slings me a look of shock rather than of gratitude that I've taken her side.

"It's not private when it's *my fiancé*."

"Jocelyn, please calm down," I say. "Whatever you're insinuating, you can't take it back."

"Why would I take it back?" Jocelyn lets out a maniacal giggle. "I was close before, wasn't I? I didn't hit the nail on the head, though. Cady *is* in love with my fiancé, but the story doesn't end there. Nope." She licks her lips. "She's also obsessively texting him. He's probably calling to tell her to back off."

"Joss—" I try, but she cuts me off again.

"You're pathetic, Cady. You know that? Like Landon would *ever* see you as anything more than my plain-looking, schoolteacher sidekick."

The words slice through the air like a swinging blade. But before they have a chance to land a blow, Cady is on her feet, napkin sliding from her lap. "Oh, wouldn't he?" she shouts, her hand knocking her fork, which flies off the table and clatters to the floor.

I shrink down in my seat. I've never heard Cady raise her voice like this, not in all of our years of friendship.

She removes her phone from her jacket pocket, hand shaking with rage as her fingers move over the keypad to unlock it. "There!" She tosses it onto the table, letting it skip along toward Jocelyn. "You wanted it? Go ahead and see how little *your* fiancé thinks of me!"

Jocelyn's delicate freckles drown in a sea of red as she snatches up the phone and starts scrolling. It's like a spinning wheel of colors as her skin goes through the gamut. Red, then pale white—even more pale than usual—followed by a sallow yellow. She sinks into the chair, dazed.

I ready myself. This is the calm before the storm if I ever saw it. Why is Cady still standing there? Doesn't she realize her head is about to be ripped off?

The moment drags out, though, Jocelyn still clutching the phone. Silent. My shoulder muscles are so taut, they could snap.

Suddenly, Jocelyn sets the phone down on the table. Without so much as a look at Cady, she says in a voice that's part resignation and part scorn, "I guess I have a call to make." She gets up, glancing around as though she can't quite remember where she is or what she brought with her. My heart aches, watching my larger-than-life, ever-confident friend stand there, looking like a lost child. Then she wanders from the room.

I realize I've barely taken a breath in minutes and inhale a dizzying gulp. "What the hell was that about, Cady?"

She stares down at her uneaten breakfast. Her lips are pursed, like she's trying to keep the truth zipped up inside.

"Cady? I've never seen Jocelyn so . . . maybe I should go check on her." I start to get up, but Cady's hand darts out, her fingers curling around my arm.

"I've been seeing Landon."

"What?" I choke on a half-laugh, even though I just witnessed the scene. All the signs pointed here. But it doesn't make any sense. Cady wouldn't do that to Jocelyn. "Is this some sort of joke? That's not . . . you're best friends."

"You don't understand," she says, finally making eye contact. "He was my boyfriend first."

I blink. What else can you really do or say in response to that? "Your *boyfriend*." Disbelief drips from the word.

"I never told Jocelyn about us, but Landon and I were together back in college. He was my first love before she came along and just"— her hand glides through the air, ending in a fist—"swooped him up." Her eyes meet mine, full of earnest grief. "He was mine, though. I had to watch those two together when really, he was mine. We couldn't be together because of *her*."

"Okay . . ." I try to wrap my mind around it, but it's like catching fish in a net full of giant holes. Those little floppy creatures keep slipping free. "So, Landon was your college boyfriend. But what about the texts?"

Cady grabs Jocelyn's unused fork and starts pushing the eggs around on her plate. "Things started up again, a few years back."

"A few *years*? This has been going on behind her back for *years*?"

"To be completely honest, we've been on and off again since college. We're in love." Her eyes well with tears as she looks at me. She believes it, that much is clear. "He only stays with her out of some sick sense of guilt."

I'm quiet for a moment. Then the question I meant to keep trapped in my mind somehow wriggles its way to freedom. "How could you do this to Jocelyn?"

Now Cady's the one laughing. A bitter chuckle. "You still see her as this perfect, loyal friend, don't you? You have no idea what she did."

An unsettling sensation twines its way up my core. "What are you talking about?"

"You and Jake."

The feeling fans out now, little shoots sprouting off in every direction. "What about me and Jake?" Twisting, creeping.

"Jake broke up with you because of *Jocelyn*. You really didn't know?"

"How did you—" I never told anyone about the breakup. I assumed he never had either. "Who told you this?"

"Jocelyn, of course. She told Jake that you hooked up with some guy at the party the three of us went to. Just a flat-out lie because she didn't want you dating her twin anymore."

I feel sick. Those two bites of egg are churning in my gut, threatening to come up. Tears sting behind my eyes. Jocelyn wanted her brother to break up with me? More than that, she fabricated some story about me to ensure that it happened? She plotted and carried out the demise of our relationship, knowing it would devastate me. Then she carried this secret with her, all these years.

"No." I can't believe this. I refuse. My best friend never could've done this.

And yet . . .

I've always known my best friend to be a liar.

The tears are still there, burning at my eyes, but I don't let them fall. Letting them fall means it's true. That I've accepted this horrible tale as reality. I want to ask Jocelyn if it's true, to make her explain it to me. But she isn't here, so I take my frustration out on Cady. "You've ruined everything."

"I'm sorry." She reaches for Jocelyn's napkin and wipes her eyes and nose. "I shouldn't have said anything."

I shrug, and it feels like I've got twenty-pound weights strapped to my shoulders. The small movement is painful. "I've always wanted to know what happened." My words sound strangely distant in my ears. "Guess I got my wish."

One wish granted.

One friend lost forever.

CHAPTER 21
CADENCE

I regret it, all of it. Coming clean to Jocelyn, ratting her out to Rowan.

But for one brief moment, I relished that look on Jocelyn's face. Her words still reverberate in my ears: *You're pathetic, Cady, you know that? Like Landon would ever see you as anything more than my plain-looking, schoolteacher sidekick.*

Seeing that sneer stripped right off her face, it felt good.

Most people who'd compare me to Jocelyn would share her sentiment. He's got her, so what could he possibly want with me? I admit, I was insecure about this for quite a while. He'd left me for her once, after all. I studied Landon long and hard. As if he were the subject of that dissertation I never quite made it to. It took many months, days, hours, until finally, I got it.

Landon is just like the rest of us. He's pretending to be something he isn't. Between his parents and his friends, he's been conditioned to believe he has to marry someone like Jocelyn. He may even believe he *wants* to marry someone like her—gorgeous, rich family, confidence bursting out her ears. That's the dream, isn't it? To end up with a girl like that.

But deep down, that was never what Landon wanted. Deep down, he wanted a girl like me. A bit hard to sell on paper. Too quiet, too plain, and way too smart for her own good. But then there are the intangible qualities. The time we spend together—fingers entwined, minds locked, souls embraced. The nights he's been frustrated with his job and Jocelyn was too self-involved to listen, so I listened. I held him. I'm the one who helped him rewrite his résumé so he could land that new corporate job she'd nagged him about. What did Jocelyn think? That he'd done it all on his own?

So yeah, for a moment, it felt good to watch it all register on Jocelyn's perfect face. *For once, you're not it, Jocelyn Elliott.* In one man's book, the whole package is Cadence Fletcher.

But that feeling could never last. By the time Jocelyn had left the breakfast room, whatever satisfaction I'd felt had turned to nausea. It's only Wednesday, and we haven't done half the things I typed into our travel itinerary; it's like I ended our trip and our friendship in one fell swoop.

"Should we get going?" I ask a dazed-looking Rowan. "It's been hours since I gave Magnus that medicine. If he manages to hitch a ride out here, we're in trouble."

Rowan shrugs, as if her will to survive has been extinguished. She hasn't shifted in her seat or taken a bite of her breakfast since I told her about Jake.

"I know things with Jocelyn are screwed up right now," I say, "but you have to get home. For Molly."

At her daughter's name, Rowan's eyes reanimate. But she shakes her head. "I can't talk to Jocelyn."

"You have to. At least until we get on that plane. Eat something." I point to her food, which has now grown cold. "I'm going to try to talk to her."

"Good luck," Rowan says, an acerbic smile on her lips.

Stomach in a knot, I gather up my things and exit the breakfast room. I've thought about this day countless times over the years. I pictured it like this phantom weight on my back being lifted off me, once and for all. Finally breathing easy. No black shadow over my every kiss with Landon. No more looking over my shoulder. No more lies.

Reality is much, much different. The Jocelyn stuff is the part I skipped over in my fantasy. I don't feel lighter having her upset with me—quite the opposite. I've done a lot to keep this relationship a secret, and this is the reason.

The reception area is empty, but my skin prickles at the sound of a car outside.

I run to the front door, which swings open, nearly knocking me over. "Oh, sorry," Jocelyn says, dragging her suitcase right past me. "Didn't see you there."

"What's going on? Why is the driver leaving?"

"Because I'm not ready to go to the airport." She struts back through the door, grabs Rowan's suitcase, and then wheels it inside the lobby.

"What about Magnus?"

She turns to face me at the base of the stairs, eyes red and puffy. "I'm going to be safely locked up inside my room, which Helen has given *me* the key to."

"So, we're not leaving?"

"There is no *we* anymore, Cady. If and when Rowan and I decide to leave, we will be doing it without you." She's changed from her wool sweater to the soft blue hoodie she wears when she wants to do nothing but watch movies and eat ice cream. Usually, when she's in one of these moods, she calls me to join her, to console her with my presence beside her on the couch. Now, all she's got left to comfort her is that hoodie.

"Joss."

"If I were you, I'd look for a safe place to stay."

The rage building up inside me bubbles over. "I told her, you know."

"Told *who* what?"

"I told Rowan that you broke her and Jake up."

She blinks, as if there's a fly flitting at her lashes. "Why the hell would you do that?"

"Because of the way she was looking at me! I needed her to see that I wasn't the only one who'd done something horrible. What you did was plain evil."

Jocelyn smiles, but there's rage in her eyes. A pit of worry plants itself in my gut. "I can't believe I ever trusted you. I deserve everything that's happened for being such an idiot. Go call your *boyfriend*." She makes a shooing motion at me. Like I'm that imaginary fly. "You better hope he isn't upset with you for all of this. But I have a feeling he's pretty upset. Oh, and Cady?" She smiles now, lips tight and eyes red rimmed, and it's the ugliest I've ever seen her. "If Magnus manages to track us down, then I hope to god he murders you the way he did those other girls." With that, she spins around and heads up the stairs, leaving me alone in the reception area.

The pain from her words radiates, more acute than the wound on my forehead. I duck out to the porch, fetching my suitcase from where it's been abandoned. Wheeling it over the threshold and back behind the front desk, I flip it over to open it. I remove Magnus's things and zip them up inside my jacket pockets.

Then I head outside, not quite sure where I'm going. I only know I can't stay in this B&B. Not with the two of them judging me. I didn't want to hurt Jocelyn. But she hurt me first, the moment she started dating Landon. Neither of those two understands.

I'm dying to call Landon and find out where his head is with all of this. But I'm afraid. If he's upset about Jocelyn finding out the truth, then I have to let him cool off. In time, he'll understand that this is the way it had to be. He couldn't have us both forever; he has to see that. I'm the one he keeps coming back to, the woman with whom he can't seem to sever ties completely.

He thinks of our stolen moments—the early morning tangle of bedsheets, the late-night kisses beneath a starless night when we aren't seeing, only feeling. The covert phone calls during lunch hours. He sees those moments the way I do. He savors them, lets his mind linger on them whenever we're apart. He desperately wishes they could be our happy normal.

They can be. I know they can be. We'll get a new place, one that has no ties to his relationship with Jocelyn. One with a yard, so I can fill my spare time with gardening. I'll need a new hobby, now that there's no sneaking around to do. The rest of the time will be spent with him, the two of us, in *our* home. Maybe even with a child of our own. Jocelyn never spoke of children, and I know that bothered Landon. He doesn't have to worry about that with me. I only want what he wants.

The sky is still clear, so I make my way to the trail. Out in the woods, I can take care of the things in my pockets. The fresh air will help to clear my head. Then I'll form a plan. I'll figure out what to do, the way I always have.

I enter the pines. For the first time, without Jocelyn whining in my ear, I see how truly enchanting these woods are. The trees are the lushest shade of green, the sunlight sparkling onto their boughs to cast a mystical aura. If I'd come here on my own, I might've simply wandered this forest all day, gazing and taking photos that would last a lifetime.

The hike is easier this time around, now that I know what to expect. My pace is leisurely, my eyes drinking in as much of the scenery as possible. Somewhere behind me, a branch snaps, and I spin around. But the coast is clear. It must've been an animal or the wind. It's stupid to worry about Magnus now.

A few minutes up the trail, I leave it, wading into the undergrowth of the forest. I push aside a large shrub and tread over the bed of pine needles and weeds. The wind kicks up a sweet, fruity scent, and I soon find the source: a blackcurrant shrub. Its bright-green pointed leaves and dark, round fruit grow around the base of a pine. Many Americans wouldn't even recognize the berries. I remember reading about them, about how they were once banned by the US Department of Agriculture because they carry a fungus that threatened our pine trees and, in effect, the entire logging industry. Part of me wants to stop and pick some, to taste the tart fruit that, still to this day, is a rarity in my country.

Instead, I trek deeper yet, looking for the perfect place to bury Magnus's things. Somewhere nondescript, where no one will ever think to look.

When I find it, a patch of land between two trees that look like all the other pines in the woods, I crouch down and start digging. There's still dirt embedded beneath my fingernails from last night, dirt I couldn't remove, no matter how much I washed in the inn's bathroom. I keep digging. More dirt seeps beneath my nail bed, pushing in and invading that delicate pink flesh. It gets beneath my jacket sleeves, cakes onto the knees of my jeans.

I hear a rustle in the brambles, but my heart barely kicks up this time. I don't have to worry about Magnus, not the way the others do. I know he isn't coming back.

Because I killed him.

CHAPTER 22
CADENCE

Jocelyn may be the queen of lies, but sometimes I lie too.

It wasn't just a sedative I put in Magnus's whiskey last night. In addition to the two crushed lorazepam, I also put two crushed oxycodone.

As someone I'd hoped was unaccustomed to these drugs, on top of the level of alcohol in his bloodstream, Magnus stood little chance. I checked to make sure he was dead—that coy little "I'll tuck you in" bit—and he didn't respond. Then I lay there with my head on his chest, listening to the way his heartbeat slowed. Waiting as his breathing went from soft and shallow to inaudible.

Then it all stopped: the heartbeat, the breathing.

I took his things and dragged him a little farther into the woods. It took all of my strength, but I did it. Then I covered him with some dirt and brambles.

The others think our race is against Magnus finding us here. In reality, our race is against someone finding that body.

I told my friends I was merely putting him to sleep in his room because they'd never understand. They aren't like me. If they knew the truth, they might've stopped me. They don't know what it means to do whatever it takes to protect yourself and the ones you love.

I do. I know what it means.

I've done it before.

CHAPTER 23
JOCELYN

I've locked myself in the room, even though the others are still out there, sitting ducks for Magnus. It's like some deep, primordial instinct has kicked in. It's me against the world now.

When I first got inside, I called Landon. I guess I hoped he'd deny everything, that some magical explanation could possibly exist. Instead, when I told him I'd seen the texts, his response was silence. An eternal moment that kept stretching.

When he finally spoke, his voice was low, but it hit me like a blast, shattering my insides. "I'm so sorry, Joss," he said. "I have no excuse. I'm an idiot."

His voice broke on the last word, followed by a sniffle that turned my stomach.

"Cady and I have a history. Back at UCSB, before you and me." The information takes the few pieces of me that are whole and crushes them into oblivion.

"But it's over," he said. "I'm ending it."

If it had been a text, I might've shoved the damned screen in front of Cady's face downstairs just so she could hurt as much as I did. But it wouldn't have been much of a victory. My cheating fiancé chose me over her. So what? I'm the fool, either way.

He kept talking. I kept listening, even as the words blended together to form meaningless sounds.

"I don't deserve you," he said at one point, and this came out crystal clear, separating from the other garbled noises. That line was what really got to me. It was what Cady always said over the years. Back when I thought she wanted the best for me.

Now, I know the real reason she said it. I know the real reason she flipped the sentence around on me yesterday too. *You don't deserve him.*

It's obvious now that we really do deserve each other, Landon and me. Now that the very thought of him makes me want to take a hammer to something. Or someone.

"But I want this marriage. I really do."

He kept talking, begging for my forgiveness. Whether he was sorry he'd done it or simply sorry he'd been caught, I'll never know. I hung up the phone and ignored the seven incoming calls that followed.

I've just been lying here ever since. One thing he said cycles through my mind on repeat. *Cady and I have a history. Back at UCSB, before you and me.*

I've always liked to think of Cady as my trusty, boring friend. The plain one. The one I could count on for her smarts but disregard as any real type of threat when it came to men. I obviously underestimated her. The man I took for granted—the one I believed loved me with his entire heart—loved her, too, possibly the entire time we'd been together.

And Cady? I don't know if she ever considered me a friend over the past decade. Maybe she was just using me to get close to Landon.

The only thing that's certain is that a bad man is out there, likely searching for a way back to us. And now, the person I trusted most to get me through this ordeal isn't that person anymore.

As if Cady's affair weren't enough, she tried to torch my relationship with Rowan on her way out the door. *I told Rowan that you broke her and Jake up.*

For some reason, that line—that confession—is bothering me. It was such a long time ago. I suppose it's possible that in my grief, I let my crime slip to Cady.

But I don't remember telling her that I'd been the one to come between Rowan and Jake. It was a horrible thing to do, too horrible to confess, even to my best friend.

One thing is certain: I have to get Rowan on my side. I can't lose everyone in my life, all in the same day. Leaving the suitcase in the room, I take the stairs down to the reception area.

"Everything okay, love?" Aunt Helen asks, scribbling something down on a pad of paper.

The tears come again when I try to answer, my throat constricting. Instead, I simply shake my head. She drops the pen and comes around the desk to embrace me.

I sob onto her shoulder, inhaling the scent of blueberry muffins. Somewhere in the recesses of my mind, a memory trickles in of my mother baking them—maybe even using the same recipe passed down from my grandmother—and her asking for my help. As Helen holds me, the memory, the feeling that I need my mother, becomes so unbearable that I have to sit down. Helen helps me to one of the chairs in the corner. "Tell me what happened, love."

"I can't. I—" It's too much. "I have to find Rowan. Have you seen her?"

She turns her head in the direction of the breakfast room. "Last I checked, she was in there."

"Thanks." I stand, struggling to get feeling back in my legs. I open the door to the breakfast room to find it empty. Our table is still cluttered with plates and wadded napkins. I glance out the long window.

The view is nothing but the pristine lawn and pine trees shivering in the breeze.

Across the table, Rowan's food appears untouched, even though she was the one who asked to eat in the first place. I sit for a moment. Maybe she'll be hungry enough to come back for a bite.

I'm too jittery to wait, though. After a few minutes, I return to the reception area, finding the desk empty. Rowan could've ducked into the fireside room to hide from me. But when I check, she isn't there either.

It's unlikely she went to the room without the key. Still, I head up there to make sure. She could be sitting out in the hall, pouting.

The second floor is eerily quiet. No sign of Rowan. I pass Magnus's old room, unable to ward off the trickle of unease. I continue to our room and unlock the door. It's empty, the linens and bathroom appearing undisturbed. I pull out my phone and send off a text to Rowan: Where are you?

Out in the hall, my eyes veer over to room one. I force myself to tiptoe up to the door and press my ear against it. My heart thumps in my rib cage so loudly I worry it will blow my cover. A clink sounds, and I jerk back, my foot snagging on a seam in the carpet.

I recover, catching my breath. The noise didn't come from this room. It came from two doors over—the Welsh couple's room.

Carefully, I pad down and knock on the door. The man answers in nothing but a pair of shorts. His hairy gut hangs over the elastic waistline, so I focus on his round, unshaven face. He frowns, clearly displeased at my presence. "Yes?"

The pungent scent of body odor tinged with a slightly herbal note wafts out of the room. I refrain from wrinkling my nose. "You didn't happen to see my friend, did you? The one with the curly brown hair?"

"Sorry, no," he answers, already shutting the door.

My hand shoots out to stop it. "Please. I'm worried about her." I attempt to peek past him into the room, but he shuffles sideways, blocking my view with his body.

What is he hiding? "Can I at least speak with your wife?" I ask, still trying to get a look inside the room.

"She isn't here."

"Well, where is she? Maybe I can talk—"

"That's none of your business," he snaps.

I flinch, his hostility hitting me like a slap. He crosses his arms. As he does, I manage a glimpse into the room. There's a stack of books on the table. I can't make out a complete title, but the small pamphlet on the top is familiar.

Before I can get a better look, he spits, "I can't help you." He shuts the door in my face, leaving me stunned.

A paralyzing sense of cold wraps around me. How could he possibly be so unfriendly about a missing girl?

As much as I want to lock myself up inside my room again, I have to find Rowan. Our relationship is the only one worth salvaging. The only relationship that may be *possible* to salvage.

When I reach the bottom step, I plop down to wait for her. I check my phone, but my text remains unanswered. She's obviously angry with me about Jake.

I should be planning my apology; instead, my mind locks on a memory from senior year of high school. That was before Jake's death, before he was dating Rowan, before college or babies—back when the worst thing I could fathom was ending up without a date to senior prom. That was exactly what happened.

I'd just broken up with Mark Hanson. He was this big shot basketball player, and none of the other guys were brave enough to chance stepping on his toes if he was still interested. As prom got closer, I started to freak out. Even Cady had managed to find a date. I couldn't miss my prom, but there was no way I could show up solo. I was on the damned prom court. Finally, I asked Jake to talk to his friends, just to see if anyone was still dateless.

The night before the dance, I still hadn't been asked. I was sitting in my room, my glittering midnight-blue dress draped over my lap, tears sprinkling down onto the fabric. That was when Rowan knocked on my bedroom door and announced that she was going to stay home and watch movies with me. "But what about Henry?" I asked. Rowan had been so excited to go with him. We'd picked out our dresses together, back when I was still dating Mark.

She shrugged. "He'll live. Guys only do these things for us, anyway."

"But what about you?" I asked, sniffling. "You only have one senior prom. You don't have to give it up for me."

"I know, but I want to. No dance or guy is as important to me as you."

It was hard to make her words fit into my finite understanding of things—of friendship, of people, of love. Rowan was willing to sacrifice the thing I valued most at that time, and she was willing to give it up for *me*.

In the end, no one had to miss prom. Jake came to the rescue with a date, and we all rented a limo together. Eventually, I let the memory of that day in my bedroom with Rowan slip away. I blocked it out, pretended like it had never happened, especially when the thing I wanted most two years later meant sacrificing her happiness.

Now, the memory has returned to me—Rowan's heart, her willingness to throw her own desires aside to help—now that it's too late.

I check my phone again, positive there's no text from Rowan because I would've heard it. It's all my fault. I blew it with Rowan years ago, and it's finally caught up to me.

Still, that little hum of unrest remains in my ear. I stand and cross the lobby to peer out the front window. Nothing's out of place, no car other than Uncle Paul's Ford Fiesta off in the dirt, half-shrouded by trees.

Even so, I can't help wondering if something bad could've happened to her.

NOW

"I don't understand," I say, following the detective through the reception area. My friend remains seated, mug in hand, eyes on me.

DI Collins heads for the front door, but I race to cut her off. "Magnus isn't dead," I say.

"I'm afraid he is." DI Collins tucks her folder beneath her arm. She seems in a hurry to leave as she finagles her free arm into a coat sleeve.

I wonder if she might lie about something like this. I've watched enough of those police procedural shows to know that sometimes these detectives can't be trusted. They resort to desperate measures to get a confession. Even a false confession. Maybe these Welsh police can't locate Magnus, so they're lying in an attempt to pin this on someone else.

As if reading my mind, DI Collins sets her folder down on the reception desk and shuffles through the papers. She plucks a photo free and slaps it on top of the stack.

I move close enough to make out the image. The pale and wrinkled flesh, already ravaged by insects and the elements, half-covered in dirt. But I recognize the face. Within the weeping folds of skin, Magnus's pale, hauntingly blue eyes are open. "How did he die?" I ask, unsure if I really want to know.

She sighs, her shoulders lowering. "A drug overdose."

I stare at the carpet, suddenly noticing the floral pattern that had always appeared to be dots when my boots trampled it, time and time again, over these past few days. "Which drug?" I finally push out.

"That's confidential." She tries to brush past me, and the coconut scent of her shampoo tickles my nose. It conjures up the image of a beach, a place I'd much rather be in this moment.

But the picture doesn't last. Like smoke, it evaporates, replaced again by the question. It wriggles there in my mind like one of the worms eating away at Magnus's rotting flesh. I can't help but ask it. "Lorazepam and oxycodone?"

DI Collins stops, her head cocking to look at me. Her deep-brown eyes narrow.

And I *know.*

I don't bother turning around to look at my friend. But I feel it, that prickling sensation of two minds sharing the same thought; my friend knows too. Those were the drugs that had shown up on the death certificate, eight years ago.

The drugs that killed Magnus were the same ones that killed Jake.

CHAPTER 24
CADENCE

The soil is compact after the rain. I keep digging, using sticks, rocks, whatever I can find to make the hole deeper. Then I remove Magnus's things—his phone, passport, wallet, keys—from my jacket pockets and dump them inside.

Before I went back to the room last night, I took all of Magnus's belongings from his room and dumped them in a trash bin behind the Starboard Inn. Between that, smashing his phone with a rock, and turning in his room key, the inn will have no idea Magnus is missing. It won't be until his family or friends back in Norway notice his failure to return that anyone will even begin to look for him.

There is the issue of the elements, however. I'm a rather small woman, and in the middle of the night, I could only do so much to hide that enormous body. It took every ounce of strength and resilience in me just to drag him out of sight. If the rain starts up again, and someone else wanders off the beaten path, we could have a problem.

If we're lucky, though, we'll be long gone before anyone finds him. No one witnessed my little meetup with Magnus last night. His death will look like a classic overdose. A guy who had a little too much fun on vacation. When he wandered too far from the inn, intoxicated, no one was there to help him. I'll be free and clear.

Just like the last time I got away with murder.

Things happened much the same way eight years ago, with Jake. Only we were inside a lit room, so I could see his eyes the moment he realized what I'd done.

By that point, it was too late. He tried to get up, but his eyelids wouldn't stay open. His limbs refused to obey him. He struggled on the bed to no avail.

That was the first time I realized that I wasn't like everyone else. That I would do whatever it took to keep myself safe. People, things, circumstances—they'll try to come in and take what's yours. But you don't have to let them.

I was Landon's first love, and he was mine. Jocelyn came along and ruined things for a while, but Landon came back to me. He and I started things up again sophomore year at UCSB. That was when he came up with my nickname. It was at the park near the university— we couldn't hang out on the grassy lawn outside the student union building like all the other couples. I felt the tickle of an insect on the back of my bare arm and went to swat it off. But Landon stopped me, gently scooping up the culprit and kissing me on the forehead. "It's only a ladybug, Cadybug." It was a term of endearment only he and I knew about.

We stole kisses behind buildings on campus, had secret midnight phone calls from the halls of our dormitories, touched fingertips in passing. Like whispers, these caresses were fleeting, but their meaning lingered for ages.

One day, we got too bold. The momentary glances and under-the-table touches were no longer enough. While Rowan and Jocelyn were out, Landon came to my room—*our* room, the one I shared with the girls. Jake, believing everyone was in the cafeteria, walked into the room to find me and Landon in a rather compromising position.

Jake's fair, freckled skin turned the color of a tomato. "Sorry, I just—Jocelyn has my chemistry notes. I'll, it's . . . sorry." He backed out of the room, shutting the door.

Landon swore to me he would fix everything and ran off after him. He returned a few minutes later, convinced that Jake wouldn't mention the incident to Jocelyn. "Guy code," Landon said with a reassuring wink.

I was anything but reassured. That evening, I did my usual stroll, stopping by Grace Ling's room to make sure she didn't need anything. Only this time, she was asleep. I used the mirror in my room to check my hair. It was the first time I'd cut my hair short, and the girls on my floor had been particularly brutal. I was constantly checking to make sure I didn't look like a mushroom. Then instead of heading to dinner, I swung by Jake's dormitory, where I cornered him in his room. I was surprised to find him seated on the bed, crying, mini spirit bottle in hand. The room reeked of alcohol, and a few empty bottles were scattered over the rug.

"What's wrong?" I asked. Perhaps the emotional turmoil over whether or not to tell Jocelyn had brought him to tears.

"Nothing," he grumbled, chugging the bottle. "What are *you* doing here?" I'd known Jake for years, and this was the first time he'd spoken to me that way.

"It doesn't look like nothing," I said, ignoring his question and sliding into my mothering-nurse role.

"It's—Jocelyn told me about Rowan."

"Oh?" I had no idea what he meant, but I was glad it had nothing to do with me.

"You were there too, right? You saw Rowan kissing some guy at the party?"

I did my best not to react. If this was something Jocelyn had told him, I couldn't deny it. I was already about to be in a lot of trouble with Joss. "I'm really sorry." I reached out to lay a hand on his arm, my attempt at comforting him.

But he jerked back, as if afraid of my touch. "I know why you're here, Cady. You're just as bad as Rowan. Joss deserves to know what her boyfriend and her *BFF* are up to."

I made my best attempt at puppy dog eyes. "Nothing happened, Jake. You told Landon you wouldn't say anything."

"Yeah, well," he said without looking me in the eye. "We'll see."

Clearly, he wasn't about to let this go. It would always be hanging over me, threatening to come down on my head. I'd developed a friendship with Jocelyn over the course of six years. I'd gotten Landon back after a year apart. It was everything—well, almost everything—I'd dreamed of. I'd waited, worked for it, earned it. I deserved this happiness.

Now, Jake was threatening to take it all away.

He had a mini refrigerator full of beers, and I asked if I could have one. "Only if you get me one too," he said, the words slurring.

"You can talk to me about Rowan, you know," I said as I opened the cans. Inside his can, I slipped the contents of my Ziploc baggie: two crushed lorazepam pills and one crushed oxycodone. The lorazepam had been prescribed to my mother for nausea during chemotherapy. She ended up changing medications, resulting in a half-full bottle in her cabinet. I'd stolen them, knowing the occasional antianxiety pill could come in useful during final exams.

The oxy had been Grace Ling's, prescribed for the post-surgery pain. I'd taken a handful from the bathroom while she was sleeping. She really didn't need the entire bottle anyway; that stuff's addictive, and she wasn't in much pain anymore.

I might've tried to spread the pills out, so Jake wouldn't taste the medication. But he was already so far gone after all the alcohol. I wasn't too worried.

I turned to see him shrug, as if indifferent. He was a tough guy who didn't need to talk to anyone. When I turned back to the beers, he said, "I thought she was the one, I really did." He let out a soft, sad laugh. "And she thought I was . . . just some guy."

"No, she didn't. Rowan loves you. She probably drank too much and made a mistake." I crossed the room and handed him the tainted can.

"I can't be with a girl who would do that to me."

"No," I said, sipping my beer. "I guess not." Of course, *Jake Elliott* couldn't be with anyone less than perfect. His standards were up there in the clouds, like his father's. Like his sister's. That was why Jake Elliott would never allow his sister to be with a guy like Landon, who would cheat on her in her own dormitory with her best friend. Jake would never allow his sister to continue being my friend and share a bunk bed with me after this betrayal.

It was why I knew I had to go through with this.

Eventually, his beer can fell from his hand and bobbled onto the bed. He mumbled about needing a nap. His eyes fell shut, and I thought it might simply be that easy.

But he pried his eyelids open. For a moment, he looked from me to the near-empty can, accusation blaring from those blue-green eyes.

He knew what I'd done. It was too late for him to tell anyone, though. Too late for him to fix what was happening to his body. His pulse slowed, and his breathing became labored. He twitched a bit. Eventually, it all stopped. The can lay there beside his unmoving hand, leaking brown liquid over the linens.

I left a couple of extra pills on the bed to make it look like an overdose. Then I took both of our cans with me and walked out the door.

Now, in the woods, I cover Magnus's things with dirt, ensuring the hole is filled. I push some leaves over the top to make it look as though this patch of land was never disturbed. I cast my digging sticks aside and wipe my filthy hands on my jeans. I'll have to change anyway.

The rustle sounds again. This time, I flinch. My gaze zips to the trees, where a pop of yellow flashes among the pine needles.

Someone's there. Someone saw me.

CHAPTER 25
ROWAN

Jocelyn calls my name from the B&B, so I speed up my steps, pushing farther into the woods. When I first came outside, I smelled smoke. That grumpy neighbor, the Welsh doctor, was sitting on his balcony, smoking a cigar with a scowl on his face. I hope he doesn't tell Jocelyn which way I went.

My phone is on silent now to keep her from tracking the noise. Still, a series of texts comes through:

I'm so sorry about Jake. I hate myself for what I did

But I never told Cady about it

How does she know, Ro?

I bite back a growl and stuff my phone into my jacket pocket. Leave it to Jocelyn to try to deflect at a time like this. To point the finger because she can never take fault.

I can't deal with her fake apology right now. I need to process the fact that my supposed best friend sabotaged the only meaningful relationship I've ever had with a guy. If Jake were still alive, would we even be together?

Or would Jocelyn have ruined it? Would I be raising Molly apart from her father?

Would I even have Molly?

I shiver at the thought. I know people wondered why I kept the baby when there were other options. After all, my decision cost me my education, my friends, my life. My parents were so disappointed; they barely talked to me until Molly was born. Despite everything, for me, it was never a choice. When Jake passed away, that little life growing inside me became the only remnant I had of him. My one true love. I couldn't get rid of it, or give it away. I wanted to have it, to hold it, to let that child fill my arms the way he once had.

But if Jake had lived—if he'd lived but *apart* from me—would I have made a different decision? I'd like to think I wouldn't have. That Molly would still be with me, growing into this smart, freckled, bubbly little person with goals and dreams enough for the both of us. I'm not sure I would've, though. I might've let the pressure, the questions, and the insinuations get to me.

They said I'd never live out my dreams. That I couldn't achieve everything I'd worked for, that I'd earned. In a way, they were right. This road has been rougher and windier in many ways. It didn't lead me to the place I'd envisioned when I enrolled in college.

But after the last eight years with Molly, I know I haven't lost anything. I only traded one dream for another.

I shove my hands into my coat pockets—*my* coat, not Magnus's. Cady left his jacket behind last night. I continue my trek, trying to clear my mind of everything. Instead, my thoughts dwell on Jocelyn's text messages.

But I never told Cady about it

How does she know, Ro?

I check my phone for more messages, but I've lost service. Who else could've known that Jocelyn was the reason for the breakup? It could've been one of Jake's friends. I always assumed he never told anyone, because no one said anything. But maybe he did. Maybe Cady heard from one of Jake's friends when he was in that state of depression before he overdosed. And Cady knew the story about me and some guy at a party wasn't true.

But if it wasn't one of his friends, that means Cady was with Jake the day he died.

Suddenly, I have to find her. I have to get to the bottom of this.

CHAPTER 26
NOW
JOCELYN

"It was Cady," I choke out, unable to feel my fingers or my toes.

"Cady?" DI Collins says, staring at me like *I'm* the one who killed Magnus. How else could I have known what killed him?

"Cady took Magnus out to the woods," I say. "Lorazepam and oxycodone—that was the exact drug combination that killed my twin brother, Jake, eight years ago."

I don't even realize I'm swaying until DI Collins reaches out to steady me.

"Breathe, just breathe," she says, steering me toward a chair.

But I can't. How can I breathe when my entire world has been upended? Jake certainly isn't breathing. My brother, my sidekick since birth, took his last breath that day.

When my best friend took his life.

I wish I could suck back up every tear I shed for her since the moment I discovered she was gone. She never deserved a single drop.

I can't bear to look at Rowan, the person I've quietly blamed for Jake's death since the day it happened.

I shut my eyes and focus on my breathing, but my mind floods with memories: All the hours Cady spent comforting me after Jake's death. The consoling words she whispered into my ears. How she accompanied me to my parents' house after we got the news. How she spent the night beside me in my childhood bed so I wouldn't be alone. My stomach curdles. I've just taken my seat, but the nausea is rising quickly. "I think I-I'm going to—"

I run outside to the porch, leaning over the railing and vomiting. Retching until I've got nothing left. Just like I did in the woods when we found the body. Only this time, I'm spilling my insides all over the flower bed.

Bet Mr. Kemble's going to love that.

A moment later, DI Collins follows me outside, placing a gentle hand on my back. When I finally pull away from the railing, she hands me a glass of water. "You've had quite a shock," she says. "We should go back inside."

She guides me back through the reception area to the fireside room.

"I'm coming too," Rowan says, hurrying after us and sitting down next to me at the table.

"Did you know about this?" I hiss, loud enough for the detective to hear. "That Cady *killed* Magnus?"

"Of course not! How can you ask me that?" Rowan reddens. "I mean, I had my suspicions yesterday about Jake, but only because of what *you* texted me! I thought Magnus was asleep in his room at the inn, same as you."

"Rowan," DI Collins says, "we were able to track your cellular phone activity from two nights ago." She slides a sheet of paper full of numbers across the table. "It shows you were there in the woods where Magnus died."

Rowan blinks, stunned. "My *phone* was there in the woods," she sputters, leaning onto the desk. "Cady took it! She probably—this has to be why she borrowed my phone in the first place. She wasn't worried for her own safety. She figured if his body was discovered, you people would pin it on me!"

"Rowan was with me that night," I say, my voice shaking. My stomach hasn't settled, and I feel weak. "She didn't kill Magnus."

Rowan slings me a look of gratitude.

I ignore it. "But she wasn't with me when Cady died," I add. "And not too long after I texted her my suspicions about Cady, I saw Rowan leave the woods." I force a swallow, the horrible, acidic taste lingering in my mouth. "Alone."

CHAPTER 27
NOW
ROWAN

I stay frozen for a moment, as if the words won't exist until I move.

But of course, they do. DI Collins perks up in her seat. "Is that true, Rowan? Were you alone in the woods yesterday?"

"You're unbelievable," I spit at Jocelyn.

"Rowan," the detective repeats, "what time were you in the woods yesterday?"

"It was hours before we found Cady," I say, bordering on tears. "Maybe around . . . I don't know, ten a.m.? I only went into the woods to get away from her!" I point at Jocelyn the way Molly used to blame other kids in the park for misbehavior when she was tiny.

"What time was it *exactly*?" DI Collins asks in a firm voice, pen in hand.

"You've got my phone." I hate how defensive I sound. "Whatever time she texted me about Jake."

The detective scribbles something on her pad and looks up at me. "I'm going to need you to stay close."

Her words shred my nerves. "I can't seriously be a suspect here. I didn't even see Cady out in the woods!"

Suddenly, I'm wishing I would've asked for a lawyer a long time ago. A *solicitor*, whatever the hell they're called in Wales. I don't have a single clue what my rights are here. "Am I under arrest?"

The thought runs through me, cold as ice. Oh god, I'm going to a Welsh prison. I'm never going to see Molly again. The feeling is dark, like the water trapped beneath a frozen pond. It winds up through my throat, filling it.

"Not at the moment," is the detective's only response. I need her to say something else. Some comforting word—just one word that this is going to be okay. Even if it's fake, like the cops in the TV shows who pretend to be friendly so you'll slip up. Clearly, DI Collins isn't going to offer me any such solace.

When I glance at Jocelyn, I might as well be looking at a porcelain doll. She's so cool and calm, her complexion as smooth as her breathing.

"Then I'm getting some air." I stand, giving my chair a shove so hard I practically knock it over. Before I leave, I slam a palm down on the table. "Jake was *her* twin, you know. And Cady? She didn't just kill Jake. She was also sleeping with Jocelyn's fiancé. That's what the second fight was about. Maybe *she's* the one you should be looking at."

I storm out of the room and through the reception area. The second the outdoor air hits me, guilt follows. I stooped to Jocelyn's level. I was backed into a corner, and I shot my way out of it, nailing my friend in the face. Not that she was acting the part of trusted friend back there. What the hell was she thinking? We're all we have left, and she throws my name to the cops? She can't possibly believe I had it in me to murder Cady.

A thought sends twin trails of goose bumps prickling over my arms: unless *she* killed Cady. What if Jocelyn threw my name to the cops in order to avert suspicion?

The tightness continues to build in my chest, only there's nothing in my path to steal. I pass two police officers on the porch and picture myself reaching over and swiping that bulky baton off the one nearest me. At the image, I let out a hysterical giggle. The thought is almost as good as the real thing. The feeling starts to fade. I gather enough oxygen into my lungs to keep moving.

I won't stray far. There's a killer out there; if it's not Magnus, it could be anyone. I just need to get away from that horrible detective. She's trying to put words in my mouth. Instead of taking the trail, I loop around the property in the other direction, toward the peak Cady wanted to hike, back when she was still breathing. That day she nearly blurted out the truth about her relationship with Landon.

All these secrets she kept have become our undoing. Dammit, Cady, you couldn't even die without taking us all down with you.

I know I deserve to be punished. Ever since high school, I've felt this guilt. I felt it for years after the valedictorian fiasco. Felt it every time I took something that wasn't mine.

And then this week, my actions sparked everything that happened. If I hadn't stolen the coat, Magnus and Valentina never would've followed us here. The three of us might've enjoyed a quiet, healing week in the countryside. Bonding over old memories and creating new ones. And Cady might still be alive. In a way, it was my fault she died.

But I didn't murder her.

And despite everything I blurted about Jocelyn, I'm not certain she did either.

Magnus is dead. He's been dead since Cady drugged him two nights ago. I don't remember Jocelyn ever going back out to the woods during all the turmoil. I'd been looking for Cady and hadn't found her. When I exited the forest, Jocelyn had this big, melodramatic reaction. "Oh thank god, Rowan. I thought Magnus had found you!"

She was only trying to make up for what she'd done to Jake and me eight years ago. I bulled past her, but she chased me up the stairs and followed me into the room.

She tried to talk to me, but we ended up sitting in silence—her too proud for an apology, me too hurt to demand one. It wasn't until it started to get dark, and there'd been no sign of Cady for hours, that our fear finally outweighed our egos. We tried her phone. Every call and text went unanswered.

Jocelyn wanted to call the cops, but I was still worried about that damned photo of the coat I'd stolen, along with the dragon figurine. Worried that if we brought Magnus into the picture, and everything with Cady turned out to be a case of paranoia, he'd report what I'd done out of revenge.

I had no idea he was already dead.

Once I'd convinced Jocelyn to calm down, we grabbed the flashlight from the bedside table drawer and took off into the woods to search for Cady.

That was when we found her body. Before that, Jocelyn had been with me in the room.

No. That's not quite true. Jocelyn did leave for an hour while I spoke to Molly. She wasn't getting anywhere with me, so she said she was going to ask Helen for some coffee.

But what if that's not how she spent that hour?

I thought I knew my friend—my *best* friend. She was a liar, but I had no idea just how cold and callous she could be. To break Jake and me apart on some selfish whim? And then whatever that was just now with the detective.

Maybe there's a darker side yet to Jocelyn Elliott. Maybe she's a killer.

She could've pretended to stumble upon Cady's body with me when, really, she'd put it there herself.

I search for a log or rock to rest on when a crackle of leaves pulls my attention to the left. *Movement.* A large shape darting through the trees. A yellow shape.

Someone's following me.

Or are they? The footsteps are too loud, too disruptive to the delicate hum of the woods. Whoever it is, they don't know I'm out here.

I stay very still for a moment, long enough for the sounds to fade. Then I follow the shape.

It vanishes behind a tree, but I head in the direction it went. I listen for the footsteps, for the rustle of branches. My hopes fall. Like pine needles in the wind, they drop to the forest floor. I've lost them. He or she must've disappeared into the trees, the sound too far off now.

Then a flash of canary yellow shifts into my periphery, and the trail is hot again.

I follow. Every time my boot lights on the twig-strewn earth, I say a silent prayer that it won't alert this person. I weave along through the trees after the figure. Skirting a large shrub, I get a clear view of the yellow, hooded jacket.

A rain slicker, to be more precise.

Suddenly, I know whose back I'm watching. I know the person who's hunched over what appears to be a stone altar, humming an old-fashioned, eerie tune.

My heartbeat accelerates. My forehead breaks out in a sheen of sweat.

This man had a reason to want to hurt Cady. Their little incident in the garden two days ago cost him his paycheck, and nearly his job. I take a step backward, my foot snapping a twig in half.

At the noise, the groundskeeper turns. He gets to his feet. His fingers are coated in red. In one hand, he holds a sharp blade that drips blood as he moves toward me.

I turn and run.

CHAPTER 28
CADENCE

The figure freezes, a canary-colored statue among the pines.

"Hello?" I call out, standing. "Who's there?"

He steps forward, leaving the cover of the trees. I flinch, despite my air of bravado. I squint into the hazy sunlight that slips through the branches.

It's that groundskeeper, Mr. Kemble, the one who grabbed my arm in the garden. At the memory, my arm begins to throb and tingle. The ghost of his fingers presses down hard. "What are you doing out here?"

"I think the question is, what are *you* doing?" He smiles with only one side of his mouth, his yellowed teeth peeking through. His accent is so thick that it takes a second for me to process the words.

"None of your business." The wool scarf I bought in town is nearly dragging in the dirt, so I loop it around my neck an extra time. "Apparently, you haven't learned your lesson about leaving Helen's guests alone."

"Guess not." He takes a step closer, a twig cracking underfoot. "You cost me my livelihood, you know."

My spine tenses. "I didn't cost you anything. You only lost a few days' pay. And *you* were the one who grabbed *me*. Jocelyn tattled on you. I had nothing to do with it."

"If you hadn't been trampling my garden, it never would've happened."

I fight the urge to check the dirt beneath me, to make certain I haven't left anything conspicuous behind. "I'm sorry about that. You were blocking the path, if you'll remember. We did try to get your attention."

"Those damned earbuds," he says, frowning. For a moment, I think everything is going to be okay. We've reached an understanding.

But he lifts his hand, and I catch a glimmer of metal. Mr. Kemble walks toward me now, holding a pair of gardening shears. "This is just the reason we have to go back to the old ways. Nothing good ever comes of newfangled inventions or beliefs. The practices of old, that's where we all need to set our eyes."

I step back. "Why do you have those?"

He smiles again, flashing those horrible, rotten teeth. "For the ritual, of course."

A thread of sick curiosity spools through me. "Ritual?"

"You're the one we need. To complete the ritual."

"I think you have the wrong idea about me," I say, my gaze never leaving the pair of blades.

"No, you're exactly the person we need. And if you help, we won't have to go back to Helen and tell her that you were out here, burying things in the dirt. Things that, I'm guessing, are valuable to someone."

"Excuse me?" I fail to resist that urge to check the burial spot, all but confirming his accusation.

Mr. Kemble picks up speed, and suddenly, Magnus's things are the least of my worries.

I have to run. But my mind is spinning and my boots are pinned to the earth.

"The stones are waiting." He closes the space between us and lifts the shears.

CHAPTER 29
NOW
JOCELYN

Rowan crashes through the front door, panting. "Where's DI Collins?"

I set my coffee down and point to the fireside room. "What happened?"

"The groundskeeper, Mr. Kemble. I saw him in the woods behind his shack. He had a blade of some sort, and he was—all that blood we saw on the stones the other day, that was him. He caught me watching and chased me back here!"

"That can't—*my god*," Helen says, leaving the desk to knock on the fireside room door.

As we wait for DI Collins, Rowan locks the front door. "He chased me," she says, moving to peer out the window. "I thought he was going to kill me. He must've been the one who killed Cady. Maybe even Valentina!"

"That's quite an accusation," DI Collins says, stepping out into the reception area.

"It was him," Rowan says. "Mr. Kemble, the groundskeeper. There was blood all over the stones, the same as with Cady."

At this, DI Collins's face goes grave. She sets her folder on the reception desk and pulls out her radio. "All units, we're looking for a white male, approximately fifty years of age. Keep the perimeter secure. One Daryn Kemble. When found, bring him straight to base for questioning."

"I think it was because of what happened with Cady in the garden," Rowan says, more to Helen than to anyone else.

DI Collins's gaze whips to mine as she returns the radio to her belt. "What happened in the garden?"

Helen helps a trembling Rowan to the table, where she pours her a cup of coffee.

"Mr. Kemble grabbed Cady out there," I say, pointing out the window. "He was upset that she'd walked on the flowers, and he yelled at her to keep off them. He was so off his rocker that Magnus had to intervene." I scratch at the nape of my neck, my fingernails probably dirty. "I told Helen about it, and she put him on a leave of absence."

DI Collins looks to Helen, whose nod confirms my story. "I relieved him of his duties until next Monday. Leave without pay, confined to his cabin. He can afford it, since I'm the one providing his room and board."

"Only I saw Mr. Kemble on the property yesterday," I say, "when we came back from the Starboard Inn. He didn't look like he was on leave at all."

Helen's shoulders stiffen. "Exactly where did you see him?"

"Just out there in the flower bed. He was working with some gardening tool." My stomach goes cold, like a hollow space has just formed inside me. "Unless it wasn't a gardening tool after all. What if it was—" I clamp a hand over my mouth.

"Maybe he was waiting for us," Rowan says, taking her coffee to the window again. Her fingers are jittery around the ceramic, her body weight shifting from one foot to the other. "Waiting to get one of us alone. The pamphlet. I—" She glances up in the direction of the stairs. "It's in my room. Some sort of cult that performs rituals at the stones. And then Cady swore she saw someone in a cloak with a torch. Remember, Joss?" Her brown eyes plead with me in desperation.

"It's true," I say, noting her use of my nickname.

"I'll need to see this pamphlet," DI Collins says, and Rowan, removing her fingers from her curls, rushes up the stairs.

As we wait for her to return, a crippling sense of shame comes over me. Rowan really had nothing to do with this. And I fed her name to DI Collins. Feet faltering and breath shallow, I wander to the reception desk to rest an elbow on it. I see the detective's folder beside me, a few photos from inside having spilled onto the desk. Partially covered by the gruesome image of Magnus's corpse is a photo I remember posing for; the one Valentina took of the three of us in front of Conwy River. DI Collins must've had her team print it from my phone's photo roll, maybe to have a photographic record of the victim. *Or,* I think with a shudder, *of the prime suspects.*

When the detective isn't looking, I tug the photo free of the others. Seeing it, my heart wrenches. We're smiling, the sun beating on our faces, a day of possibilities ahead of us.

Now, there's nothing but hopelessness ahead of me. In the photo, I'm standing in between my two best friends, one of whom has since died; the other, I placed directly onto the chopping block today. My desperate attempt to throw the suspicion off myself.

But I think it was more than that. I think I was already feeling so low, knowing what Cady did to me—what she did to my twin—that I started to toy with the idea of making myself feel worse. To see if I'd actually reached my lowest low, or if I could possibly drop another notch.

It turns out, I wasn't at my lowest low. That level is here, now. Watching my one remaining friend fear for her life, knowing that if Rowan hadn't stumbled upon the groundskeeper in the woods just now, she might've actually gone to prison for this. She might've been taken away from Molly, all because of some maniacal whim I'd had.

Cady and I really did deserve each other.

Rowan races back down the stairs, handing the tattered pamphlet to the detective, who uses gloves to place it in an evidence bag.

"It was damaged like that when we found it," Rowan explains.

A muffled voice breaks the brittle silence, and DI Collins wrangles her radio from her belt. "DI Collins here."

"We have the suspect in custody," the voice says.

"Bring him inside." DI Collins adds the bag to her folder and moves to turn the latch on the front door.

At the click, Rowan backs away from the window so quickly, coffee sloshes over the rim of her mug onto the carpet.

The detective pulls open the door, and a red-faced Mr. Kemble is shoved along inside the B&B. His hands are cuffed behind his back, and his beady eyes scan the room. When they land on Rowan, he snarls like a wild animal.

The sight sends a shiver through me. This man could've done it. He could've taken Cady's life.

"In here," DI Collins says, flicking her head toward her makeshift office.

They're shut inside, one officer with them, the other stationed out here with his back against the door.

That silence returns, filling the room like thick smoke.

A moment later, Helen stirs at the desk. "I didn't know," she says, tugging at her collar. "I knew he had a temper. I saw it the day some rabbits ate up his lettuce patch, the way he chased after them. But his family had owned the land for a century. I really thought I was helping out a local, letting him stay on and make a living. I should've done a more thorough background check. But I thought"—she lets out a strangled sound—"it was just *gardening*. The land he kept spoke for itself. What sorts of references could I possibly need?"

"It isn't your fault, Helen," I say, though the words sound vacant and insincere. I should go over there and comfort her. After all, she's done it for me countless times. But I don't have it in me. I'll get Paul; he'd be better at it. He's out in the garden, doing what Mr. Kemble would be doing if we hadn't shown up and managed to turn my aunt's and uncle's lives upside down.

Rowan is back at her chair, feet tapping nervously. "I need my phone back," she mutters to herself. "I have to call Molly."

"You can use the one at my desk," Helen offers. "It's a landline."

Rowan looks up at her, gratitude washing over her face at this small kindness. It's something she hasn't received from anyone else. "Are you sure? It would be long distance."

Helen smiles. "Don't you worry about it. This is a terrible thing that's happened, and you need to hear the voice of the most important person in your life. It's cordless. Take it into the breakfast room for some privacy."

"Thank you." Rowan wipes the tears from her eyes and leaves with the phone.

I get the sudden instinctive need to call Landon, which is soon replaced by the crushing realization that Landon isn't mine anymore. I took off my ring during our phone call and packed it up in my suitcase. I told him to go be with Cady.

Cady, who's now dead.

I bet Landon doesn't even know about her. I certainly can't be the one to tell him.

After Rowan ran off earlier, DI Collins was extremely interested in the little tidbit she'd left about the love triangle. It did, as Rowan insinuated so kindly, provide a motive. I had to go back to the fireside room with the detective. I'd barely had the chance to wrap my mind around the affair before we found Cady's body, yet there I was, rehashing all of it.

I told the truth, plain and simple. Cady had a yearslong affair with my fiancé. We argued at the breakfast table, and I stormed off. I never saw her again.

Not alive, that is.

"Jocelyn." Helen waves, trying to get my attention. "I canceled the bookings for next week. I can't have visitors while this place is a crime scene."

"Oh, right."

"That means your room will be empty. However long the detective needs you to stay, you have a place here."

"Thanks, Helen." I can't bear the thought of staying here for even one more night. After the way Rowan and I cast each other to the wolves, though, there's no way DI Collins will let us fly home. We haven't been labeled persons of interest—not yet.

But if Mr. Kemble manages to chop his way out of this the way he does the garden hedges, there will only be two names left.

This can't be real. This is one of those things that happens to other people, but never to *you*. They happen in the movies, in television docuseries, or to some poor sap you'll only read about in a newspaper. Not to *you*.

"I'm off to find Paul," Helen says, heading outside and leaving me alone with my nerves.

They eat away at me, leaving me raw like the skin at the back of my neck. I can't stop scratching, even when my fingertips start to slip over the broken skin. I pull my hand away, finding blood beneath the nails.

I wonder if they found anything beneath Cady's fingernails. At the thought, I feel queasy. DI Collins took a thorough scan of my hands and face yesterday. Does that mean Cady fought her killer?

If she did, they'd only have to do a DNA test. If Mr. Kemble is the killer, they could test him and see if it's a match.

Rowan wanders back into the room, replacing the phone on the base. I hide my bloodied fingers beneath the tabletop. As she takes the chair nearest mine, a memory of the two of us sitting side by side at a coffee shop surfaces. We were freshmen in college, and Cady was off with some study partner that I now realize was likely Landon. I'd been scratching at my neck that day too. Stress over upcoming final exams weighed on me. Rowan and I headed to a Starbucks to study, and we made very little progress because we couldn't stop talking. We'd been whispering about the hot barista—the main reason we studied at that particular Starbucks. We kept inventing scenarios to get him to talk to us, the more outlandish the better. Eventually, our Frappuccinos melted, my stomach ached from nonstop giggling, and my knowledge of history remained the same as the moment I'd walked through the door.

But I'd stopped scratching. Being with my best friend had been the perfect salve for my frazzled nerves.

Now, I can barely look at Rowan, much less joke with her. She winds a spiral of hair around her finger. When I move to touch my own hair, I discover that I've been scratching again. My fingernails no longer catch skin at this point; they're merely swirling the blood around, creating a muddled mess. Rowan's presence is the exact opposite of a salve; it's lemon juice drizzled onto a wound. The things I did to her can no longer be denied or banished to the depths of my mind. Now, they're ever present.

Our friendship is just as dead as Cady.

In my periphery, the fireside room door swings open. DI Collins walks out first, followed by Mr. Kemble and the guard.

"Did he confess?" Rowan asks, standing.

DI Collins is calm, as always. "Afraid not. They're meeting my superior at the station for further questioning. He is officially a person of interest."

Mr. Kemble shuffles his feet, his eyes on the ground. He clears his throat and, without looking up, mutters, "I didn't do nothin' to that rotten girl. I tried to warn her." The officer yanks him along, out the door.

"What did he mean by that?" Rowan asks. "How did he explain the knife? The blood?"

"It was just a rabbit!" Mr. Kemble shouts, resisting the officer's nudges. "Didn't want Helen to know that I've been killing 'em. She doesn't understand the nuisance they pose. Thinks they're cute."

DI Collins ushers the two men along and shuts the door. "It appears Mr. Kemble has been killing the pests that are destroying the garden. According to him, Helen doesn't like to see the blood, so he takes the animals up into the woods, using the stones as a sort of . . . operating table for the skinning and cleaning."

"You mean he eats them," I say, gagging at the thought.

"I believe it's about more than the mess or Helen's delicate sensibilities here," DI Collins says. "I suspect Mr. Kemble's been involved in some illegal hunting in these woods. Killing some of the park's protected wildlife. The crime would explain his reluctance to tell us the truth concerning his whereabouts yesterday when we first questioned him."

"So, you don't think he killed Cady?" I ask. "You believe that bullshit about killing rabbits? This is unbelievable. That man had a motive. And what about the pamphlet? Was it his?"

DI Collins's gaze diverts to the carpet. "Mr. Kemble had some things to say about all of that too."

"*Some things?*" Rowan looks like she might grab that mug off the table and chuck it at the detective's head. "Cady was killed with something sharp, right? I saw him with those gardening shears."

I think of all the blood dripping over the stones last night, and my stomach turns.

"As I mentioned," DI Collins says, "they'll continue to question him at the station. Meanwhile, we're obtaining a warrant to search his cabin and the grounds for anything that could tie him to Cady's murder. We have the shears. If Cady's DNA turns up on them, we'll have a case."

I can't help but notice the way she says all of this. Like she doesn't think they will have a case. "Why don't you believe he's the guy?" I ask, moving closer, ready to get in her face if I have to.

"He very well could be," DI Collins says, glancing from me to Rowan. "But he told me something rather interesting. Something that—if verified—would mean we have the wrong person in custody."

CHAPTER 30
CADENCE

"Wait!" Mr. Kemble calls after me.

My legs are finally working. Breathing in the copper-tinged air, I'm sprinting. I can't stop until I get him far away from that burial spot.

"I'm not going to hurt you! I only want your help!"

I keep going until the voice fades, the pounding of my boots against the earth drowning it out. But something snags my eye, and my feet come to a halt, boots kicking up pine needles.

It's a stone circle. The slab nearest me is coated in blood, something dead splayed open upon it. There's a tang to the air as I inch forward, finding white tufts of fur painted pink and a set of tiny claws dangling from one side of the stone. Mr. Kemble's footsteps draw nearer, and his words find their way inside my ears with sudden clarity. "There's someone after you! I saw her! The one who was rooming with the blond man!"

I stay with my gaze fixed on the stone. "What did you say?"

"She was talking to the blond man in the woods the day after you all arrived. They were hiking. I followed them because they were getting too close"—he clears his throat—"to my stones."

Like a rodent in the underbrush, I'm listening. Slowly, I turn to face the man who holds the dripping gardening shears. "Drop them," I say, and he glances at the pair of blades as though they suddenly appeared in his hands. "You never did explain what you were doing with those."

He crosses his arms, refusing to let go of them. "Guess I didn't."

"Well, you'd better start talking. Helen will do a lot more than put you on leave when she hears about what you did just now. What were you going on about with the stones?"

He rolls his neck, like he's bored of this conversation. "I do some trapping up here. Skinning and cleaning too."

"And I take it you don't have permission to set these traps."

He doesn't respond, only clamps a decayed tooth onto his lowered lip. "I eat what I trap. Never bothered a soul. They keep away from me, and I keep away from them."

"But not Magnus and Valentina. They came up here and started snooping around your . . ." I frown. "What exactly *do* you use the stones for? You said something back there." Something I found rather interesting. "That the stones were waiting."

"My family lived on this land long before Helen and Paul purchased it. We practice the *old* religion. That's why we have the orchards, even though the neighboring farms never harvest a single fruit. We planted the trees ourselves, foraged for berries and wild garlic and herbs in these woods. I'm the one who got Helen's vegetable garden thriving. I've been blessed by the gods of old for my faithfulness. The land always grants me what I need. Harvest, animals to hunt." His lips twist in scorn. "Then you come and stomp all over the plants, and I get sent to my cabin. The garden's been suffering in my absence. There's only one way to restore balance."

"Well, you can forget about it. I'm not becoming your sacrificial lamb."

His forehead crinkles, so I point to the dead rabbit on the slab.

He shakes his head. "The rabbit isn't a *sacrifice*. That's not what the old religion practices. We believe in honoring nature. That's why we come to the stones, to pay tribute and connect to the ancient gods."

It all makes sense now. "That tract, the one about the stones—that was yours. Does Helen know about your . . . *religious* practices?"

"If she understood our practices, she never would've allowed me to neglect the land. Everything I do is to help Helen and Paul—to help the land. There's only one way to fix this. Together, we have to light the fire in the center of the stones in an act of penance."

"Why the hell would you want *me* to do it? Don't you have your church friends for that?"

"You're the one who owes penance," he says. "And the gods delivered you to this very place."

"No, that's not—forget it. I'm not doing it." Does he honestly think he can get me to take part in his pagan cult? "I'm in a hurry here. Just tell me more about this person you claim is after me."

He skews his brows. "What about the ritual?"

I clench my teeth and take a deep breath. "Fine. I'll light a fire and do your psychotic little dance." Whatever it takes to shut this guy up and find out what he knows. "But drop those disgusting things," I say, indicating the shears, "and tell me what I want to know."

He hesitates, running his slimy tongue over cracked lips. "The girl," he says finally, letting the tool fall to the forest floor. "She told the guy they should follow you to town. She said she was enjoying getting into your heads. Making you squirm."

I feel a flicker of validation. Valentina *was* the one driving the psychological warfare. I'd known ever since the first night when she just happened to be holding on to my missing phone. The way she kept prying, stirring up drama between the three of us. "And what makes you think this girl is after me now?"

"She's been sneaking around, in the woods and about the property."

Magnus was right. Valentina never left. She's simply been . . . *around.* "Did you tell Helen?"

Mr. Kemble's gaze lowers. "I can't get involved. You said it yourself. If I mess up again, she'll fire me. She's letting me stay in that cabin. I can't lose it all by sticking my nose where it doesn't belong."

Valentina really did steal my phone to start trouble. And then, once she'd successfully scared us off, she simply put it back in the room along with my passport and wallet. That way, I'd be forced to return here. Where she's waiting for me.

She's been successfully stringing us along this entire time. All because of what Rowan did.

But why did she and Magnus split up? Did he fail to play the part of pretty sidekick?

A horrible thought strikes me like a fist to the gut: maybe they never split up at all. What if it was a ruse—another part of Valentina's master plan? To help Magnus get a little closer to one of us. If Valentina was here all along, watching my every move, then she knows what I did to Magnus.

And if she was willing to terrorize us over a coat and some cash, what will she do about me murdering her travel companion? I remember the way her eyes trailed after him, her pained expression the night he followed Jocelyn out the door. He was more than a traveling companion. He was her boyfriend, her lover, her *obsession*.

"Where did you last see her?" I ask, trying to grind my fear down into a fine dust.

I have to protect myself, the way I've always protected myself.

My friends think that because I'm shy and soft-spoken, I'm also weak.

But I am not weak. I will do what it takes to make sure no one ever finds out what really happened to Magnus.

Mr. Kemble shrugs. "The last I saw, she was skulking around behind the B&B."

"When was this?"

He shakes his head. "I can't remember."

"Well, try."

"I guess it was . . . I know she was wearing a dark-blue coat."

Valentina's coat. The one she was wearing earlier this week. The one Jocelyn found in the room with her things. Valentina did come back for her bag. But something still nags at me. "Why should I believe you? You practically admitted to following all of us ever since we got here."

"I try not to use technology too much. The gods don't seem to approve. It always comes back to bite you in the end." He pulls an Android phone from the back pocket of his ratty work jeans. "But I've got a smartphone like everybody else. And I snapped this on it."

He holds up the screen, but I don't fall for it. There's no way I'm getting any closer to this man. "Toss it over," I say.

He does, skimming it over a patch of pine needles. I tell him to take a step back. When he reluctantly obeys, I pick up the phone and look at the photo he's opened, dated this morning at 9:46 a.m. It's a figure in a navy-blue coat, just as he said. She's crouched outside what looks like the breakfast room window, her hood pulled up over her head. "This is hardly proof," I say, ready to throw the phone back at him. "This could be a man, for all I know." But then I see it. On the subject's free hand, dangling at her side. A big silver butterfly ring, rhinestones glinting beneath a sliver of sunlight.

Valentina has been here this entire time.

That means Magnus never killed her. He likely never killed Lisa Granger—never even went near her—for that matter.

He was just along for the ride, a pawn in Valentina's sadistic games. Valentina was the one who targeted us from the get-go, and I just killed the man she loves.

And she may be targeting me now.

CHAPTER 31
NOW
ROWAN

"Doctor and Mrs. Pearce have corroborated Mr. Kemble's account." DI Collins leans back in her chair in the fireside room, hands folded over the closed file on the table.

"That's because they're part of it!" Jocelyn shouts, throwing a hand up. "I saw one of those tracts in the Pearces' room when I was looking for Rowan."

DI Collins nods patiently. "They got it from Mr. Kemble. Apparently, he has a habit of proselytizing to the guests."

Jocelyn sits back in her chair, lips parted in awe. I think back to that heated, hushed conversation between Mr. Kemble and Dr. Pearce yesterday in front of the B&B. Were they merely discussing the tracts?

"There has to be more to it," Jocelyn argues. "The doctor refused to speak with me when I was looking for Rowan, almost like he was trying to keep me out of the room. What if it was because he'd done something to Cady?"

DI Collins lifts an eyebrow, the glimmer of a smirk on her lips. "I was able to speak to *Mrs.* Pearce for a moment, one-on-one. Apparently, the woman caught her husband paying . . . a little too much attention to you girls. It caused an argument and a bit of tension for the newlyweds the rest of their stay. My guess is that's the reason Dr. Pearce wasn't too keen to be seen speaking with you, much less allow you into the room while his wife was out."

That explains why they'd both acted so unfriendly toward us. "But why does any of this mean we have the wrong person in custody? None of this proves that Mr. Kemble is innocent."

"The Pearces claim to have seen someone in a dark-blue hooded coat walking around the property yesterday," DI Collins continues.

A dark-blue coat? That isn't right. Valentina is dead.

Except we believed that Magnus was a killer, and now he's dead too.

I get a shiver. Was Valentina spying on Cady the whole time? On all of us? I think back to the woods, when we found Cady's body at the stones. I'd felt something out there. *Someone.* Was Cady's killer watching us, even then?

"We followed up on Mr. Kemble's report about Cadence having buried something in the woods, and we recovered Magnus Larsen's rental car keys, wallet, and passport. Kemble's story checks out."

I rub at my temple. "So then, if Valentina was following Cady, she would've known what happened to Magnus. She may have wanted revenge. But why go to all the trouble to make it look like she'd left in the first place?"

"She's unhinged," Jocelyn says, eyes wide. She sips her coffee with her head tucked into her shoulders like an owl. "I can't believe we ever worried about her. First, she toyed with us in plain sight. Then, she decided to escalate things by doing it in secret. She probably sent Magnus after us when we fled to the inn."

"So, where's she been staying, then?" I ask. "It's cold. It's been two days since Valentina faked heading home. Where's she been this whole time?"

"That's what we're trying to find out," DI Collins says. "Police are currently scouring the area. There are a few abandoned shacks in walking distance."

"The one we passed on the hike," I say, looking at Jocelyn. "It looked abandoned. Maybe Valentina's been hiding out there."

"Can you take us to it?" DI Collins asks.

"I can try, but Valentina was the one leading the way."

DI Collins straightens her papers and shuts the file. "I'll get some officers to accompany us. You two, grab whatever gear you need and meet me back here in five minutes."

It's late afternoon when we start out. The trail is cast in shadows, and I can't seem to get warm, no matter how quickly I move. I worry we won't be able to find the shack again. Discovering it the first time was such a fluke.

Hiking the same steps we took with Cady only three days ago is like picking at an old wound. Everything has changed since then. Instead of Valentina leading the way, it's DI Collins, with her severe, slick-backed bun and black peacoat. She walks far ahead, seemingly antsy about this lead. Every few minutes, she seems to remember us, stopping to ask if we're okay and if we recognize anything yet.

There was always a chasm between Cady and me—I'd just assumed it was jealousy over Jocelyn. Turns out there were other reasons Cady could never really get close to me. She was probably never truly close to Jocelyn either. How could she have been, when she'd murdered Jake?

I think of the moments we did share and feel sick. Cady, always the mother of the group, always there to bring a cup of soup or to lend a listening ear. The baby shower she forced Jocelyn to throw. The presents she brought for Molly every birthday and Christmas. Had it really all been an act?

"I don't understand why I have to be here," Jocelyn grumbles behind me. "I have no sense of direction, and I hate hikes."

I drop back until I'm nearly at her side. "You know why," I whisper. "She's keeping an eye on us. If they don't find Valentina, they're going to try to pin this on one of us."

"No thanks to you," she says.

"You started it," I retort, which shuts her up.

DI Collins passes beneath the large shadow in the shape of a bird. It isn't an enormous bird, of course. It's the mountainside above us—a tree on the rocky overhead ledge with two long branches, its shadow seemingly stretching out like wings. I remember that ledge, that specter bird. More than that, I remember the shrub growing from the side of the trail, its large leaves the color of Cady's blood.

"Stop!" I call out, turning my back to the plant and the tree and inching toward the woods. "It was through there. We passed the shack on the way to the stones."

"Lead the way." DI Collins presses closer to the mountainside, allowing us to slip by.

I do, trekking through the trees until I hear water. That creek we crossed. The shack was earlier, though. It should be—*bingo*. "There." I point to the dilapidated one-room cabin.

"Wait here," she tells us, using her radio to call in a unit. She rattles off the coordinates and heads inside the shack.

Jocelyn spares no time before slumping down onto a boulder. "Oh my god, I swear, I will never hike again when this is over."

I'd love to tell her to stop being such a baby. But I'm beginning to see her point. It's one thing when the end goal is a mammoth waterfall or a gorgeous view from the highest peak. It's quite another when you've come to see a rotten old building for no other reason than to seek answers to the most horrible question you've ever asked.

Is Cady's murderer hiding out inside this shack?

The minutes tick by, and my hopes fade. My throat is dry, my muscles cramping. Something nudges my arm, and I startle. It's Jocelyn. She pushes her water bottle at me. "Here, you look thirsty."

I want to refuse it, to live out the rest of my life without ever accepting a single thing from Jocelyn Elliott again. No more dinners ending in her slapping down her credit card. Never another "let me get this" in the department store. And above all, no more free vacations.

She's right, though. My throat is dry, and my muscles are cramping. But I don't thank her when I take it and gulp some down.

Fifteen minutes later, DI Collins exits the shack and finds the leader of the crime scene unit. They begin whispering, and it starts to feel like worms are crawling around in my intestines. After sending the unit inside, DI Collins heads toward Jocelyn and me. "She was most likely here. Looks like she left in a hurry. We found remnants of meals, blankets she must've stolen from the B&B. Some toiletries. Nothing appears to have been left for too long." She takes a deep breath and lets it out, lips nearly forming a smile. "Well done, you two."

"How will you find her?" A phantom tickle grazes my neck, and I glance over my shoulder. "You think she left, but what if she didn't? What if she's still out here?"

"Valentina was last spotted yesterday near the B&B. The most plausible scenario is that she carried out her intended crime and then fled."

"But you weren't able to find her," I press, "even after giving her name and destination to all the airports and train stations."

"Ladies, this may take more time than we'd hoped. It's likely that Valentina wasn't really Valentina at all."

"What do you mean?" Jocelyn looks from her to me.

"I mean that if a woman named *Valentina* had boarded a plane to Argentina or had even checked into an airport, we'd know about it. We've done searches on the name, on employees in the marketing field in Argentina." Her free hand signs a zero. "No hits. So, we have to consider the possibility that the name she gave you was a pseudonym. She may not have even been from Argentina."

"She used a fake identity?" I ask. "So then, she's some sort of convict?"

"Possibly," DI Collins says. "But sometimes, people just want to disappear. They come out all this way and simply decide never to return to their old lives. Maybe Valentina—or whoever she is—decided before she ever arrived in the UK that she wanted to stay untraceable."

"Did you at least find enough to make a case?" I ask. "Assuming you can track her down?"

"I can't disclose that information at the moment," DI Collins says, and my stomach clenches into a tight ball. We hiked all the way up here, did everything she asked of us, and now she won't share the one thing that can clear us of all suspicion and allow me to go home to Molly. "I have to keep certain aspects of this investigation private if we're going to nail this person."

I open my mouth to argue, but catch the glimmer in her brown eyes. They narrow with something like satisfaction. It's barely perceptible, the nod.

Jocelyn looks at me, her lips parted in awe, and I know.

They found something.

CHAPTER 32
CADENCE

"Thank you for showing me." I toss the phone back, missing Mr. Kemble by a few feet. He scowls and turns to dig it from the leaves.

"Oops," I say sweetly, moving for the shears the moment his back is turned.

Once he realizes what I've done, he charges me.

"I don't think so," I say, pointing the bloody blades at him. "Step back."

His eyes widen. "What about the ritual?"

"We'll have to do it later." I wave him off.

"We'll do it *now*. You think you can just come on my land, trample everything I've put my sweat and blood into, and then take off? Maybe it's time to talk about what it is you buried out here."

At his words, a tremor runs through me. "What?"

"I saw you put something into the ground. People don't do that unless they've got something to hide."

"You saw wrong," I say, my fists curled at my side. "I just dropped an earring and had to look for it." *Dammit.* Now I've got to find my way back to that hole, dig everything up, and start all over again.

"I don't think I did." He sneers. "You're going to help me with the ritual, or I'll tell Helen what you've been doing out here."

I roll my eyes. "Go ahead and tell." He didn't see anything, did he? He can't possibly know what I've got buried in the ground out here.

"What about that ginger-haired bitch? I'll bet you care if I tell her. Miss High and Mighty, *do you know who I am?*" He does a poor impersonation of an American accent.

Or I could just take care of Mr. Kemble, the way I did Magnus.

I deliberate a moment. I consider my weapon, consider his utter lack of one. It would be messy. And there isn't time. I've got bigger problems than this creep. Valentina is out here, stalking me, hunting me the way Mr. Kemble hunts his wild beasts. If he thinks I can't play his game, he's sorely mistaken.

"You're forgetting something, dear Mr. Kemble." I match his smile. "*You've* been hunting on Helen's property. *You've* been threatening one of her guests for the second time." I tap a filthy index finger to my chin. "Hmm, if one strike was suspension, I wonder what two strikes will be."

His smug expression falters. His ugly, worn boots fidget over the dried pine needles.

I take an empowered step toward him, my hand dropping to my hip. "Go back to your shack and leave me the hell alone. If you don't, I'll march straight to the B&B to tell Helen—who I've known for many years, and who loves me like a daughter, by the way—that you threatened me with these shears. After the way you grabbed me in the garden like a lunatic, it won't be very difficult to believe."

He grimaces. "You're rotten, you know that. I can tell. You probably deserve whatever this girl has in store for you. I hope she finds you."

I look down at the tool in my grip, and when I look up, terror floods his pale eyes. When he takes a step back, this time, it's of his own volition.

"I hope so too," I say. And I mean it. Valentina has no idea what I'm capable of. I just need to get back to the B&B so I can find a way to defend myself.

First, I've got to take care of Magnus's things.

"Go on, get out of here," I say, jabbing my weapon in his direction.

Mr. Kemble flinches, then scratches at his ear with a blood-coated hand, lets out a grunt, and takes off through the trees.

When his lumbering footsteps fade, I drop the nasty shears where I stand and try to retrace my own steps to where I buried Magnus's things. I was in such a state of panic that I hardly remember. I should've marked the place or at least made a note somehow, in case I ever needed to find it. But that son of a bitch came up behind me, and I stopped thinking clearly.

I keep moving, panic building, pushing down on my lungs like an iron clamp. Everything looks the same. I did too damn good of a job making the spot look inconspicuous, and now I'll never find it. But *he* knows.

He'll find it. Dig it up. Eventually, they'll discover Magnus's body. It'll all be over for this middle school English teacher.

I spot a patch of leaves in front of a familiar-looking rock and crouch down. Digging my fingernails into the dirt, I scoop up heaps of it. But there's nothing down here; it's not the spot.

Growling, I stand and take in my surroundings. I breathe in, slow and steady. It'll be okay. I will find it. I couldn't have run too far after Mr. Kemble showed up.

When the familiar sweet scent hits my nostrils, I hurry until I spot the pointed green leaves of the blackcurrant shrub. They wave like a flag marker in the breeze. *This is it.* The location is nearby.

I continue on, finding another patch where the dirt looks a little darker, like it's been disturbed. I push aside the leaves and start digging. I mine the earth until my fingers bleed and my nails tear. Just when I'm about to give up, the corner of a leather wallet pokes through.

I feel a flutter of relief.

But a crunch sounds behind me, and the relief is quickly replaced by a fiery rage. "What the hell did I tell you?" I snap.

I spin on my haunches, only it isn't Mr. Kemble and his yellow rain slicker.

Instead, a thin-framed figure stands in the shadow beneath a tree, wearing a dark-blue coat.

Valentina.

Her hood is cinched tightly to cover her hair and most of her face. When she lifts the Swiss Army knife, the familiar ring on her finger glints beneath a ray of sunlight.

I stand, abandoning the hole. My eyes dart in every direction, taking in my surroundings. The way back to the B&B should be straight ahead—right through Valentina. I'm already tired from the hike and in no shape to attempt running past her. Instead, I curse myself for not keeping those gardening shears and turn back the way I came. I'll have to lose her in the trees and then loop back around.

She's insane. If I scream for help, anyone could stumble upon Magnus's things before I get the chance to cover them back up. I hurry, and her footsteps crackle over the forest floor behind me.

I round a tree and check over my shoulder for her. But intense pain crashes over me. Stemming from my shins, the feeling vibrates down to my toes. I let out a groan.

My vision is mottled and cracked through, like broken glass. But I see the standing stones in front of me. I must've run straight into one of them. Staggering, I pivot just in time and spot Valentina behind me.

I attempt to recover, but she's on me in a flash, the knife raised high. I let out a yelp, throwing up my hands to shield myself from the blade.

The moment it slashes down at my neck, the hood falls back.

CHAPTER 33
NOW
ROWAN

Back in the B&B, Jocelyn and I head to the room to wash up. DI Collins returned our phones, and now we're waiting on more news, hopefully the green light to head home in the next couple of days. After everything that's happened, all I want to do is hold Molly tightly. I need her sweet little voice to drown out the stories that will forever haunt my mind.

After my shower, I dig around in my bag, trying to find a pair of clean socks. My hand lights instead on the little ceramic corgi I took from Helen's bookcase.

A tendril of guilt curls through my chest. I don't want to be this person anymore. *I can't be.* What if Molly ever found out about my nasty habit? That her mom deals with stress by taking precious things from other people, even people as lovely as Helen and Paul.

I'm going to therapy when I get back. This whole nightmare of an experience has been my wake-up call. The first step in my new direction will be making one thing right. I shrug on a hoodie and slide the figurine inside its pocket.

When I finish getting ready, Jocelyn's shower is still running. I duck into the hall and take the stairs down to the reception area. Both the desk and the front door are unattended; the officers normally stationed there must be out on the porch. I peek into the fireside room and, finding it empty, slip inside. The fire is still blazing, flames flickering over the walls. Crossing the rug to the bookcase, I remove the figurine from my pocket and place it back on the shelf.

Immediately, the tension in my chest eases. I take a long-needed, unimpeded breath. It feels good. Right. I'm about to spin around and head back out when I notice the way the firelight dances over the shelf, illuminating the mounds of dust. This bookshelf hasn't been cleaned in ages. But it's a mark in the dust that catches my eye. A distinct path has been carved out, the wood wiped clean, as if the book behind it was recently removed.

The book is an ancient encyclopedia, not something a guest would likely pick up for pleasure reading. I pull it free and let the thick leather cover follow the previously blazed trail through the dust. Taking the book to the wing-back chair, I attempt to flip it open on my lap.

Only it won't open. A thick layer of tape covers the fore edges, and something is stuck beneath the tape. I squint at the object, realizing what I'm seeing with a sickening turn of my stomach.

My vision blurs. The blue of the cover melts into the blue of my jeans. I'm not seeing this. I'm not seeing anything. I try to get up, but my legs are numb.

The object taped to the fore edge of the book is a silver butterfly ring.

I can't make sense of it. I try to move, to force my vision to clear and my legs to support me. Why would

Valentina's ring be *here*? She's been roaming the property with it on her finger. My breathing is labored, my arms working to hold the book as I stand and take one shaky step toward the bookcase.

"I am sorry you had to find that," comes a familiar voice from behind me.

My breath hitches as the door clicks shut.

CHAPTER 34
NOW
JOCELYN

When I get out of the shower, Rowan is gone.

I get dressed and find six missed calls from Cady's mother on my phone. She must've arrived at the train station. As soon as she was notified about Cady's death, she booked a plane ticket to come out here. It was hard enough speaking to Mrs. Fletcher on the phone this morning. I don't know how I'm going to look her in the eyes.

I've been no stranger to guilt. I felt it for years after betraying Rowan and Jake. Felt it every time I cheated on Landon. Then it came crashing down one hundredfold after we found Cady's body on the stones. *Guilty, guilty, guilty.* It's been a constant echo. This was *my* bachelorette trip. Cady died on my watch.

And then there's the thing no one else knows: the last thing I told Cady was that I wished she were dead.

Sure, there was something wrong with her, something of which none of us knew the full extent. Now, her mother is about to learn all about it too.

The last thing that poor woman needs is a two-hundred-pound taxi fee. I'd better see if Paul can pick her up. DI Collins instructed him to stick around the B&B today, so he's probably outside doing chores.

I head downstairs and toward the front door. When I pass the reception desk, voices from the fireside room stop me in my tracks. Usually, I'm the one getting interviewed. So what's going on in there? Did they find Valentina?

I should mind my own business. I should continue outside, as planned. Except there isn't an officer standing guard right now. The itch to eavesdrop worsens, and I tip-toe closer, pressing my ear to the door and listening for that familiar Spanish accent.

Instead, I hear Rowan's voice. "Please, I didn't mean to. I won't tell anyone!"

She's in trouble. What the hell is that detective—I push open the door, finding that Rowan isn't with DI Collins; she's standing face-to-face with my aunt.

At the creak of the door, Helen shrinks back from Rowan, making a show of straightening her blouse.

"What's going on in here?" I ask, shutting the door behind me.

"Nothing." Rowan tucks a still-damp curl behind her ear. But I hear the tremor in her voice.

"You won't tell anyone *what?*" I say, the room suddenly cold despite the fire.

"I suppose I should come clean," Helen says softly, wandering over to the couch. She settles down and then motions for us to follow suit. "She found the ring."

"Ring?" I ask, struggling to make sense of what she's saying as I find the nearest chair.

"Valentina's ring. The one they used in Mr. Kemble's photo to help identify her." Helen rolls her shoulders and moves her neck, showing her age. "It's not what you're thinking. I didn't kill Valentina." She stares down at her wrinkled hands, unable to meet our eyes. "But I did kill Cadence."

I nearly laugh, the declaration is so preposterous.

"What?" Rowan stands with her back pressed up against the bookcase. Like she's too afraid to move. "Why?"

"Because Mr. Kemble was right," she says, tears welling in her eyes. "Cadence was rotten. I knew the moment I figured out what she'd done to Jake. I was cleaning your bathroom, and spotted the pills in her overnight case. They weren't labeled, but they looked familiar. So I googled the imprint codes, along with the size and shape, and I came up with lorazepam and oxycodone. The drugs from Jake's death certificate. My sister had spent countless hours researching the drugs, trying to figure out how Jake had gotten hold of them, why he took them when he'd never had a problem with pills. She shared the research as well as her theories with me." Helen rubs her hands together, fingertips nervously tracing over the lines and folds. She's so used to serving people, and now, she doesn't seem to know what to do with her hands. "I'll admit, it all seemed outlandish at the time. Conspiracies—mostly about you, Rowan. That something must've happened between you and Jake, so you'd drugged him."

I swallow, and it sounds like an explosion. That was *my* theory. I let it slip to my mother one evening in a fit of grief. I had no idea she'd taken it seriously. That she'd started looking into it.

"They were the exact drugs that killed Jake—drugs Cadence had no business possessing. I dug around her things until I found a photograph hidden in an inside pocket of her travel wallet. It was a selfie, taken by Cady while Landon kissed her on the cheek. Naturally, I started wondering how she'd have such a photo. And then it dawned on me. Cady's hair was short in the photo, just like it was at Jake's funeral. In all the time I've known Cady, her hair was only short once."

Nausea starts to roil in my stomach. I want to tell her to stop talking, but I'm afraid more than words will come up.

"And I knew that meant Cady had been seeing Landon while he was with *you*," my aunt continues, still fixated on her hands. "She'd kept this horrible secret from you, and Jake must've found out." Helen finally meets my eyes. "She'd stolen your twin, Jocelyn. My nephew. She'd *ruined* my sister's life. Teresa—your mother—*died* the day Jake did. At least, the version of her we knew and loved." Now, I'm the one who has to look away. She's right. I've been living without my brother for eight years, but I've also been living without my mother. "Once I put it all together, I couldn't think of anything else. That girl had murdered Jake, and she was just gallivanting around, pretending to be your closest friend. I began to obsess over what to do about it. If there was a way to get her out of your lives for good. If I could make her pay."

With a shiver, I picture Cady sprawled out on the stones, skin pale and eyes unblinking. All that blood.

"And then you three started throwing all these accusations around—that Magnus and Valentina were stalking you." Helen points a bony finger at us. "That she'd stolen Cadence's phone and that she was harassing you. It turns out you were right about most of that. So when Valentina disappeared, I thought I had my scapegoat. But then you asked me to call the cops, and I worried everything would be ruined."

There's a knot in my throat, but I push the question past it. "You didn't call, did you?"

She shakes her head. "I never followed through with it."

An acute pain shoots through me at my aunt's betrayal.

"You don't understand," she says, voice strained. "I didn't call the authorities because I'd seen Valentina leave. I knew that no crime had been committed."

"What?" I ask in a strangled cry. If I could scream without alerting the cops out on the porch, I would. "Why didn't you just say so?"

"I couldn't," Helen says. "Before the sun was up Tuesday morning, while I was preparing the breakfast room, I heard voices coming from the reception area. It was odd at that hour, so I moved closer to listen—just to make sure there wasn't an issue. It was Magnus and Valentina, but it took me a moment to recognize Valentina's voice. The girl was speaking with an English accent, not Spanish. And when Magnus addressed her, it was by a different name, only I didn't catch it. Maybe Sofie, or Sofia—all I know is it was *not* Valentina."

Rowan shakes her head. "No, that's not—she was from Argentina. She spoke Spanish to me." She steps forward, gripping the back of the wingback chair, her brown eyes wide. "She was—oh my god."

Helen attempts a half smile that looks more like a grimace. "Magnus was drunk and upset. He said he deserved to have some fun with you girls after what Rowan did to him. He wanted to send the photos out, as punishment. Or at least the ones of Rowan robbing the toy shop."

I glance at Rowan, whose gaze never leaves the rug.

"Valentina—or whatever her name was—argued," Helen continues. "She said he'd had more than enough fun. They'd gathered all the intel they needed, and now, they had to be smart. Jocelyn was loaded. Cady had mentioned a rich father who pays for everything. Jocelyn would find the money to cover up her"—my aunt reddens—"*indiscretion.*"

My palms start to sweat. My aunt knew all about the kiss and the photo. She even knew about Rowan's bad habit. This whole time, she's been keeping all of our dirty secrets.

"Magnus's voice was sharp when he insisted that *Rowan* was the target. Valentina had promised that he'd get to mess with the girls, and then on their way out, they'd blackmail Rowan for three times as much money as she stole from him. But Valentina didn't like this at all. She told Magnus he was getting sloppy. They had to stay under the radar. He had to let her run the operation. Jocelyn was the better mark. Once they used the photos of her and Magnus to drain her dry, they'd disappear to a new land, in search of a new target. If Magnus let his emotions get in the way—if he got sloppy—then they'd be caught.

"Magnus raised his voice then, snapping that Valentina was *not* running the operation. He said they were going to blackmail all three girls. They'd screenshotted some texts between Landon and Cady, proving they were having an affair. It confirmed one of my suspicions about her.

"I heard a thump then, like something large knocking against the wall. That's when I pushed open the door, walking into the reception area and interrupting their conversation. I feigned surprise to see them there and carried on with my chores."

Helen lifts her hands, like the meek, frail woman I'd always believed she was. "Magnus trudged off, back upstairs, but Valentina didn't follow. She stayed behind, watching me as I pretended to work at the desk. She stood there until I got the horrible feeling she was going to *do* something to me. I asked if everything was okay, but she merely stared me down. 'We weren't going to hurt them, you know,' she finally said, causing my heart to beat so fast and hard that I nearly shouted for Paul. 'It was only about the money.'

"I said I didn't know what she was talking about and I had work to do, but she marched to the desk and stood right in front of me, forcing me to look at her. She told me she'd leave, that she'd walk right out that door, as long as I swore not to tell anyone what I'd heard. I could see tears well up in her eyes, and I wasn't sure if it was out of repentance or fear. She said, 'All I need is a nod that we understand each other, and I'm out that door. Forever.'

"'What about *him?*' I asked, flicking my head in the direction of the stairs.

"Valentina only laughed and said, 'Magnus? He's a handsome, harmless idiot. He won't try anything without me.' For whatever reason, I believed her. Or maybe I just wanted her gone because of the unsettling way she looked at me. The second I nodded, she headed toward the front door.

"I asked about her things, the ones she'd left up in the room. But she said she couldn't go back up there or he'd follow her. And she was done with him. She wanted me to get rid of her bag for her. I think she was also a bit wary of me, that I'd go back on my word and call the police on her while she was upstairs. Anyway, she patted her shoulder satchel and said she had everything she needed right there. She begged me not to tell Magnus she'd left the property."

My head starts to ache. I let my hair down from its bedraggled ponytail, going through the motions in a zombielike state. I try to follow Helen's words, but I'm failing to match her face to that of a murderer.

"As much as I wanted her to leave, it was chilly out there. I told her to at least take one of my coats," Helen continues. "She smiled, grateful, and I headed back upstairs to rustle up something. By the time I made it back downstairs, though, she was gone. Valentina, whoever she was, had slipped out into the dark fog. Clearly, she never wanted to be found again. Not by me, not by Magnus, and especially not by the police. Who knows how many victims of her cons would've come forward if I turned her in?"

My aunt looks at me now, her hands held out beseechingly. "I need you to know, my dear, I don't wish for someone else to go down for my crime. That was never my intention. But I knew if I could pin Cadence's death on Valentina, it would be like pinning the murder on a ghost. Don't you see? *Valentina* never existed. The girl standing in my reception area would vanish, and authorities would never learn the whole truth." Helen's face has never reminded me of my own mother's more than now, with her eyes and nose red, tears streaming down her puffy cheeks.

She sniffles. "The next afternoon, I created a bit of a credit card issue for Magnus, forcing him to come down to the desk and sort things out with Paul. That's when I did as Valentina asked. I snuck into their room and took her bag from beneath the bed. Later, I found Cadence's things buried at the bottom of it—Jocelyn, you must've been too caught up in the fact that her bag was in the room to search it thoroughly. I knew Cadence would have to come back for her passport. Even then, I wasn't certain I could actually go through with it. Until I saw you crying in the reception area, Jocelyn. I knew that Cady was the type of person who takes and takes, and would continue to take unless someone put a stop to it."

I'm dizzy, sick to my stomach. I can't listen to this anymore.

"Before I took Valentina's belongings to the shack in the woods, I removed a couple of items—things that would be easily identified—and wore them around the property. I wanted the guests in room three to witness a woman wearing the coat and the ring before Cadence's death. Your accounts would've been meaningless. Theirs, on the other hand, were just what the police needed to believe Valentina had never left."

Helen starts to twist her gold wedding band around her finger. *One loop. Two.* "Once it was done, I cleaned my prints off the Swiss Army knife I found in her bag, leaving Cady's blood on the blade. Then I stashed it in the shack along with the rest of her things." *Three loops. Four.* My vision swirls, mimicking the motion. "Only I didn't leave the ring there. I thought it might seem strange, her leaving without the ring on her finger."

My neck starts to itch where my hair brushes the skin. I reach back to scratch at it. "You could've called the police back home and left a tip about Jake's murder. You didn't have to throw away your own life over Cady."

"Maybe I should've called," Helen says, her eyes glossy. "I worried that, after all these years, they wouldn't be able to prove it. That maybe they wouldn't even care about proving it. That the do-gooder middle school teacher would get away with everything. They'd already ruled Jake's death an accidental drug overdose. Finding the same pills isn't exactly hard evidence. This was the only way to make certain she got what she deserved."

"But you're not a killer, Helen," Rowan says, echoing my own thought.

A sad smile forms on Helen's lips. "I'll find DI Collins and confess."

"What?" I glance at Rowan, a sudden jolt of panic hitting me. I rush toward my aunt, throwing my arms around her. I breathe in her sugary scent, and it all hits me—everything she did to avenge Jake, to protect Rowan and me from a friend whose existence was nothing but a layer of rot upon our lives. She'd never forgotten about my mother, not even for a day. She'd never abandoned her. "I don't want you to confess, Aunt Helen."

"Neither do I." Rowan crosses the room to slide the encyclopedia back onto the shelf. "The only thing I want is for everyone to learn what Cady did to Jake. Her name can't be touted as some sort of angelic victim for years to come. People should know who she really was."

"We'll stick with the Valentina story," I say, though the gravity of the suggestion digs into my abdomen like talons. "The cops must've found the Swiss Army knife. We saw the look on DI Collins's face. She was convinced they'd found the culprit."

"We'll take it to the grave," Rowan says solemnly.

Helen wipes her eyes. "You don't have to lie for me."

"We can't lie," Rowan says.

"Because we don't know anything," I add with a nod. "All we know is that Valentina was unhinged. She enjoyed toying with us, like we were her little puppets. And when Cady killed her boyfriend, Valentina got her revenge."

Helen looks at us with some mixture of gratitude and uncertainty before adding, "And like a gwyllgi on a dark rural road, she vanished."

CHAPTER 35
NOW
ROWAN

DI Collins stares at me again, only this time it's through the fuzzy television screen Paul set up in the corner of our room. "We are now searching for a con woman named Valentina, who is suspected in the homicide of twenty-eight-year-old American, Cadence Fletcher. Though Valentina is thought to be of Argentine citizenship, not much is known about the woman, who has allegedly been funding her globe-trotting by scamming other travelers and leaving no trace. We suspect there may be other victims." A sketch, which we provided the police, shows a young woman whose physical features bear no resemblance to the Valentina we knew—apart from her brown eyes.

"Good luck, detective," Jocelyn says, turning off the television.

Now that investigators have their sights set on Valentina, Jocelyn and I are free to leave the country. I'm desperate to get back to Molly, but we couldn't get our plane tickets moved any earlier; we have to leave tomorrow. My parents are terrified, believing the crazed murderer is still out there, and that she could return to the

B&B to finish what she started. I did my best to appease them. I told them about the officers standing guard at the B&B and that the rest are busy tracking Valentina down.

The guests in room three checked out, understandably. Helen offered the room to Cady's mother. I feel bad for Mrs. Fletcher, I really do. When she heard about Jake, she realized Cady must've stolen the lorazepam from her back when she was going through chemotherapy. It was prescribed for the nausea, but she rarely used it and never noticed when her daughter stole a handful of pills. With Cady gone, the weight of responsibility has fallen completely on her shoulders.

I know how she feels. Hell, every time Molly so much as pinched a kid in preschool, I felt as guilty as if I'd done it myself. To think that one day she could turn into something as monstrous as Cady—it makes me afraid to let her out of my sight.

But we can't be with our kids every second of every day. And deep down, I know that Molly is nothing like Cady.

Cady always knew the perfect reaction, the perfect thing to say. It was all an act, though. I realize that now. Cady had studied up on empathy the same way she'd studied for her college exams. Everything was calculated. She was merely playing a part. Because Cady never actually felt a thing for anyone other than herself. The people in her life existed only to help her achieve her goals, and if those people couldn't play along—if they posed any sort of threat to her desires—she had them removed.

The only hang-up she'd ever had was Jocelyn. No matter how much Cady loved or obsessed over Landon, she couldn't stand the thought of losing Jocelyn. She couldn't *deal* with her the way she did the others. Joss was her weakness. I can relate.

"Ready?" Jocelyn asks, grabbing her backpack. She didn't do her makeup today, and unlike on the plane ride over here, she looks terrible without it. Her eyes are red-rimmed, skin blotchy. Apparently, Jocelyn Elliott can appear less than perfect under exactly the wrong circumstances.

"Yeah." I pull my curls up into a bun and check for my wallet and phone.

Jocelyn is still somewhat in denial about everything. It's a harder pill for her to swallow. That sounded wrong. What I mean is, she and Cady had been close for years. It's going to take some time for her to deconstruct the myth of Cady as her caring, loving best friend.

Despite everything, Jocelyn has planned a little excursion to Caernarfon today in Cady's honor. I think it's more of a show for Cady's mother—take photos of us doing things Cady would be doing if she were alive—in which case, I'm proud of Joss. That woman has had enough torn away from her—not only her daughter, but the perfect picture she held of Cady too. I imagine that all the Student of the Month awards and Mother's Day cards must be flashing through her mind on a constant, tormenting loop. We can allow her to believe, for one day, that Cady is truly loved and missed.

It will be good to get away from the B&B, even if it means spending the day with Jocelyn. After our chat with Helen two nights ago, Jocelyn attempted an apology. Not the fake kind she gave me when Cady ratted her out about Jake and the breakup. This time, she seemed genuine. "I know you can't forgive me, Ro," she said into the darkness. The mattress springs creaked, and I knew she was sitting up on her bed as I lay in mine, pretending to sleep. "Even *I* don't forgive me. I just . . . when I found out that Cady was responsible for taking Jake from me, my world imploded all over again. That detective was staring us down, and suddenly, I lost my grip on reality. I couldn't trust anyone— not even you." Her voice quivered. "I knew you'd been in the woods the day Cady died. In that moment, sitting in front of DI Collins, I realized that if *I'd* been with Cady in the woods . . . I might've killed her. I could see myself losing it. So, I must've extended that logic to you."

It was hard to hear. The length she might've gone to in her grief if she'd found herself face-to-face with Cady. Maybe it was hard to hear because it resonated a bit with me. I honestly don't know what I would've done to Cady had I tracked her down as planned.

I'm not even angry about what Jocelyn said to DI Collins anymore. She panicked. I get it. One could say I did the same thing by throwing her name to the detective.

But it doesn't explain the secret she kept from me for eight years. The relationship she destroyed on purpose.

"I know, Joss" was the only thing I could say before turning over to face another night of sleeplessness. They were the only words I had the emotional capacity to push out.

Jocelyn had once provided a sense of safety. The sole thing I'd counted on in high school and hoped I could one day count on again was her having my back. Now, that hope has been utterly demolished, and I don't think there's any way to restore it.

Deep down, I want to forgive her. One day, I believe I will. We're not just friends; we're family, bound together for life by Molly. But it's not something I can do today.

For today, I'm going to pretend like she never betrayed me. I'm going to remember that friend who protected me at the cabin all those years ago, the one who always stuck up for Cady when the kids bullied her. I'm going to remember the girl I followed to college because I couldn't imagine life without her. Today, we're going to tour the castle at Caernarfon like friends, even though we aren't friends. We'll tour it in Cady's honor, even though she was the opposite of honorable.

We knock on the door to room three before heading out, and Cady's mother comes to the door, her hair disheveled, eyes swollen. "Are you sure you don't want to come with us?" Jocelyn asks. "It's finally sunny out. The vitamin D might be good for you. The sights might . . ."

She's about to say *take your mind off things*, like she did when she pitched me the idea; it's obviously in poor taste here. Not a minute will pass that Mrs. Fletcher doesn't think about Cady's horrible fate for a very long time.

"Thanks, girls, but I'm going to stay in." Mrs. Fletcher looks down, unable to face us after what her daughter did.

"Can we bring you anything from town?" I ask.

She starts to shake her head, her hand already on the door. "Actually," she says, cheeks flushing, "I could use a bottle of something. Anything, really. I hate to trouble Helen with all she's done."

"Of course." Jocelyn offers a sympathetic smile.

On the staircase, Jocelyn whispers, "That's how it starts, you know. I saw it with my mother when Jake passed away. It starts with them asking for just one bottle to help numb the pain."

"What can we do?"

"Nothing. You can't tell a grieving mother how to cope."

"How did you cope?" I ask. "When Jake passed away."

She still hasn't answered when we're out the front door, spring sunlight warm on our skin. I assume she's ignored me until her voice drifts over, soft and childlike. "I found someone to blame." She clears her throat, rubbing at it like there's something lodged in there. "Only it was the wrong person."

We continue down the driveway to where Phylip is waiting for us.

The drive to Caernarfon is quiet. I have nothing to say to Jocelyn. I take in the scenery, marveling at the green landscape. It looks the same as it did the day we arrived, though our entire world has turned upside down.

"Look, Rowan," Jocelyn says as Phylip's taxi rolls away, leaving us in front of the castle entrance. "I'm not using the excuse that I was a kid, because I know it's not an excuse. I own who I was back then. I am sorry. I never should've come between you and Jake."

I follow her up the steps to the ticket window. "Why did you?" The twins were always close, but they weren't codependent. Jocelyn had boyfriends; Jake had girlfriends. Joss would do the catty-gossip thing in an attempt to rattle Jake—"Did you hear Megan dated a twenty-five-year-old last year?"— but it never reached the point of blatant sabotage.

She pauses at the top of the steps. "In my mind, the two of you together meant I'd lost you both. The two people most important to me. I didn't understand how you felt about each other, not really. I never imagined you'd end up . . ." She tucks a strand of hair behind her ear. "I didn't know about the baby."

My stomach twists. "Thanks to Cady, Jake never did either."

She reaches for my hand, then thinks better of it. "I know he would've been an amazing dad. I know you two would've made great parents together." She gets in line to purchase our tickets, and I wait off to the side, leaning up against the gate.

"You know," I force out when she returns, handing me a ticket, "what hurts isn't just seeing Molly miss out on having her dad."

"What do you mean?" She looks up from rearranging credit cards in her wallet.

Now that I've begun, I don't want to finish. This isn't the type of thing I should have to say. She should just know. If I say it, I'll always hate myself for it. I'll hate her for making me say it.

But if our relationship is ever going to improve, I'll have to break it all the way first. "I mean that it hurts to see *you* missing from Molly's life. I used to tell myself that everything would be okay once Molly came, because we'd have Auntie Jocelyn. Molly's spitting image. The two of you were supposed to run around looking like mother and daughter, and I would cherish your close relationship. I loved the"—the words catch in my throat—"the *picture* I'd painted of the two of you. Of the three of us. And then, you never showed up. I thought you were just taking your time grieving. But Molly's eight, and you never came around."

Jocelyn stares down at the mossy stone steps for a moment that stretches on. Without a word, she walks over to the attendant, hands over her ticket, and passes through the gate.

It feels like a blow to the windpipe. To pour it all out, to give Jocelyn yet one more chance she didn't deserve, and have it trampled on.

I don't want to go inside, but the attendant is holding out her hand, waiting for my ticket. I step forward and pass it to her. "Diolch," she says, handing me a map. "Have a nice day."

"Diolch," I mumble, finding myself in the open plaza with the castle surrounding me. Jocelyn has vanished, not that I'm looking for her. The courtyard is crowded, the spring breakers apparently having found this place too. Rather than checking the map, I head straight for the archway nearest me. I navigate around a tour group to find myself in a dark stone chamber. When I take the narrow stairwell up, there's a tap on my shoulder.

I flinch and turn around. Jocelyn is there, eyes flooded with tears. "It was like looking at *him*," she says. "Every second with Molly feels like that part of my soul is being ripped away all over again."

My eyes sting, but I force the tears back. "I know."

"How could she do this to us?" She's sobbing now, nose red and dripping. An elderly couple comes up behind us in the stairwell. I start to nudge Jocelyn, but the couple turns right around and heads back down, wanting nothing to do with our emotional confrontation.

"She wasn't right," I say, torn between comforting her and letting her suffer. She's earned a little taste of the sadness and loneliness I've endured. "She had us all fooled."

Jocelyn lets out a dry laugh between sniffles. "I have no one left. Not her, not Landon." She glances up at me. "Not you."

I can't tell her what she wants to hear. Instead, I dig a travel pack of tissues from my bag. I hand one over, and she wipes her face. "Let's just get through today, okay?"

She nods and heads back down the stairs. I watch her go, knowing we'll never be what we were, once upon a time. Then again, I'm not the person I was back then either.

Maybe we're both in need of a different sort of friend now.

EPILOGUE
HELEN

I wave goodbye to the girls from the porch. Paul's car drives off down the dirt road, headed to the airport. Cadence's mother is also in the car, so I'm alone at the B&B. Well, apart from Mr. Kemble.

When the girls discovered what I'd done to Cady, I hoped they'd take my side. I never counted on it, though. Even Paul had been horrified when I told him what I'd done. But he'd seen the effects of Cady's actions, the way the life drained from my sister after Jake passed. In the end, he supported me. He even helped to cover up my crime.

He's my husband, though, my other half. I couldn't expect the same support or understanding from Jocelyn and her friend. So, when Rowan looked me dead in the eye and said, "We'll take it to the grave," relief ran through me. We're bound, the three of us. I trust them with my life now, even if I didn't when I confessed to them three days ago, back in the fireside room.

Three days ago, I told the girls the truth, but not the whole truth.

I wanted to trust them, but Cadence had done a lot of brainwashing over the years. I wasn't sure how far they'd been dragged into her pit of lies.

I had my gwyllgi, that mythical beast standing on a rural road. Valentina had appeared to us and then vanished so quickly, she almost made you question if she was ever here at all.

If I was going to pin this murder on a ghost, there was one fact I had to keep to myself: it seemed like Valentina was never here at all because she never was. Not at the beginning of the week, not on the day of Cady's murder.

Early the morning Valentina disappeared, I did overhear a conversation between her and Magnus. But it wasn't an English accent I'd heard; it was American. The wheels in my head had started to spin. For three days, something had nagged at me about Valentina. Something vaguely familiar that I could never quite put my finger on.

And then, I overheard the part I left out of my account in the fireside room. Magnus called the woman by a new name—neither Valentina, nor some name that sounded like *Sofie* or *Sofia*.

That was the moment it all came together. I interrupted their spat, and Magnus stormed off. Valentina stayed in the reception area, only she was anything but menacing. In fact, I don't think she realized how much I'd heard. She shook with rage or frustration, and I told her to sit a minute in the reception area while I brought out some tea. "Thank you," she said, back to the Spanish accent.

As she sat across from me, sipping her chamomile, I saw Valentina for who she really was. "I won't tell anyone your secret," I offered softly.

Blinking, she set the cup down. "I don't know what you're talking about."

"You've straightened your hair, and the eyes are different from the ones on the news. Are those brown contacts?" I added a sugar cube to my own cup. "Anyway, I won't tell anyone it's you, Lisa. As long as you leave, right now."

She paled and pushed her chair back. "I would appreciate that very much," Lisa said, in what I knew from the news was a Texas twang, standing up. "It was only about the money, you know. I-I just couldn't go back to my old life. Please don't tell Magnus we spoke."

The rest played out much as it did in my account to the girls. When I asked Lisa about her belongings, she frowned. "I hate all that stuff. I got it to become Valentina. Now, it's time to become someone else." Her smile was somber as she patted the shoulder satchel. "Besides, I have everything I need right here."

Lisa tugged the butterfly ring off her finger and placed it on the desk. "Get rid of this for me too." Then she left, too desperate to ditch her accomplice, maybe too worried I'd report what she'd attempted to do to my niece and her friends.

Too scared I'd break my word and tell someone I'd spotted Lisa Granger.

But no one was looking for Lisa Granger anymore. She was a grown woman who'd run away from her home in Texas, just like her friend had said on the news. Never in a million years would the authorities peg Lisa Granger for Cadence Fletcher's murder.

All I had to do was make it look like Valentina had stuck around on my property an extra day and that she'd committed the crime.

Afterward, when the girls found that ring, I couldn't tell them about Lisa. The authorities could search for Valentina. They could even search for some girl named Sofie from England. But I could never let them connect Lisa to this case or even to this B&B. That was a secret I intended to keep.

And so, I did what I had to do. I lied.

THE END

Acknowledgments

Publishing this book has been a dream come true, and I have so many people to thank for making it happen. To my wonderful editor, Alexandra Torrealba—thank you for loving this story and taking a chance on it!

To my fabulous agent, Uwe Stender—for your belief in my writing and unwavering support along the way. I am always grateful to have you in my corner.

A huge thanks to the team at Thomas & Mercer, and a special shout-out to Nicole Burns-Ascue and Andrea Nauta for their close work with me on this project. Thank you to James Iacobelli for the perfectly eerie cover. To my developmental editor, Wendy Murali—working with you was a delight and truly made this story shine.

I am forever grateful to my dear friends and critique partners, Julie Abe and Laura Kadner. And to my early readers, Laura Kadner, MK Pagano, and Meredith Adamo—thank you for your honest feedback and encouragement!

To Courtney, Leah, and Bethany, to whom this book is dedicated—maybe it wasn't a bachelorette trip and maybe our friendship wasn't quite this complicated, but thanks for the trip that would one day inspire this story.

To my parents, George and Rebecca Kienzle—for listening and cheerleading through all of the publishing highs and lows. Mom, thank you for being one of my first readers. To my Ichaso and Lewis families, your support means the world.

To my husband, Matias—for always being my first reader and the person who talks me through every single new idea or plot struggle. I couldn't do this without you.

Kaylie, Jude, and Camryn—keep writing your stories. You have far more imagination than I ever did at your age. Thank you for thinking that my job is cool and for being the best people ever.

To the book bloggers and influencers—thank you for supporting my books. Every post and photo means so much to me.

And of course, thank you, dear reader! You're the reason I get to keep writing, and I'm endlessly grateful that you picked up this book.

Finally, all gratitude and praise to my Lord and Savior, Jesus Christ.

About the Author

Photo © Jen Alvarez

Chelsea Ichaso writes twisty thrillers for young adults, including *Dead Girls Can't Tell Secrets*, *They're Watching You*, and *The Summer She Went Missing*. A former high school English teacher, Chelsea currently resides in Southern California with her husband and children. She likes to think she plays guitar and would succeed on a survival television show, though neither is actually true.